Miss Thornfield's Daring Bargain

The Troublemakers Trilogy
Book 1

by
Addy Du Lac

© Copyright 2025 by Addy Du Lac
Text by Addy Du Lac
Cover by Dar Albert

Dragonblade Publishing, Inc. is an imprint of Kathryn Le Veque Novels, Inc.
P.O. Box 23
Moreno Valley, CA 92556
ceo@dragonbladepublishing.com

Produced in the United States of America

First Edition March 2025
Trade Paperback Edition

Reproduction of any kind except where it pertains to short quotes in relation to advertising or promotion is strictly prohibited.

All Rights Reserved.

The characters and events portrayed in this book are fictitious. Any similarity to real persons, living or dead, is purely coincidental and not intended by the author.

ARE YOU SIGNED UP FOR DRAGONBLADE'S BLOG?

You'll get the latest news and information on exclusive giveaways, exclusive excerpts, coming releases, sales, free books, cover reveals and more.

Check out our complete list of authors, too!

No spam, no junk. That's a promise!

Sign Up Here
www.dragonbladepublishing.com

Dearest Reader;

Thank you for your support of a small press. At Dragonblade Publishing, we strive to bring you the highest quality Historical Romance from some of the best authors in the business. Without your support, there is no 'us', so we sincerely hope you adore these stories and find some new favorite authors along the way.

Happy Reading!

CEO, Dragonblade Publishing

PROLOGUE

Miss Pollitt's School for Young Ladies
Hertfordshire, 1846

SHE HAD TO run. Though it went against every rule of conduct Ada had been taught in her fifteen years of life, running was the only option now. When their parents died at sea, her brother Zhenyi had decided to send her to school. Taking over the family business so unexpectedly had largely monopolized his time so in the interest of her being around more girls her age, he'd sent her to Miss Pollitt's, an exclusive boarding school for the girls in the ton. The idea was to help her socialize with other girls from affluent and connected families.

Ada had been excited at first, but ever since she'd begun boarding there, she'd been a target. She had certainly tried to fit in. When that failed, she tried to make herself invisible. However, with the features her Chinese mother had given her, there was nowhere for Ada to blend in or hide.

Sarah Hill had set her sights on Ada the minute she'd been introduced to the other students. Within a week, Sarah's vitriolic attacks began. But Ada was nothing if not resourceful, and she knew how to make herself scarce. Today, the mail had been delivered and Ada had received a letter from her brother, Zhenyi. Sarah, as fate would have it, had received a letter from no one. Ada watched as the little harpy's brown eyes had narrowed their envious gaze at her and knew today was going to be another day for hiding.

The music room was always empty after lunch, so Ada made a sharp left down a hallway and ducked into the room. She scampered behind a curtain and hoped she would go unnoticed again. She held her breath as the voices and footsteps came closer, pressing her body against the window as hard as she could.

"Are you certain she came in here?" she heard a girl say.

"Lottie said she always hides in here," Sarah replied, and Ada closed her eyes in resignation. Stupid Lottie. The mousey redhead Ada shared her rooms with had no doubt been attempting to protect herself, but it still felt like a betrayal. The closer the footsteps came to her hiding spot, the more she held her breath, praying desperately that none of them would check behind the curtains.

A moment later, her hopes were crushed as the heavy brown drape was yanked to the side and she came face to face with her tormentor.

"Look who I found hiding like a little rat," Sarah said before grabbing Ada by the wrist and jerking her forward. Beside her stood Claire Stanton, the dark-haired sycophant who never came for Ada alone but was always there to lend Sarah a hand when it came to tormenting Ada. And she wasn't alone. Charlotte Balfe, or Lottie as she was called, refused to meet her eyes and Aliana Ricker, another blonde was standing just behind her. Probably to keep her from bolting now that her duty was done.

"Sarah!" Ada steeled herself with a breath, knowing what was sure to come.

"Didn't you hear us calling you? It's rude to ignore people."

"I wasn't ignoring you."

"And to lie. But then I always knew you'd be a liar. Your kind are always liars."

"Let go of my arm," Ada said, refusing to acknowledge the slanderous words. Her brother had always told her it was best to remain calm, to find a way forward without escalating the situation. Judging by the grip Sarah had on her arm, she wasn't certain she'd get the chance to avoid a fight.

"You come here to our country and our school and then have the audacity to demand anything?" Sarah hissed, tightening her hold until it was painful.

"I didn't come anywhere," Ada replied in what she hoped was a reasonable tone. "I was born here the same as you were."

"You are nothing like me. You have no right to anything here."

"Let go of my arm."

"And if I don't? You can't tell me what to do."

She would try one more time for peace; after that she would use her nails. "Sarah…"

The shove came abruptly, and it sent Ada crashing into the wall, then a second blow to her head forced her to her knees with her ears ringing.

I'm sorry, brother, she thought to herself.

"Where is it?" Their hands forced her head down until it touched the ground while others rooted in the pockets of her blue cambric skirt. She struggled against their hold even while they pulled her brother's letter from her pocket. "Give it to me, Claire."

As soon as she was released, she looked up to see Sarah peering at the envelope. Watching it in Sarah's hands evoked an unexpectedly extreme reaction within Ada. That letter was everything, her father's warm smile, her mother's laugh and loving eyes, her brother's teasing affection. She'd never receive another letter from her parents, and she hadn't seen her brother in months. The idea of that bully holding her brother's precious words to her made her livid. "Give that back to me," she said, unable to keep the tremor from her voice.

"Who on earth would write to you?"

"Give it back!" She lunged forward and Sarah snatched it out of her grasp.

"Hold her back girls."

Ada's eyes stung against furious tears as she tried to fight off the grasp of the three girls with Sarah. "That's from my brother; give it back to me."

"Brother? I don't think so, it must be from a lover." Aliana's eyes gleamed wickedly, "I should report it to Miss Harding."

"No, give it back to me!" Miss Harding hated Ada. She'd only been at the school a week and the woman had already taken to singling Ada out for unwarranted criticism. Who knew what she'd do?

"I'll read it first, of course." Sarah broke the seal on the envelope and pulled out sheets of rich paper covered in neat Mandarin characters.

There was a vicious delight in watching the incomprehension on Sarah's face as her eyes scanned the pages. "What does it say?" Ada asked smugly.

"You little—"

"Is that you, Miss Hill, causing all that noise?" came another voice.

Sarah turned and Ada caught a glimpse of another girl. She was slim and dark-skinned with the bearing of a dowager despite looking no older than Ada. Her bounteous tightly coiled dark hair was twisted into a top knot. She stepped forward, her dark eyes brushing over Ada and her captors to the letter in Sarah's hand. They had never spoken before, and Ada could barely place her name. Was her last name Harrow? Harrod?

"Stealing letters again? Can't you get your family to send you one of your own?"

"Shut your mouth you little n—" The slap rang out through the silent room before Sarah went crashing to the ground. Ada watched the dark girl with wide eyes as she crouched down elegantly to pick up the scattered sheets of paper on the ground.

"I'd let her go now if I were you unless you all would like to go a round as well," she said coolly to the other girls holding Ada captive, ignoring Sarah's whimpers from her place on the floor. Within moments Ada was free and the room was empty except for her and the girl who had saved her. "My name is Miss Elodia

Hawthorne, what is yours?"

Hawthorne, that was it. Her father was a viscount if Ada remembered correctly. "Miss Adelaide Thornfield."

Elodia handed Ada back her letter and smiled. "Very pleased to meet you, Miss Thornfield."

"I can't believe you hit her," Ada said, wondering at Elodia's courage.

"I've been aching to thrash her for over a month."

"Won't you get into trouble?"

"Oh, undoubtedly," she replied with a wolfish grin. "But the worst punishment would be worth watching that vile witch hit the ground like a sack of flour."

"I'm glad to offer the opportunity," Ada joked. "Thank you again, Miss Hawthorne." She gave her a small curtsey.

"That is far too formal for fellow combatants. You can call me Ellie," she said hooking her arm with Ada's.

"Elodia Hawthorne!" a shrill voice called out and Elodia turned to face the emaciated woman standing in the doorway. "Did you strike a fellow student?"

"I most certainly did," Elodia replied, lifting her chin in defiance. Her unshakable spirit gave Ada the courage to meet the eyes of the teacher who had made herself the bane of Ada's existence.

"She was helping me, Miss Harding," Ada spoke up as the woman approached with Sarah and her minions behind her.

"Helping you to break the rules?"

"No, Miss Harding. I was trying to read my letter and—"

Miss Harding snatched the paper out of Ada's hand and sneered down at it. "You mean this nonsense?"

"It's a letter from my brother," Ada explained.

"You are in England now, Miss Thornfield. English girls in English boarding schools read English letters." With that, as Ada watched in horror, she ripped the pages first in half and then into quarters, before throwing the pieces onto the ground. Ada fell to her knees gathering up the fragments as best she could. "Leave it, girl," Miss Harding commanded, grabbing Ada by her arm and yanking her up to her feet.

Elodia looked ready to explode, "You—"

"And you, Miss Hawthorne, will remember that it is only by civilizing your brutish nature that you will find a place in England, regardless of who your father is."

"And what about Miss Hill's brutish nature?" Elodia replied, "Is she allowed to steal and bully others?"

"I didn't steal anything," Sarah whimpered while her eyes gleamed in triumph.

Elodia's eyes narrowed on her. "You loathsome little—"

"Enough!" Miss Harding snapped. "You two will both come with me," she replied before looking at Sarah and her cronies. "You all return to your rooms."

"Yes, Miss Harding," they chorused before following the smug Sarah out of the room.

Ada numbly followed Miss Harding, and Elodia walked beside her in furious silence until they reached Miss Harding's classroom.

"Miss Hawthorne, you will receive twenty strokes of the cane on your hand so you remember not to use it against others," she said snatching the thin cane that hung by the door and taking Elodia's dark slender hand in hers, forcing her palm to face up.

The force of the strikes as she carried out the punishment had Ada flinching, but Elodia only stared mutinously at the older woman, refusing to cry out no matter how hard the cane came down.

On the fifth strike, the door to the room opened and the headmistress entered followed by a dark-skinned Indian girl who wore an expression of grim satisfaction. Ada let out a small sigh of relief at the sight of her. Headmistress Pollitt was a stern woman but not unkind. Her curvy figure was bound by the severe lines of her dark green dress and her auburn hair was swept back into a utilitarian bun at the nape of her neck.

"Miss Harding," Headmistress Pollitt called out as she approached. "I've heard there was some trouble. What exactly is going on here?"

"This girl struck another student; I was simply disciplining her as our Lord Jesus dictates. 'If thy right hand causeth you to sin,' and so forth."

"According to Miss Mason here," Headmistress Pollitt said gesturing to the brown-skinned girl, "Our new student was being attacked by Miss Hill. Is that an inaccurate statement?"

"Well—"

"No, it isn't, Headmistress Pollitt," Ada replied, mustering up what courage she had. "It's true."

"Miss Harding, see to it that all four girls who attacked Miss Thornfield receive the same punishment as Miss Hawthorne."

"Yes, Headmistress."

"Miss Hawthorne, Miss Thornfield, Miss Mason, come along with me," the headmistress said and ushered them from the room. Ada wasn't certain what she'd expected when they all reached the headmistress's office, but a chocolate biscuit wasn't it.

Headmistress Pollitt watched them for a moment as they ate their biscuits before heaving a sigh. "Miss Hawthorne, you know that I'm going to have to account for your behavior, however warranted it was."

Elodia looked up at her in surprise "But—"

"Even in defense of another student," she cut in. "Striking a peer is unacceptable."

"What about Miss Harding?" Ada interjected, unable to keep quiet anymore.

"She is a capable teacher," the headmistress replied.

"She ripped up my letter."

"What?" Her brown eyes went wide with shock.

Ada pulled the fragments she'd managed to grab from her pocket and showed them. "I tried to explain that Miss Hawthorne was trying to get back my brother's letter and she ripped it to shreds."

"I didn't know about that," she glanced at Miss Hawthorne

who confirmed with a nod, before turning to Miss Mason.

"I'd already run to get you, Headmistress," she replied in lightly accented English.

Mrs. Pollitt closed her eyes and took a deep breath before shaking her head. When her eyes opened again her jaw twitched in frustration. "I am sorry for that, Miss Thornfield. I know how important letters are when you're away from home for the first time." Her warm brown eyes flicked over each of the girls before she smiled. "I think it best that you three stick together from now on. I could allow you three to share Miss Hawthorne's room if that is agreeable to you all. It was built to hold four girls so it should be up to the task."

"Really?" Elodia asked eagerly.

"Yes, under the strict understanding that you start no more fights with students no matter what words they use." Headmistress Pollitt stared at Elodia, her face a firm mask. "Do we have an agreement?"

"Yes!" Miss Mason said before glancing at them nervously. "I mean…"

"We have an agreement," Elodia replied.

"Excellent. Take your new dorm mates to your room Miss Hawthorne. I will arrange for your things to be transferred Miss Thornfield and Miss Mason."

"Thank you."

Ada stood and left the office with her two accomplices. When the day began, she never imagined she'd end it with two new friends. She glanced at Miss Mason and offered a smile.

"Thank you, I don't know what we would have done if you hadn't thought to get the headmistress."

"Sarah Hill is a menace," she replied shaking her head. "I didn't want to fight her, but I certainly wasn't going to let her get away with what she'd done."

"Your timing was impeccable."

"It wasn't much at all."

"Nonsense. A little back up at the right moment can go a long way." Elodia stuck out her hand to Miss Mason. "Miss Elodia Hawthorne, the one you helped save is Miss Adelaide Thornfield. And you are?"

"Miss Regina Mason."

"Very pleased to meet you. Welcome to the troublesome triumvirate." Elodia hooked her arms with Regina and Adelaide's before continuing down the hall with them side by side.

"Proud to be a member," Regina replied with a mischievous grin.

"Speaking of, do you really think we can avoid any more altercations while we are here?" Ada asked. Even with the inducement of staying close to these delightful girls, it seemed an impossible thing to promise.

"Well, strictly speaking we never promised not to get into any more fights with Sarah," Elodia began, shooting a smirk at Ada that reminded her of her brother for the briefest moment. A look he always wore before he sprung a trap she had been too slow-witted to discern.

"Indeed, we promised not to start them," Regina finished with a wink.

CHAPTER ONE

Thornfield House
London, May 1851

BRIGHTON. ADA STARED at the letter in her hands from Regina inviting her to accompany her, her parents—the Captain and Mrs. Mason—and Elodia to the seaside for a mini break and sea bathing. According to Regina, her parents had offered the invitation as a way to make up for the fact that she wouldn't be able to fully partake in the season.

Ada had never been to Brighton, and the idea of sea bathing sounded wonderful. She knew better than to ask her brother to take her. She didn't know if it was due to their parents dying in a shipwreck or too many storms at sea when he went to China with their father, but Zhenyi hated the ocean and staying by the seaside. If she was lucky and he was feeling generous, however, she could get his permission to go without him. After all it wasn't as if she would be unchaperoned. She looked down at the letter again and reread it. It said they were leaving the day after tomorrow. It had arrived yesterday…

Damn, they were leaving tomorrow. Regina had her own strategy for her parents and it tended towards ambush. Ada rolled her eyes and headed from the family sitting room to her brother's study. He'd need to be distracted or in a good mood for him to give his permission on such short notice.

She peeked around the open door and saw him perched on

the large oak desk, reading a letter. He was a handsome man, from his high cheekbones and wide heavily lashed eyes to his olive toned skin and the wealth of dark hair he always wore a touch too long. His slim, elegant frame was clothed in a dark green brocade waistcoat and a snow-white shirt with a copper paisley cravat and fitted brown trousers. As usual his jacket was missing.

He wasn't frowning, which was usually a good sign. The sweet faced sister approach would likely be effective. She clasped her hands behind her back and walked towards him.

"Brother," she asked in their mother's language, Mandarin. They always spoke it whenever they were alone together. He hummed in acknowledgement, but his eyes didn't move from the paper. "Do you have a moment?"

"Exactly a moment, I'm meeting Basil for lunch."

His friend from school? She remembered a skinny boy with kind blue eyes. "Oh, that's nice."

"What is it A'Wei?" he asked. She was always A'Wei to him. His mèimei. Never Adelaide or Ada.

"May I go with Ellie and Gigi to Brighton?"

That earned his attention for a moment as he glanced up at her. "Brighton?"

"Yes, Gigi's parents are taking her, and they've extended an invitation to Ellie and me."

"Captain Mason certainly has a strong constitution if he is able to cope with all of you," Zhenyi commented, moving around to sit behind his desk.

Ada flopped heavily into a chair fighting back waves of irritation. No one was more infuriating than her brother when he was in the mood to tease.

"It is certainly true what the poets say, sister," he continued as he opened the tome of a ledger and flipped to the marked page. "Nothing is lighter than a woman."

She pulled an unladylike face at him, and he smiled knowingly although his eyes stayed on his book. He always knew too much as if he could see everything. "You have no reason to say 'no', Gigi's parents will be there."

"Silly girl, I don't need a reason," he replied giving her a pitying look.

"You said that you were going on a trip in a few days. I'm twenty years old after all, there is no reason for me to stay here by myself."

"It's unseemly for a young girl to be so out and about. Aren't you all meant to be quiet and unseen?" he asked, opening a second letter.

She rolled her eyes, "Not in the middle of the season, brother."

"If you are in your season, then why are you running away to Brighton?"

"Well Gigi already has a fiancé, and we want to keep her company because she is in low spirits." He didn't comment on that. "You're meant to be escorting me around. Why are you leaving me behind?"

"Because with a personality such as yours, getting you married will be expensive," he replied glibly, and her mouth dropped open in outrage. Just as she was about to retort, he frowned and rose to his feet slowly, eyes fixed on the paper in front of him. "I have to go."

"But what about Brighton?" she asked as he grabbed his dark brown jacket from the back of his chair and started for the door. "Zhenyi!" she cried, stomping her foot in exasperation. He paused in the doorway and turned slowly, a disconcertingly stern look on his face.

"Come here to me," he said evenly. Ada watched him for a moment, wondering if he was playing a trick on her. She'd lost count of the times he'd made her believe he was angry just to get her to concede quickly. He tilted his head expectantly and lifted one eyebrow. There was no humor in those dark eyes, or the sharp angles of his face. No, he wasn't joking this time. Other than being her elder, Zhenyi was her guardian. Their mother would never have countenanced her disrespecting him by calling him by his name, especially their family name, but he was goading her on purpose.

Perhaps she had gone too far. It was never easy to tell with him.

Ada clasped her hands behind her back and walked over to stand before him, her eyes fixed on the floor. His hands came up and a moment too late she realized his intent. He cupped her face in both his palms and pressed her cheeks firmly between them. She cried out, her hands grabbing on his wrists futilely as his frown deepened comically. *Damn.*

"What did you call me?" he asked.

"Let go!" she cried out, her speech garbled. She had always hated when he did this even as a child. He'd grab hold of her face and squeeze it or pinch her cheeks until she conceded.

"Answer me first, think it over well." He exerted a touch more effort.

"Zhenyi, I called you Zhenyi," she muttered.

"And what am I to you?" he raised one imperious eyebrow.

"My brother, you're my elder brother!" she cried.

He released her face and gave her a smug nod. "That's correct."

She frowned at him and cupped her tender cheeks in her palms while she pouted. "I hate when you do that."

"And you never see it coming," he replied with a wistful sigh. "Can Miss Mason take you to the concert tonight?"

"Are you not coming?" she asked, still holding her face.

"I'll have to meet you there, sister, there is something I need to see to first."

"Is something wrong?" she glanced at the letter in his hand.

"Nothing to worry you. I'm sure it's a misunderstanding; I'll have it cleared up in no time." He kissed her forehead and patted her hair in a gentle loving gesture.

"Alright."

"And you may let Miss Mason know that you will be joining

her at Brighton," he added with a wink.

She smiled and nodded, finally dropping her hands. He was a pest and a brat but he was still the best brother in the world.

She followed him to the door and watched as he jogged down the front steps. He gave her a small wave and a smile once he reached the street, a tradition of theirs, before setting off at a brisk pace.

When he never joined her at the concert hall that night, she imagined his work had kept him away. Normally he sent notes when he would be late or absent, but she decided that it wasn't a true cause for alarm.

When Ada woke up the next morning, she began packing for Brighton. She hadn't been sea bathing in years, not since before her parents passed away. She missed the crisp, salty sea air and the immensity of the cool water. Mostly she was excited about the uninterrupted time with her two school friends Elodia and Regina. Ever since that first meeting at school they had indeed stuck together as Headmistress Pollitt had suggested. The result had been a true friendship that continued to be a source of comfort and joy even now, years later. If they tended to get into trouble upon occasion due to a shared determination to reject the unavoidable judgments of society, well, then… that was fate.

After picking out the clothing she planned to wear, she went downstairs to breakfast. Her brother never made an appearance, but that in and of itself was nothing to be alarmed about either. She didn't know when he'd arrived the night before. He was a grown man of thirty-two, and a bachelor despite his care with her.

It wasn't until she was dressed in her Prussian blue travel costume and waiting next to her trunks that news came in the form of the mill's foreman, Mr. Trent. He had been the foreman at the main branch of Durant Mills since before Ada was born.

He was introduced by the footman as she waited in the front receiving room, named the 'Plum Room' for the hand-painted plum blossoms on the wallpaper.

From his average height, pale grey eyes, and brown hair to the brown suit he wore, Mr. Trent was a familiar sight for Ada. As a little girl, whenever her father would bring her to visit the mill, Mr. Trent would always give her candies, or carry her whenever she grew too tired to keep up with their long legs. He'd been more of an uncle to her then her father's younger brother, Uncle Simon, who had never made a secret of his dislike and resentment of Ada, Zhenyi and their mother.

"Good afternoon to you, Miss Thornfield," he said as he entered, and she rose to greet him.

"And to you, Mr. Trent. I thought you were overlooking things in Cheshire. To what do I owe this surprise?"

"Begging your pardon, Miss, but I'm looking for the master."

"Richard?" Outside of their home and family he was always Richard, the name their father had given him. Only she and their mother called him Zhenyi, just as only he and their mother had called her A'Wei or Xiuwei.

"Aye, I was wondering if you'd seen him since yesterday."

"I haven't," she replied before meeting the eyes of the footman. "Thomas, did Mr. Thornfield return as yet?"

"Not since yesterday, Miss," he replied gravely.

At those words, a knot formed in Ada's stomach. Missing an engagement was one thing, but not returning home was another. Their parents had died at sea on a journey they'd taken several times. Since then, Zhenyi always made a point of making his location known. "Thank you, Thomas," she said before turning back to Mr. Trent. "What do you know?"

"I was supposed to meet him, Miss, but I saw him get snatched up and thrown into a carriage."

"That is not possible." Ada fought back a bubble of incredulous laughter.

"I'm telling you, Miss. He came out of a tea shop, and I saw them take him."

With every word the knot tightened further. Snatched and taken away with no one to help him. How had her brother fallen into such a situation? "People don't simply get snatched off the street. Why didn't you go to the police with this, Mr. Trent?"

"I thought someone could be having a laugh, so I wanted to check if he'd made it home."

She couldn't process that chain of logic. Richard didn't have many friends and none of them were the type to do such a thing as a joke. "Are you telling me that my brother was kidnapped at midday in the middle of London and the first person to bring me word of it was you?"

"I can only tell you what I saw, Miss."

Ada collapsed onto the chair as her entire body went numb. "I cannot..." she kept shaking her head. "This cannot be real. It cannot be. Grown men do not simply get snatched up like a parcel."

"London is a dangerous place, Miss. It happens more often than you'd think."

"I have to go to the constabulary."

"No, Miss. What you want is a runner. I'll look into it on your behalf, Miss. It's not good for the likes of you to be over there."

"But the constable—"

"People like this always get spooked by a copper; it could make 'em desperate and master will pay the price."

Pay the price? Ada could feel the blood drain from her face. "I hadn't thought of that."

"Best to play it safe, Miss. I'll take care of this, and I'll let you know what happens."

"Miss Hawthorne is here to see you, Miss," the footman announced before Elodia strode in, resplendent in a cobalt blue and cream traveling costume, her thick, dark curls twisted into a low chignon under her hat.

She took one look at Ada and the smile on her face melted away. "Ada, what on earth is the matter?" she walked past Mr. Trent and sat beside her on the settee, taking her hands in her own. "Your hands are like ice."

Ada pressed her forehead to Elodia's shoulder hoping her

brain would stop spinning. It was like a nightmare. How had she ended up all alone? "Ellie, it's unimaginable. Richard has been taken."

"Taken?" The word was like the crack of a whip. Ada lifted her head and saw the alarm settling over Elodia's face.

"Aye, Miss, he was taken only yesterday," Mr. Trent chimed in.

Elodia stared at her in stunned silence, her mouth opening and closing against words that wouldn't come. "Taken by whom? The Faeries?" she finally asked incredulously.

"Some thugs in a carriage. They threw him in and drove off." Taking him to God only knew where with no doubt the worst of intentions. Zhenyi wasn't a helpless man, but he was still only one person against who knew how many.

Elodia blinked in disbelief and looked over at Trent. "I can't believe this. Random kidnappings in the middle of the street? It doesn't make any sense."

"He's a wealthy man, Miss. There's a lot of people who'd take advantage if they saw a good opportunity."

"And you are?" Elodia asked, watching him carefully.

"Trent, Miss. Mr. Donald Trent."

"He's the foreman at our main silk mill, Ellie," Ada said.

"I see." She turned to Ada again. "What is being done to recover Richard?"

"Mr. Trent is going to engage a runner to track him down," Ada said.

"Not Scotland Yard? Why are they there in heaven's name?"

"Safer with a runner, Miss. Can't have them getting spooked," Trent said.

Elodia watched him for a long moment, an inscrutable expression on her face before turning to Ada, "I think you should come home with me, Ada."

"I can't leave now! What if Richard comes back? What if—"

"Consider this: the men who took your brother must have known that he was worth a good deal of money. If they know that, then they could know about you. You should be with friends. Your bags are already packed, just come home with me and stay until we know more."

"Do you think your father would mind?"

"Not if he knew the truth."

The truth. With her protector gone the viscount wouldn't waste any time contacting her Uncle Simon. The one person whose clutches she dreaded the most. They'd avoided him for most of Ada's childhood and had never given them a reason to change that habit. "I wouldn't want him to know the truth, Ellie. Mr. Trent doesn't think we should do anything to tip-off anyone, and your father might raise an alarm. I can't risk my brother."

"What do you think then?" Elodia took Ada's hand, silently urging her to keep calm.

"Where were you off to, Miss?" Trent asked.

"Brighton," Elodia replied.

"I'd go if I was you."

"I can't go to Brighton with my brother missing!" Ada replied, her eyes burning with tears. The helplessness and fear were building into a wave that threatened to overwhelm her at any moment. Everything inside her was screaming to go to the police, but what if Trent was correct? What if Trent was wrong and she wasted precious time? As an unmarried young woman of twenty, what could she even do in the end?

"Business as usual is best. By the time you come back, I'll have more for ya."

"You can't stay here alone, Ada. Come with us. It won't be for long." Elodia squeezed her hand gently. "There's nothing to be done until we know more."

"Perhaps you could stay with your uncle, Miss. Until we know more. He's in town for the season and I'd be happy to escort you there. It's good to be with family at a time like this."

The idea of Brighton was no longer as scintillating as it had been even an hour ago, but the thought of being with Uncle Simon and her insufferable cousins was unbearable. She needed

Elodia and Regina's warmth and good humor, not Uncle Simon's thinly veiled distaste, or heaven forbid, excitement over his possible good fortune. He'd want nothing else than to gain control over their family assets and remove Ada at a moment's notice. And he certainly wouldn't give a damn about finding Zhenyi. "Alright Ellie, I'll go with you."

"Excellent, I'll have the footman put your things in the Tilbury," Elodia replied before rising to her feet, "Good afternoon, Mr. Trent. I hope you are successful in your search."

"I hope so too, Miss," he replied giving her a small bow. He turned to Ada, "I'll take my leave, Miss Ada."

"Yes, of course, Mr. Trent," she replied, her mind racing with a thousand thoughts at once. "Thank you for letting me know. And let's keep this quiet for now. No need to alert my uncle to this situation for the moment."

He smiled slowly. "No problem, Miss. You and master are like family to me." He gave her a nod and left.

Giltspur Street Compter, Debtor's Prison
London, May 1851

WHEN BASIL THOMPSON had started his week, he'd expected to catch up with his old friend, Richard Thornfield, for a light lunch and good conversation. Probably acquire some advice about his upcoming nuptials. He was a reasonable man. By all accounts he was considered even-tempered and rational in his approach to most things.

In this instant, however, he was ready to ram his fist through the smug guard's face and see if he would smirk so much with half his teeth missing. Seeing Richard snatched up and carted off to Giltspur Street Compter debtors' prison was one thing, but the utter lack of due process was another. He'd followed closely behind, hoping to get a chance to speak to Richard and get an idea of what was happening, but his entry had been barred by this smug fucking jackass for the last three days.

"Let me in," he repeated, keeping his voice as level as possible. Richard always teased him about his tendency towards condescension whenever he was annoyed. If the man was going to help, the last thing Basil needed to do was talk down to him.

"Piss off, guv," the man sneered back.

Breathe Basil. Breathe. "He has a right to visitors."

"Not today he don't."

Maybe if he tried a different approach. "How much does he owe?"

"None of your business."

"I'm making it my business, you arrogant little shit."

"He stays 'ere until I hear otherwise, and he gets guests when I say he do, and today he don't. Got it?"

Basil stared at him for an enraged moment. What kind of debtor's prison took new inmates without a court order or even a basic attempt at recovering funds for the injured parties? It didn't make any sense. But he wasn't going to get anywhere with this ingrate. His only chance was to wait until someone else was on shift. Someone less enraging. If that didn't work he was prepared to take it to a magistrate himself. "I'll be back."

"And I'll be here."

Basil rolled his eyes and walked away a few steps, his mind racing over what to do. The idea of Richard being in debt was ridiculous, but he was a proud man. Was it possible he had kept it to himself? It wasn't as if Basil was better off than he was. If Richard couldn't pay the debt, Basil sure as hell couldn't make a dent in it himself, but if it had come this far there would have been no way to keep it a secret. Magistrates would have been involved, to say nothing of the newspapers and scandal sheets. Richard was many things, but careless wasn't one of them. Durant Mills had existed in one way or another for centuries from the arrival of the first Huguenot refugees in England. The Thornfield name in the textile manufacturing business had been around for well over a century. Richard's pride alone would ensure his scrupulousness with his family legacy.

"Mr. Thompson?" he heard a voice call him.

Looking over his shoulder, he saw the foreman of Durant Mills, Mr. Trent. "Mr. Trent, are you here for Richard?"

"For master?" He tilted his head in confusion.

"Yes." Had he not noticed that Richard had been missing the last few days? Richard had been bouncing between Durant and Thornfield House for weeks with the new changes he'd been pushing with housing for the workers. He'd been due for a visit within the last few days.

"The master ain't here, Lad." The older man shook his head with a small smile.

Basil blinked for a moment in confusion. "I saw them bring him through those doors."

"You're mistaken."

Basil turned and pointed to the guard who was watching them with interest. "Go and ask that smirking little shit over there, ask him if he's holding Richard Thornfield."

"All right, Lad, settle down." Trent patted Basil on the shoulder and ambled over to the guard. They exchanged a few words before Trent heaved a deep sigh and walked back over to Basil. "He said he ain't ever heard of him."

Basil saw red. "You little fucker!" he cried charging forward. Trent grabbed hold of him, yanking him back from the gate as the city guards patrolling the street took an interest. Never heard of him? What the fuck was he playing at?

"Let it go, Lad. Let it go."

He felt like he was losing his mind. Did he have the wrong prison? Had he been mistaken this whole time? No, that was impossible. The guard knew who Basil was talking about, but now he was claiming ignorance of his existence. What was happening here? "Richard is in there."

"I believe ya, but we won't get in like this. Let me handle it."

The red haze cleared for a moment as Basil turned his attention back to Trent. At the end of the day, no matter how close Trent had been to the late Mr. Thornfield, Richard was only Trent's employer, not his brother or friend. Basil wasn't so naïve as to imagine that professional loyalty translated into personal investment. The man was too calm by half. As if the news didn't strike him as odd or even surprising. Basil's suspicious nature was beginning to take hold. "You'll get him out?"

"I have some connections here; I'll work them and get more information on it. Then I'll meet up with you and we'll put our heads together."

Far, far too calm. He hadn't even blinked when he heard the news, as if it wasn't a surprise to him at all. There was no sense of urgency in him to match his words. If he was trying to placate Basil and appear reassuring, he was failing spectacularly. "Why are you here then, Mr. Trent?"

"What?" The man blinked as if the question was confusing.

"If you aren't here for Richard, who were you coming to visit?"

"No one, I was just passing by."

It took every ounce of self-control Basil had to keep his growing suspicion from his face. Just passing by a debtor's prison clear across town and far from where he lived or worked. Nothing suspicious there. "Ah, understood. A walk is good exercise I'm told."

"Right you are, sir. It is must be providence that I found you here."

Basil took a deep breath and nodded in agreement. Whatever had befallen Richard, Trent was almost certainly at the center of it. Who knew how long it would have taken for him to piece this together if he hadn't seen him here? Basil wasn't in a hurry to let him out of his sight, but he was very keen to keep every point of recourse squarely in his hands. Trent had made the first move, but Basil now had the element of surprise. *Providence indeed.* "You are right, I suppose. You'll probably have more luck than I at this point."

"Just leave it to me, sir."

"Very good, Trent." Basil tipped his hat and walked away, feeling the beady eyes of Trent burning into his back until he turned the corner. Then he stopped and backtracked until the gate to the prison was in view. He needed a visual confirmation of what he suspected. Trent was indeed speaking to the guard again, but this time they were far more friendly with each other. Then he patted the man on the back and walked through the gate.

Right... Basil turned and walked away. He needed reinforcements.

CHAPTER TWO

"So where'd you put him, Oliver?" Trent asked the guard, after checking to make sure Basil Thompson was gone.

"Ian's got him in the empty storeroom," Oliver replied. "Nobody'll be there for at least a week."

Trent nodded and began to walk away but Oliver grabbed his arm. "What?" Trent asked, keeping the annoyance out of his voice. Who did this little shit think he was, putting his hands on him?

"Who's that toff? Is he gonna be a problem?"

"Nah. He ain't nothin," he assured him. And if he became a problem, he'd be easy enough to deal with. Skinny men like him, like Thornfield, with soft hands and posh accents broke easily against real men. Men with dirt under their nails.

"I don't want no trouble."

"And there won't be. Just follow my lead, eh?"

Oliver nodded and released his arm. Trent adjusted his jacket and walked on, crossing the inner courtyard and heading for the back rooms. The unit in question was on the far side of the prison. It was quiet. Quieter than he'd been expecting if he was honest. Thornfield was a proud man. He'd expected him to be shouting his innocence and demanding an audience with magistrates to clear his name.

When he opened the door, he found Thornfield sitting on the floor, his back straight and his eyes closed. He didn't even look upset. Had to be some kind of heathen practice. When the dim light hit his face, Thornfield's eyes opened and fixed on him. There was no surprise there, no reaction other than the slow breath he released. The little bastard was trying to rattle him.

Fat chance. "Well, fancy seeing you here," Trent said, closing the door behind him and leaning against the wall.

Thornfield's dark eyes burned with anger, but he said nothing.

"I'll bet you never saw this coming, did ya? Don't look at me like that. It's your own fault I did this. I've been working under your type, running your businesses all my life, and you think you can take that money and piss it away on workers? As if they deserve it more than me. Your father knew better than to waste his money, but you... you're a bleedin' heart just like the rest of those jumped-up toffs with their middle-class morality and their high and mighty ideals."

Still, Thornfield remained silent, watching him with seething contempt. As if he had the right to judge him when he was too stupid to see him coming. His father had been too caught up in his wife and two brats to notice what Trent had skimmed off the surface. This narrow-eyed crossbreed was another matter altogether. He'd been trusting enough the first couple years but those dark eyes missed nothing once they started looking. Soon after the questions had begun, Trent had to ease off rather than risk more scrutiny. But there were others who understood Trent's position, who were ready to help Trent get the respect and compensation he deserved.

"It's fine though, I'll get mine anyway. All I have to do is keep your little sis out the way while I handle business. Once I get my money from your offices, I'll be free and clear."

"Will you?" When Thornfield finally spoke, his voice was almost curious. Something else was there instead of anger. Was he amused?

"Will I what?" he asked.

"Be 'free and clear'?"

"You think I don't have a plan? I've got friends in high places same as you. We've been cooking this up ever since you started with those weavers from Ireland. No one knows you're even missing and the ones that do, don't even know you're here."

"For now."

For now? What was that supposed to mean? Why wasn't he more anxious? Did he think he was going to get away easily? Did he think that Trent wasn't ready for anything? "You think you have the run of this town, don'tcha? Cause you got money? This here is my town boy, my London, my England. Ain't no one's gonna notice you're missing or care about where you a

"Except for Ada."

"That little miss is the least of my worries. I have her eating out of my hand."

Thornfield's slow smile was an unspoken challenge. "Despite what you clearly think, I will get out of here. I will hunt you down. And if you hurt a hair on my sister's head, I will dispose of you piece by piece."

Something about him had Trent's stomach twisting in alarm. It wasn't natural. He'd already been beaten, only a fool didn't know when to admit defeat. "Tough talk from a man in shackles," Trent replied before leaving the room and slamming the door shut behind him. That little shit wasn't going to rattle him. Everything was in hand, all he needed was a fortnight to get the money from his simple crossbred sister to his debtors. A fortnight and he would be living the life he was always meant to have.

CHAPTER THREE

1811 Garret Street
Pimlico, London

BASIL NEEDED HELP fast, and there was only one person he trusted: his and Richard's friend from Cambridge, Leo. They had formed a formidable friendship over the years. Richard and Leo's mothers had always left their homes open even when Basil's parents had proven to be less welcoming. After school, Leo had gone into the military and served in India before returning home to join The Metropolitan Police Force. He'd left the police force only a year before to work as a private investigator. Establishing himself quickly meant he was busy, so catching him at home with his mother was a matter of luck. If this gamble didn't work out, then he'd have to wait to speak to him.

Basil knocked on the familiar grey door and waited impatiently until it opened to reveal the housekeeper, a slim stern-faced woman named Mrs. Kemp. Her blue eyes fell on him and narrowed playfully even as they warmed.

"Trouble," she grumbled, shaking her head.

"Mrs. Kemp," he took her by the arms, "Is Leo home?"

"Aye, just. He's in the front sitting room with the Missus," she said stepping aside for him to enter. He handed her his hat and gloves and walked down the hall and up the stairs to the family sitting room. The house was immaculate as always and modestly furnished, but there were small paintings everywhere, done by Leo's late father, of meadows, of his family, and of a large stone house near a lake with a yellow door.

Leo sat beside his mother, Naomi Kingston, on the blue sofa having tea. Based on the coat flung across the back of a chair, Leo had just returned. Naomi would never have allowed discarded clothing to clutter her otherwise immaculate sitting room for long. She had always been a proud and warm-hearted woman, wrapping her coarse hair with bright turbans which, while unfashionable, always matched her dresses perfectly. He knocked on the doorframe and her hazel brown eyes found him first.

"So you still remember to come see me?" Naomi asked, shaking her head with a pursed mouth.

Despite his anxiety over Richard, Basil couldn't help the small chuckle or the bittersweet mix of fondness and guilt that welled up in him at the sight of her. It was true, he didn't visit her nearly as often as he should now that Leo was more often than not away from home. She'd been like a second mother to him, ceremony was no excuse. He crossed over to her and kissed both her cheeks before raising her hand to his mouth and pressing a kiss on the back of it. "My apologies, my lady."

"It will take more than that for my forgiveness," she replied but her grip on his hand tightened in an affectionate squeeze. "Sit down, boy. I'll fix you a cup of tea."

"Don't. I can't stay for long."

"Something's wrong?" Leo was still seated, watching him carefully with his mother's light brown eyes. He wasn't smiling or frowning, and he didn't offer any other greeting. Leo knew this wasn't a social call.

"How could you possibly know that?" Basil asked.

"You look more uptight than usual. It seems impending marriage doesn't agree with everyone." He shot a pointed look at his mother who shook her head in bemusement.

It wasn't exactly a criticism, but Basil still fought the instinct to argue against the notion that he was high strung as a matter of course. "This has nothing to do with Miss Ashwood, thank you very much Leo, and I am not an uptight person."

"I beg to differ. Don't argue, Bas, just tell me what's wrong."

He hated when he did that, but there were more important things to discuss. Like their friend's abduction. "It's Richard. He's been taken."

"What do you mean taken?" Leo asked, sitting up straighter in his seat.

"I mean he got rounded up by two men, thrown into a wagon, and taken away to Giltspur."

"When was this?"

"Three days ago," Basil said.

"That rich boy got sent to debtor's prison?" Naomi asked incredulously, glancing at Leo.

"He was put there, but I don't know that he was sent there, exactly," Basil said.

She turned back to Basil. "What's the difference?"

"No one ends up in debtor's prison without creditors making an attempt to get money first. Loudly. There has to be court order given by magistrates," Leo explained, a slight frown the only indication of his concern. That cool head under pressure had saved them and no doubt him countless times before, and Basil was counting on it to find a solution again.

"Exactly," Basil said. "There's been no hint of that at all. They supposedly just came for him."

Leo stood and began pacing, his arms crossed over his torso and one hand collaring his bronzed neck, rubbing at it absentmindedly. "And you are sure he's at Giltspur?" he asked.

"Positive. I grabbed a hackney and followed the wagon all the way there. I watched it pass through the gates. I've been trying to get in there ever since but the guard wouldn't allow me in to see him. Today, he denied knowledge of Richard's existence entirely."

"Now that is interesting."

"Sit down, boy, you're breaking my neck," she complained and Basil immediately sat in a chair, leaning forward with his elbows on his knees to keep his feet from tapping with nervous energy.

"Did they see you following them?"

"No. I don't think so. Trent was there, but I feel as though he's involved somehow."

"Trent." Leo paused and glanced at Basil. "Isn't he at one of the mills? The foreman Richard fell out with?"

"Yes."

"What's his story?"

"I have no idea. I assumed he was there to help at first."

"But?"

"But he barely reacted at all to Richard being detained. He just denied it, calm as you like, and walked in to find out more. When I asked him what he was doing there if he wasn't there for Richard, he spun a story about simply going for a walk."

"Past a debtor's prison?" Naomi asked skeptically.

"As one does," Leo replied, his tone bone dry. Their incredulous expressions were a balm to Basil's nerves. He'd known he wasn't delusional but if Leo and Naomi Kingston smelt a rat, something was rotten.

"You think the guards are working with Trent?" Naomi asked Basil.

"I don't know. All I know is I need Leo to help me look into it and find out if there is an order for him to be sent there, and if there isn't, what the hell is going on. We have to get him out." He looked at Leo. "I know you're always busy but are you free to help me?"

"I am for this," Leo replied, and the relief that flooded Basil was nearly overwhelming. He didn't know what he would have done if Leo wasn't able to help. "First things first, assuming Trent's after money or worse, Richard's sister is vulnerable."

"Adelaide?"

"Yes. Is she in London?"

"I have no idea. Why would she be in London?"

Leo stared at him for a long moment. "For the season Basil."

"What?" The season? She was far too young to be out in society already. "She's only sixteen isn't she? Seventeen?"

Leo shook his head as if mystified by Basil's ignorance. "She'd be twenty by now, if not already past it."

Twenty? How had she gotten to that age? Try as he might, he couldn't conjure an image of Richard's sister as a woman. The last image of her in his mind was of a skinny, pale girl with wide, dark eyes and an expressive face running after Richard like a shadow. She had been effervescent and sweet as a girl. He couldn't remember if he'd seen her past their parents' funeral. "Ah. It's rude to dwell upon a lady's age."

Leo took a deep breath and continued to speak. "We have to consider he may have reached out to her already. She's young, relatively sheltered, and entirely alone to say nothing of the fact that she has no idea he isn't trustworthy. She is a prime target to extract money. Do you know where she is?"

"No, but I suppose I'll start with Richard's London house and make my way from there."

"Find her and get her to safety." He turned to his mother and rested a hand on her shoulder, "Mother will you send a note with my apologies to Mr. Willis? I have to move his case back."

"Of course," she replied, patting his hand.

He looked to Basil again, "I'll put out feelers on my end and see what I can find out for you. Meet me back here tomorrow."

Basil stood and walked over to him, clasping his forearm in a grateful grip. "Thank you,"

"Don't. He is my friend too."

Melbroke House
Brighton, three days later

ADA WAS FIGHTING to keep her spirits up. She didn't know if she was succeeding or if her friends were making a point of ignoring her silences. She wanted silence, but she was terrified of being alone with her thoughts. Everything was focusing and refocusing on her brother. Who could have a grudge against him? Who would wish to harm him to this level?

It's true there were always those like her bullies at school who despised her mixed heritage and resented the wealth and privilege she enjoyed despite it. But hurtful pranks were different to kidnapping someone and subjecting them to all kinds of humiliations. Zhenyi had always looked after her. He'd comforted her when she was afraid, defended and protected her from harm or her parents' censure. After their parents' deaths, he'd always taken time to visit her at school, bring her treats or gifts, write to her so she didn't feel lonely. Who could protect him now? Was he cold or hungry? Every day that passed dawned with fresh dread in her heart at the ominous silence from Trent. A light touch on her arm brought her attention to Elodia who was watching her expectantly. How long had she been waiting?

"I'm sorry, Ellie. What did you say?" she asked.

"More tea?" Elodia looked down at the now stone-cold oolong in the bone china clutched between Ada's hands.

"I—" she stopped herself. She'd only waste it at this point. "Perhaps not, Ellie. I don't think a fresh cup would fare better than this one."

Elodia nodded and topped off her own cup.

"What were we discussing?" Ada asked, trying to make an effort to participate.

"Well, I wanted to go for another walk on the shore, but Miss Regina here," she paused to glare playfully at Regina, "refuses because when we went five days ago she apparently saw a gentleman in the altogether and didn't say a word about it."

Ada looked over at her South Asian friend in surprise. What naked man? How had she missed that? "Was he handsome?"

"I don't know. I wasn't looking at his face."

Ada choked back a laugh and placed down her cup and saucer. Regina had a way with words that bordered on obscene without even trying.

"What exactly had caught your attention Miss Mason?" Elodia asked fluttering her eyelashes.

"Nothing, I was too busy getting out of there," Regina replied frankly, cradling her cup of tea. "What if he'd seen us? I would die of mortification."

"What if you met him again?" Elodia said, "How would you be able to form an acquaintance if you don't recognize him?"

"What if he recognized me and I had to face that circumstance. I'd rather swim in the Thames," she said with a shudder.

"What if he were the one you were meant to marry?" Elodia asked.

"I know who I'm going to marry," Regina replied rolling her eyes. "I've known since I was sixteen. I don't think my mother and father would allow me to marry anyone else at this point. The minute Lord Reginald Starkley returns from the continent, I will become his baroness."

"Nonsense. We'll steal you away before we let you marry that walrus, won't we Ada?" Elodia said before turning to Ada expectantly.

Ada gave her a small smile and nodded. She felt ungrateful. Her friends were doing everything they could to distract her from her brother's troubles, but she was unable to keep her mind from him for long. Elodia and Regina had been particularly mischievous over the past few days at Brighton. It had nearly driven the captain and his Maharashtrian wife to distraction. The sea-bathing had been truly wonderful, and when they were splashing in the ocean, Ada could allow her mind to drift. But times like now or at night, it was harder to forget that her brother was gone and that she may never get him back.

"Ada?" Regina called her name again and she snapped to attention, noticing the expectant gazes of her two friends.

"What?"

"Ellie invited us to the opera with her and her father when we return to London. They're playing *Lucia di Lammermoor*."

"Oh, thank you. That will be wonderful." She tried to smile but from the eyebrow Regina raised in response, her attempt was in vain.

"Will it? You look as though we're trying to take you to the dentist for a tooth pulling."

"No, I mean it. I'll be happy to go. Thank you for thinking of me, Ellie." She tried to smile again. Elodia nodded and squeezed her hand.

"Frankly, I don't see the point of pretending everything is all right anymore." Regina said setting down her tea cup and flopping backwards in the chair.

"Gigi," Elodia hissed.

"Well, it's not as if it's working, and no one is here to overhear."

"Wait…" Ada said as the sound of raised voices filtered through. "Do you hear that?"

She stood and walked over to the parlor door, opening it a sliver. The scene before her was something out of a comic opera. Ingsley, the butler, and another footman were physically restraining a tall, brown-haired man who was having little success in freeing himself.

"Let me in," the man growled.

"Your name and business, sir," Ingsley said, sneaking his arm around the man's neck.

"I've already told as much to that selectively mute footman over there, now let me pass."

"I'm afraid that won't be possible, sir."

"Is Miss Thornfield here?" the man asked.

At that, she shrank back in caution. How did he know her? Had the kidnappers come for her? Where was Mr. Trent?

"I beg your pardon?" Ingsley blinked in confusion and that was all the man needed to wriggle an arm free and plant his elbow in Ingsley's side, creating an opening for him to jerk out of his and the footman's grasp.

He let out a frustrated huff and dragged his hands back

through his hair. "Miss Adelaide Thornfield, is she here?" The footman started forward and the man's hands came up to fend off the attack.

Wait. She knew that voice. Her mind raced trying to place him, but she could hardly see his face, especially now that he was moving, trying to avoid being pinned between the footman and the wall despite once again being caught in his clutches. She knew she had heard his voice before, but she couldn't be certain until she saw him.

"Who is Harris fighting?" Elodia asked.

"I don't know but he knows who I am," Ada replied, making a decision. She wouldn't hide away like a mouse. Even if he proved to be untrustworthy, she was safe enough. If he couldn't get past Ingsley or Harris all she needed to do was stay far enough away. She pushed open the door and stepped out into the hallway.

"Don't go out there, Ada!" Elodia hissed, but Ada ignored her. At her appearance, the men froze and turned to her. Once she saw the unknown gentleman's face her eyes widened in shock. *Basil.* He was older, but that sharp, pale face was unmistakable even if his jaw was now covered with a light beard and his hair was a touch longer. It was him.

"It's all right, Harris. I know him," she said.

Harris halted immediately, and Basil threw him off with a force that was... unexpected. Ada didn't know what to make of it, or the effect it had on her, but she stumbled out of the way when Basil strode down the hall and past her into the room. She followed him in and watched in alarm as he slammed the door in Harris's face.

"Basil, what is the meaning of this?"

He turned to face her and she was struck by the intensity and color of his eyes. Crystal blue almost the color of a summer sky. "I apologize for my behavior, but it is paramount that I speak with you. I've been trying to find you for three days." He scanned the room and took in the two other young women who were staring at him with a mix of fascination and alarm. "Miss Mason, Miss Hawthorne," he greeted, giving them each a slight bow. Regina's mouth had fallen open slightly, her doe eyes going even wider. "How do you know who we are?" Elodia asked.

"I've heard stories about the three of you from Richard." He turned back to Ada. "Do you know where your brother is?"

"I know that he's missing," Ada replied, glancing at Elodia and Regina.

"Missing?" His eyes narrowed in consternation.

Did he know something? "Do you know his whereabouts?" Ada asked, crossing over to him and clutching his arm with unwitting candor. "Oh, it's good that you are here. I've been desperate for news about him. Mr. Trent has been looking but—"

"Mr. Trent told you that your brother was *missing*?" Basil asked, his words slow and deliberate.

"Yes... is something wrong?" she asked, apprehension flooding her with each passing moment.

He shook his head, the concern on his face turning grim. "You cannot trust Trent, Ada."

Her head was shaking in rejection of those words before he could finish the sentence. Trent was the closest thing she had to an ally. He was working with her, not against her. "I've known him all my life," she argued. "Longer than I've known you in fact."

"I understand that, but—"

The door opened again, and they turned to see Ingsley standing in the doorway watching them carefully. "A Mr. Trent here to see you, Miss," Ingsley said.

Basil gripped her arms in his hands, his touch firm but not uncomfortable, drawing Ada's attention back to him. "Please, Ada. Please trust me this once, and I will explain everything later."

It took her a moment of staring into his eyes before she nodded her consent. Basil had long been a friend to her brother, as close as Elodia or Regina to her. The chances that he would be working against Zhenyi were low and the anxiety on his face was making her nervous.

Mr. Trent had been a fixture in her life from the time she could understand. Her parents never let her or her brother forget the source of their wealth and prestige, or the people who made it possible. But from what little she remembered of Basil, he wasn't a man given to theatrics. If he was this worried it was only because there was something to be worried about. Could Mr. Trent have become so bitter and confused as to turn on her and her brother?

"Ingsley, wait a few minutes and then let Mr. Trent in," Ada said, and Basil gave her a grateful nod.

"Very good, Miss," Ingsley replied.

"Ingsley, does Mr. Trent know that Mr. Thompson is here?" Regina asked.

"No, Miss Mason."

"Keep it that way for now," she said.

"As you say, Miss." He gave her a nod and left.

"Gigi, I think we had better show Mr. Thompson into the next room," Elodia said.

"We can't leave her alone with Mr. Trent if he's a blaggard!"

"Then you go with Mr. Thompson. It will be less suspicious if I stay here with her. Trent has met me before."

"Nonsense, you go with Mr. Thompson. My mother would skin me alive if she found me alone with another man. And after all, it is my father's house."

"Why don't you both stay with her," Basil suggested.

Elodia nodded and stood. "Right then, come along Mr. Thompson," she said, escorting Basil over to the adjoining door, shutting it behind him.

Ada walked over to the door and opened it before seating herself between Regina and Elodia.

Moments later Trent entered.

Ada smiled at him and gestured for him to sit.

"Mr. Trent, what an unexpected surprise to see you here."

"Yes... I'd hoped to have good news when I saw you next, Miss, but I cannot give you satisfaction there." He sat down in the chair, leaning back comfortably.

"Your constable has found nothing?" Ada asked, paying attention to his posture.

"Nothing at all. And it's been days now."

Was he too arrogant or did he think she would be too overwrought to notice? "That is concerning. And there is no one at all that we could call on? Who have you spoken to?"

"I've been trying to manage things during your brother's absence. I haven't had time for too many inquiries." He rubbed his forehead, shaking his head wearily.

"Richard is hardly unknown. He's been running the business for at least six years now, Mr. Trent, and even before that he wasn't exactly hidden away." Ada was getting a horrible feeling that he was checking off a list of possible concerns she could have instead of showing worry for her predicament.

"This is true," he said turning his attention to her as if he'd never considered the possibility. Or perhaps he hadn't considered her before. It had never occurred to her before now, but it was clear Trent underestimated her.

"The owner of a hundred- and fifty-year-old business does not go missing without a trace. What is the name of your runner? I will make inquiries myself."

"Best to leave it to me, Miss. It's dangerous work that, it's not for the likes of you."

"You cannot expect me to sit here and do nothing." Regina's hand closed around Ada's in a silent warning. If she pushed too far or showed a blatant distrust for him it would put him on his guard. Ada drew a deep calming breath and released it.

"Perhaps it's time for my father to make inquiries, Ada," Elodia said. Ada looked at her, noted the chill in her eyes. Elodia wasn't one who excelled at games or pretending, and she was losing patience with Trent and his evasions.

"Your father?" Trent scoffed. Elodia stiffened, and Ada's hand grabbed hers reflexively.

"The Viscount Melbroke will surely have more access to resources than you, Mr. Trent," Regina replied, while Ada studied him with new awareness. It was terrifying to see how manufactured his behavior was when only an hour ago she would have believed all of it.

"Oh, begging your pardon, Miss. In my day viscounts' daughters didn't look like you." Trent replied with a meekness that Ada almost believed, if it wasn't for the sickening feeling in her stomach coloring his every action and word with suspicion.

"I assure you, Mr. Trent, there have always been viscounts with daughters like me, even in your day," Elodia replied with a regal hint of steel in her voice. "In any event, I will speak to my father about this and see if he cannot do better."

"I couldn't advise it, Miss," Trent replied, his eyes fixing on Elodia explicitly. "Men like this, they ain't the kind to let a titled gent get in their way. What if he went missing and all? You'd all be in danger then."

It was meant to sound reasonable but somehow it felt like a threat. The small smile on Trent's face had a sharp chill creeping up Ada's spine like frost on a window. What had he done? Who did he have on his side that would result in this level of boldness?

"I don't imagine the Viscount Melbroke means to engage in a round of fisticuffs with a criminal, Mr. Trent," she replied, hoping her anxiety didn't show in her voice.

"That's fair enough, I suppose," he replied, watching her closely as if he were sizing her up again and taking note of things he'd missed before. "I was only thinking of master and getting him back safely to you and all. Have you heard anything, Miss?"

The question seemed sudden. Her mind raced for an innocent explanation as to why he would ask it, desperate for a reason to believe in him but nothing was coming. "Anything about what?" she asked.

"Any rumors flying about? Anyone asking questions?"

Was he fishing for information? Did he know Basil was here?

"No. No one is aware Richard is missing outside of the present company."

"Anyone reached out to you about a ransom or anything?"

"Do you imagine the kidnappers are aware that I am in Brighton with friends?" she asked.

"Well, people will talk, Miss. You can't pay heed to everything. I wonder if it would be better if you were with your uncle."

"Why?" Ada asked carefully, while alarm bells sounded in her head.

"Well, I'll need to leave London soon for Cheshire. It would be easier on my conscience if knew you were with family."

"I don't think there's any reason for you to be concerned for my safety, Mr. Trent."

"With respect, Miss, I didn't think I needed to be concerned about your brother either until recently. Always better to err on the side of caution I say. Wouldn't want anything bad to happen to you as well, especially with the culprits on the loose."

Indeed. "That is true, but you needn't concern yourself to deliver me to him, Mr. Trent. The viscount would be more than equal to the task in the event that it is deemed necessary."

"I believe it would be best if I take you, Miss. Wouldn't want to arouse any suspicion. If they can get your brother, you can be sure they know all about you. They'll be watching you."

"Then they should take note that while I may be novel, I am hardly friendless," Ada replied, giving him what she hoped was a sincere-looking smile. She rose to her feet on unsteady legs. "You would of course, be welcome to visit me at my uncle's home, Mr. Trent," she said.

"We can be ready by tomorrow," Elodia said rising to her feet as well.

"Oh, I'd need a bit more than that, Miss," Trent said rising to his feet. She gestured to the door and took his arm, leading him from the room. Elodia stood but one look from her kept her friend where she was. She was sure of herself now as she led Trent to the front door. She needed to get as far away from Trent as possible or find a way to protect herself from whatever he was planning.

"How long will it take for you to conclude your business in London, Mr. Trent?"

"Few days, a week at most," he replied easily.

A week at most. A lot could happen in a week. Ada smiled, the first real smile she'd given since he entered the room. "Perfect. I'll look forward to receiving you at my uncle's estate."

He nodded, ceding the battle and left.

Chapter Four

When Ada returned to the sitting room, Regina and Elodia were seated together on the sofa. Basil was pacing back and forth. Where would she be if he hadn't come to warn her? She wanted to believe she would have noticed something was wrong on her own, but she couldn't be sure. So much was still unknown. When he saw her return, he paused, his arms dropping to his sides. In his face was the concern and anxiety Trent had failed to show.

"Are you all right?" he asked.

She walked over to the window overlooking the street and wrapped her arms around her torso. She watched Trent walk down the sidewalk, tipping his hat cordially to passersby, as if he wasn't at the center of her latest nightmare.

She didn't want to sit with this strange feeling sparking inside her, didn't want anyone holding her hand just yet. She wasn't just anxious anymore or afraid. Something frightening was rising within her chest and until she could name it or control it, she didn't want to look at anyone. Whatever came, she wanted to hear it on her feet. "Basil. Tell me what you know," she said.

He let out a short sigh behind her, "Your brother isn't missing, exactly, Ada."

"Then why did Mr. Trent say he was snatched off the streets?"

"Because he was. I saw him taken in a carriage with the name of a debtors' prison on it."

"My brother is in debtors' prison?"

"Yes and no. He is currently at Giltspur Common, but there was never a court order to send him there. We believe Trent has used his connection at Giltspur to keep Richard there for the time being."

Ada couldn't unlock her jaw to speak. Her brother had been taken to a debtors' prison and left there for days. Out of the corner of her burning eyes she saw Basil walk up next to her. He didn't touch her, just stared at her with those same worried eyes. She could feel the heat from his lithe but powerful body, reminding her he was there with her. As if she'd forgotten.

"I have a friend—an actual private investigator—who has been looking into this. His name is Leo Kingston. Richard and I went to school with him."

She remembered him, warm brown skin, light brown eyes, and a serious face. She nodded in acknowledgement.

"He's been trying to track down your brother these past few days."

"What do you know about Mr. Trent?" she finally asked.

"What I know for certain is Mr. Trent never approached the police."

"He said he engaged a runner."

A gust of warm breath fluttered past her neck as Basil let out a tired sigh. "Ada, there haven't been runners for over twenty years now. It's private investigators or the Metropolitan Police."

Another lie. Another lie she'd been too ignorant to understand while Trent was biding his time and making his plans. While Zhenyi was waiting. The feeling sparked again but this time she understood it. *Rage.* She wanted to scream and beat her fists against the wall. She wanted to break something.

"He isn't looking for your brother. When I told him I thought he was in prison, he didn't look surprised or concerned in the least."

"What are you saying?"

"I think you know. Whatever befell your brother, Trent is part of it. I don't know if you're aware Ada, but Richard has been taking a stronger stance on social issues like workers' rights, housing, education, and food safety."

"Yes, he spoke to me about building a school and the plans for improved housing."

"He's hired contractors to build the houses and the school, and Mr. Trent was meant to be in charge of paying them."

"Do you mean to say he hasn't been?"

"I have no idea what he's been doing with the money, Ada, but he has most certainly not been using it as Richard intended. That's probably why Richard confronted him."

"I didn't know they had been at odds. But why would he be involved in something like this? He's worked for us so loyally for so long," Ada replied, pressing her fingertips to the bridge of her nose. A headache was brewing behind her eyes.

"Mr. Trent likes to live according to the station he believes he's entitled to. He's incurred large debts that he can't pay now. I think he plans to use Richard to rectify the situation, but—"

"How much?" she interrupted, turning towards him. Money was nothing compared to her brother's safety.

"Whatever the cost, you don't have it either, Ada," he said patiently.

"I have my dowry."

"Which is inaccessible without a husband. But frankly, we can't be bothered about that now. Do you know who is listed as your next of kin, Ada? The person most likely to be your legal guardian if your brother isn't there?"

Ada felt dizzy at the implication. She could feel all the blood drain out of her body as she stared at Basil in horror. Her uncle. Uncle Simon. "My uncle, Mr. Simon Thornfield."

"We need to get you to him."

Her head was shaking before he finished speaking. "No. No, he won't try to help Richard or me. He hates us."

"Wouldn't he inherit the factory?" Regina said her face more somber than anything Ada had ever seen.

"He would get everything or at the very least he would try to. The factory, the money, the houses. He would sell me off in a moment to the highest bidder and make sure Richard never returned."

"You don't know that for certain," Basil said.

Her throat was growing tighter by the minute. She couldn't go to that man. It was clear that Trent wanted nothing more than to put her in the hands of the man who would ensure she stayed out of his way. "I know enough to understand that I cannot trust him."

"We are due back in London within a week," Regina said. "Whether you go to him or not your uncle is going to come looking for you, Ada. You need a protector."

"You can stay with my father and me," Elodia chimed in.

Basil was shaking his head before she could finish. "If what Ada is saying is true, once her uncle knows Richard is missing he will insist on taking custody of Ada. Your father won't be able to protect her, Miss Hawthorne."

The idea of being shut away was something Ada couldn't countenance. What would she do in an ivory tower, where she could safely fret herself into derangement. "We need to find my brother. He is my best protector."

"Yes, we need to find Richard. But we cannot wait until he is found to ensure your safety, Ada. You need to disappear."

"That's hardly a long-term solution. What is to happen to the business while Trent and Simon Thornfield are running amok with no one to restrain them?" Elodia said.

What would happen? Trent and her uncle would erase any trace of her brother or any of the policies he tried to implement. And then Ada would have nothing left of her family but memories. They would make sure she and Zhenyi were forgotten aberrations in the Thornfield family legacy.

The thought made her ill. Her head was spinning.

Shakily, she walked over to the sofa and sat down beside

Regina. There was no one left to fight for her family but her. As terrified as she was, she couldn't give in.

"I can't hide," Ada said, her voice sounding weak to her ears. "If my brother is missing, then it all comes to me. I can't stay hidden, Basil, and let him destroy my family legacy."

"She must marry," Regina said with a sigh. "It's the only way to secure both you and the business. Then at least you would have your husband and a chance to fight and keep control of the business if it came to that."

"But marry who exactly?" Elodia chimed in. "She barely has a week to find a husband and marry him."

"There's you," Regina said to Basil. The shocked outrage on his face would have been insulting if it didn't fill Ada with relief. Clearly, that had not been an angle he was looking at. Did it mean she could trust him as much as she would need to before this was all over?

"I beg your pardon?" he asked.

"Gigi, you are a genius. It's perfect," Elodia exclaimed before turning to Basil. "You care about Mr. Thornfield enough to ensure to his discovery and release—"

"Of course, but—" he shot Ada a panicked glance and it almost made her smile.

"And you care about Ada enough to marry her and keep her out of her uncle's clutches to ensure she has a chance to fight back," Gigi finished.

Basil shook his head sharply, no doubt struggling to understand what he'd gotten himself into. "Yes, but I was thinking more along the lines of hiding Ada somewhere," he argued.

"Haven't you been listening? Ada needs more than that," Elodia continued. "She needs legal protection. If she marries you, she'll have the protection of your family while you get Mr. Thornfield and prevent Mr. Trent from embezzling more money from the business, or her uncle from ruining her and her brother's life."

"Miss Hawthorne—"

"And it's less of a legal hassle to get a divorce or annulment for a marriage performed in Scotland than it is in England, even if it's still a bit expensive," Regina added.

There was a pregnant pause as they all turned to look at her. Honestly, the things she was aware of never ceased to set Ada back on her heels.

"How do you know about marital laws in Scotland?" Ada asked.

"When you're trying to avoid marrying an ugly baron, you get curious about your options," Regina replied with a shrug before taking Ada's hand. "Well, I'm glad that is settled—"

"Wait a bloody minute. Ada and I aren't going to marry," Basil interjected, his eyes flitting wildly from girl to girl as if he were a cornered beast.

"Oh, come now," Elodia remarked, "Surely it isn't beyond you to marry Ada long enough for both of you to achieve an outcome you both want."

Basil let out an aggravated breath and closed his eyes, likely praying for patience. "Would you two ladies give Ada and me the room?"

"I beg your pardon!" Elodia rose to her feet to argue but it was clear Basil was no longer in an accommodating mood. When his eyes opened again the irritation and resolve in them told Ada his patience and goodwill were running low.

"Whatever is decided here concerns Ada and me and doesn't require an audience. Give us the room."

Ada watched him face down her two friends, knowing that neither party would give in any time soon. Time was running out and they had precious little of it. Perhaps if she ceded this to Basil, he would be more likely to see things her way. "Ellie, Gigi, please."

They glanced at her, and Regina pouted. "Really?" she asked.

"I'm in no danger from Basil. Please just give us a moment."

Elodia looked like she wanted to argue as she glanced back and forth between Ada and Basil's mutinous face. Then she rolled her eyes and hooked her arm with Regina's. "Let's go, Gigi."

Basil waited until they left before he sat down on the sofa beside Ada and let out a sharp breath, rubbing his face roughly with his hands. "Ada, please tell me you are not actually considering this."

"We could get to Gretna Green and be back in London as husband and wife within a few days, Basil," she said.

He stared at her in disbelief. "Yes, just in time for your brother to murder me."

It wasn't a bad issue to take, but—"It would only be long enough to free him, Basil. After that, we can have it annulled and go our separate ways."

He shook his head, and his eyes grew wider. "And what exactly do you think he'll do when we tell him we plan to annul the marriage barely a week later."

"I know it's a great imposition on you. I know I am not the sort of person you planned to marry. I don't want to force you to stay with me, and I don't want to stop you from finding your own love match."

"That's very kind of you, but what about your reputation? Your plan would work short term to secure your family business and help your brother, I grant you, but have you considered that an annulment would not leave you unscathed? Your reputation would be affected by a failed marriage."

"Annulment is not divorce, Basil."

"It is close enough. You cannot make this decision rashly. You have to understand the risk of this choice. If you go into hiding, your reputation will still be intact. Choose this and you may not ever find a decent husband when this is over."

"What good will my reputation be if it is left intact only for me to endure a life of loneliness and humiliation orchestrated by my uncle? The business my family built, the people it employs, what happens to them? Trent has already done so much damage with my brother and father there, what will he be able to do now?"

"Richard would not want you to risk your reputation any more than I do, and I have obligations of my own."

"Is that your only objection?" she asked. "Your concern for my reputation if we annul this marriage?"

"The elopement would be scandal enough, frankly, but at least you'd be wed. An annulment would destroy it entirely."

"That's my business." She took his hand and he looked at her in surprise, his fingers flexing under her own as if fighting the urge to pull away. "Basil, I'm begging you. He has looked after me for longer than I can remember. He's the only family I have. I cannot be selfish when I can save him now. You are doing a duty to your friend by trying to keep me safe; I understand that. This is how you keep me safe, how I keep my family legacy safe. This is how we save him."

She held his gaze, calling on all her resolve, determined not to look away first. He had to say yes. If he walked away, she didn't know what she would do. He looked down at their intertwined hands, and she nearly pulled hers back. It was presumptuous indeed, especially without gloves, but she didn't know what else to do. Would he think her shameless?

"What are your terms exactly?"

"Marriage."

He nodded, a ghost of a smile curving his mouth. "Yes, noted. What else?"

"After we get back, we meet with your investigator, Mr. Kingston, to see if he has located Richard. If he has no leads, then we go to my late father's solicitor to arrange for my dowry to be signed over to you. I'll need your help to take over the ownership of the mill. Everything else can be organized as we go. I know it's not as perfect as Ellie and Gigi claim, but it's a start. Isn't it?"

He looked away and heaved a sigh, the muscle in his jaw working restlessly. She couldn't tell if he was annoyed with her or not. Nothing on his face indicated that he was appeased, but he hadn't moved his hand from hers yet. "Is it truly a bad plan, Basil? Can you not help me?"

He let out a short, frustrated breath and buried his face in his hands, pressing his fingertips into his eyes. It was strange how lonely her hand felt when his was no longer in it. Was it because it belonged to him? She'd never held hands with a man other than Zhenyi before. Did she merely miss the security her brother had given?

Then Basil's voice came, tired and resigned. "There's a train for London that leaves tomorrow morning at ten sharp. Can you be on it?"

The tears of relief caught Ada by surprise. "Thank you, Basil," she whispered past her burning throat.

"Don't thank me yet," he snapped, glaring at her. "This could still endanger Richard, you realize? We don't know if it's Trent or his money lenders who have taken Richard and you can be sure neither will take this counterattack lightly."

She wanted to hug him, but considering how irritated he seemed it was probably best not to. "They can't kill him if they want money. At least this mitigates the harm Trent can do."

"As far as we can tell at the moment, yes."

The door burst open and Elodia stood with Regina with wide expectant eyes and almost manic grins. "So do we go to Gretna Green?"

"Apparently," Basil replied, rising to his feet.

"I can telegraph the housekeeper at Lodge Hall, Mrs. Watson, to send a carriage to the station," Ada said. She didn't need to know that they wouldn't be back for a few days.

"We'll need to pack a bag," Elodia added.

"I'll get my mother to make snacks," Regina said bouncing on her toes before turning to run out the door. "We'll need it for our special picnic tomorrow," she called over her shoulder.

"What are you talking about? You are all coming?" Basil asked, his expression somewhere between amusement and exasperation.

"Absolutely," Elodia replied archly. "Ada may know you well enough to call you by your Christian name, Mr. Thompson, but we do not."

The Road to Gretna Green

HIS FATHER WAS going to kill him.

Especially considering he had it on good authority that his father was in the process of finalizing a marriage for him. Basil had even met the girl, a perfectly fine Miss Felicity Ashwood.

There was a part of Basil that knew he'd find the situation amusing in retrospect. Lord only knew Leo would never let him live it down. The idea of being bundled into a reasonably sized carriage with his impromptu fiancée and her two gutsy friends was not something that he had anticipated when he'd visited Ada. He couldn't explain how he'd managed to be railroaded into his current situation, even if he saw the logic in it. Ada needed protection and the best protection she could get was with a husband. Only he was never meant to be her husband.

He almost felt sorry for the unfortunate footman who met them at the station once Ada explained to him that he was not returning them to the house in Cheshire, but that he was about to drive them to Gretna Green. He'd ridden in the carriage at first. Ada's friends were spirited to be sure, but they weren't bad sorts, and they certainly weren't as annoying as they could have been in his experience. Miss Hawthorne was exactly as Richard had described her over the years, sharp-minded, loyal, and fierce. Miss Mason was a little less terrifying, but the ease with which she could spin a lie was almost impressive. She didn't strike him as unafraid of consequences, but rather at peace with a calculated risk.

Ada... Ada was the one he hadn't anticipated. He'd known her growing up, but that had been a little girl with dark flyaway hair who always found herself tricked by her brother. He remembered an adorable little sprite who whimpered and complained when her brother squeezed her cheeks between his palms and sought comfort shamelessly from anyone available.

But the composed ebony-haired beauty with dark, intelligent eyes was new.

The news of her brother had affected her deeply, he'd seen that. The knowledge of Trent's betrayal had shaken her but instead of tears, she'd started looking for solutions. He hadn't been prepared for the way his heart started racing while she stared into his eyes with frank appraisal instead of maidenly modesty. He was also positive her clothing had never clung in such a distracting way before, to say nothing of the curves of her mouth.

There was so much of her brother in her, but Richard's steady gaze had never elicited a response like that from him. Sitting in the carriage with her two friends had seemed safe enough until she fell asleep. She was a cuddler when she slept. He hadn't known that little detail when he'd elected to sit beside her in the carriage. Waking up to her slender body pressed against his side and her cheek on his chest had been alarming. Partly because it was highly improper, and partly because he wanted to pull her closer. It had seemed so harmless to lean his head against hers and drift off. No one would have blamed him for doing it. Then the arm she'd flung around his stomach in a hug fell and her hand landed heavily on his hip. Well, mostly his hip, and a little bit somewhere else. That was bad enough, but when his immediate response was to hold her hand, and tangle their fingers together he knew he was in trouble.

At that point he'd elected to ride with the footman. The stated reason he gave was to allow the poor man a chance to rest for an hour or so while he drove the horses. The actual reason was that the cool air as they moved further north calmed his blood and sent it along its regular route instead of decidedly south. The last thing he needed to do was think about Ada as a woman, let alone *his* woman. This scheme was meant to save Richard and, outside of the very real possibility of Richard killing him the moment he was free, it was a solid plan.

As her husband, he'd be able to protect her until her brother was able to do so again. She wasn't a child and her affectionate nature was not something he could take advantage of, or confuse with something more. He couldn't afford to consider what it would be like to have those embraces readily available, or see himself as a true suitor for her hand.

He couldn't imagine the shame his family would face over what he was about to do, even though he had no intention of backtracking now. He doubted Miss Ashwood would be so forgiving as to overlook his elopement with a friend's sister followed by a divorce. The shame it would bring her would be almost insurmountable. No doubt his parents would have to make huge concessions to smooth over that slight, and Basil could forget about their help with anything moving forward. Finding a wife would be even more difficult for him once Richard was found and Ada was free.

Ada... he'd been ready to turn her down a third time but there had been something in her eyes that stilled his tongue. She didn't realize how he was ruining himself and hurting an innocent woman to help her. He'd always prided himself on his logical, practical nature. He didn't act or spend money if he could avoid it. There wasn't anything Basil hated so much as injustice or a change of plans. Until roughly twenty-four hours ago, there wasn't a person alive who had managed to make him deviate from a decided course of action, even as a child. Then Ada had taken his hand in both of hers and begged him to agree to her plan and in a moment he'd upended his life for the sake of those glistening dark eyes. She'd seemed so strong up until then, but in that moment with the terrified girl holding onto him he'd known that refusing her would break not only her but himself. He had a horrible feeling it wouldn't be the last time he acquiesced to her will before this was all over.

Now he'd have to go to France or, heaven forbid, America to find a woman who wouldn't have heard about his unsteady and reckless character. So why didn't he mind? Miss Felicity Ashwood would never have been able to influence him as he now knew

Ada could. He would never have to worry about his careful plans being upended by her cheerful blue eyes. Why didn't the ominous road ahead fill him with dread or resentment?

He didn't even have a place to put Ada once they returned. She couldn't stay at his home could she? He tried not to think too much about his limited lodgings in the city. In London, he had purchased an unfinished three-bedroom terrace in dire need of decoration on the edge of the fashionable part of town. The building itself was structurally sound and complete but the original owner had run out of money before finishing the inside. They were respectable, thanks to a few clever investments on his part, but they were nothing compared to what she was used to. He'd expected to have more time to finish it during a four-month engagement period.

As the second son, Basil had received an allowance all his life, but he'd never intended to live off his family's purse strings forever. Before he graduated from Cambridge, he'd begun investing, first on small ventures and then as he gained more familiarity, bolder schemes. He lived well within his means, saved the rest, and invested what he could afford to lose. It had allowed him a measure of independence and the opportunity to purchase his own properties without strings attached from his father or brother. His home in the country was certainly a work in progress, but it was coming along nicely.

Now, he supposed he would be left with all the time in the world to finish it. Provided Richard didn't shoot him dead in the near future. As he drove further and further north, he forced himself to think about his modest country estate and the improvements he'd make to it, instead of the bright, deep eyes of his best friend's younger sister, the scent of violets that seemed to always surround her or the strange feeling taking residence behind his ribs that was too inconvenient to name.

Gretna Green
Scotland, May 1851

THERE HAD BEEN many times in her life when Ada had been extremely grateful to have her friends. She knew that they were rare people all on their own to say nothing of their shared 'otherness'. It wasn't usual to have people who would drop everything to accompany you on an emergency jaunt to another country. Now, however, she wanted to wring their necks. What had seemed like a very slapdash social convention upon their arrival was morphing into something real. Flowers and a white dress and lord knew what else.

It was building anticipation in her as if this were her real wedding, and Basil was going to be her husband for the rest of her life instead of the next month or however long it took to rescue her brother and family business from ruin.

"I have to say, Ada, I'm surprised at you," Elodia said as she styled Ada's long dark hair. They had set themselves up in one of the two rooms Basil had been able to procure once they reached Gretna Green. Only two had been available when they arrived at midday. Ada was doing her best not to think about what that would mean come nightfall.

"At me?"

"How is it that we haven't heard anything about this Mr. Thompson? Where have you been hiding him?" Regina asked.

"Hiding him?" She'd barely seen him since her parents' funeral and then it was always in passing. How could she have known how blue his eyes were, how deep and soft his voice was? She'd already found herself staring when he wasn't looking at her. Her eyes seemed fascinated with the height of his cheekbones, the steep slope of his nose, the shape of his hands. His hands were another issue. His fingers were long and slender but she'd felt the strength of them when he'd gripped her arms.

"We haven't even met him or heard of him," Elodia commented as she finished a sleek braid and pinned it to crown around Ada's head.

"And you are familiar enough with each other to be on a first-name basis," Regina added as she skillfully arranged a group of wildflowers into a modest bouquet.

"He's my brother's friend from school. He's one of his only friends, really."

"Say more."

"That's all there is to say. He was always around. My mother liked him," Ada said, remembering how at home he had been whenever he visited them in the country. He'd always sat on the floor to make sure her mother could sit in a chair, and she always remembered he couldn't eat strawberries when she arranged fruit for him and Richard.

"What's not to like?" Regina replied, winking at Ada in the mirror.

"He's a bit slender but he can certainly handle himself based on how he managed Harris the other day. And he's very handsome and intelligent," Elodia commented.

"And honorable by all accounts and with excellent posture and manners," Regina added.

"And that voice!"

That voice was deep, smooth, and crisp. She could listen to him talk for hours on end about absolutely anything. Ada kept her eyes on the vanity table before her. If she looked them in the eye she'd blush and they'd never leave her alone.

"Not a bad prospect at all, unless he isn't well off financially." Regina held up the bouquet for a critical examination.

"He isn't fabulously wealthy, but I don't believe that he is without prospects," Ada murmured, hideously embarrassed by the turn the conversation had taken. Why had she answered them?

"A fine catch to be sure." Regina smirked and picked up a red ribbon to tie around the stems.

"Are you trying to catch him, Gigi?" Ada asked, desperate to turn their attention away from her.

Regina tied off a perfect bow and held up the bouquet again. "I'm always looking for reasonable alternatives to the dreaded baron my mother is trying to sell me off to. If you could put in a word for me, Ada, when you're finished with Mr. Thompson."

"I'll do that, Gigi." Ada couldn't help but roll her eyes. When she was finished with him, as though he were a book or a bonnet she could lend out for convenience. She didn't know why, but it annoyed her to hear Regina speak of him in such a way. Perhaps it was out of loyalty. He was helping her and her brother. He didn't deserve to be reduced in such a manner, even if their description of him echoed her own thoughts. It couldn't be out of possessiveness, could it?

"Unless, of course, you were considering keeping him for yourself," Elodia commented.

"What are you talking about?" Ada asked, as her cheeks caught fire, her hands jerking in her lap.

"I'm talking about the handsome, dashing, gentleman you are about to marry. The one who is about to help you save your brother," Regina said, handing Ada the small bouquet.

"Mr. Thompson is my brother's friend. He's helping me and then he is going to annul our marriage, return my dowry, and marry someone else. And I will also be free to marry someone else."

"Who?"

"I don't know, and I'd rather not discuss it right now." *Or at all.*

Ada rose to her feet and caught her reflection in the mirror. She looked somewhat like a bride, between her white, muslin evening gown, and the bouquet in her hands. But now she kept wishing that she had her mother's red coral hairpins. No. That should be saved for her true wedding. The one with the husband she kept. She'd all but bamboozled poor Basil into this arrangement and even though he'd agreed and had behaved with good humor, she knew he'd be all too grateful to get out of it as soon as possible. His kindness and honor should be met in kind. It was how she had been raised and it was no less than he deserved.

Elodia fastened a pair of sapphire earbobs to Ada's earlobes. "There's your old, borrowed, and blue." She said, "They used to belong to my mother."

Ada fought back a sudden onslaught of tears. It wasn't the same as her mother's hairpins, but it was something warmed with maternal love. "Ellie, you shouldn't have brought them here for me."

"Nonsense," she kissed Ada's temple and then smoothed her hair, "It's simply a loan for one of my two dearest friends, the first of us to marry."

"It's not even a real wedding," Ada murmured in a watery voice. It couldn't be. It didn't matter how well he suited her or how safe he made her feel. He was a beautiful thing on loan for a short period of time. Like Elodia's mother's earrings.

"If it needs a real divorce, then it's a real wedding," Regina replied walking up to the other side to squeeze her between them in a warm embrace. "Now stop crying. The red ribbons are for happiness and prosperity, not bloodshot eyes."

Ada gave a laugh and accepted the comfort they offered her. It wasn't a hug from her mother, but it was full of love, just as they were. A knock sounded on the door, and she closed her eyes and took a deep breath, hoping her courage didn't fail her.

"It's just as well," Elodia said. "Time's up."

THE CEREMONY, IF it could be called that, was an odd arrangement. She'd always heard of Gretna Green weddings over an anvil, but the actual experience was truly strange. Only she would manage to have a marriage of convenience at Gretna Green.

She'd walked into The Blacksmith's Shop flanked by Elodia and Regina to where Basil stood waiting, and her heart began racing. All through the ceremony, she couldn't help noticing the things that Elodia and Regina had mentioned. The lean angles of his face, his height, the rich timbre of his voice, his kind crystalline blue eyes. Like her brother, he wasn't a particularly large man, but there was a power and a presence about him that gave an impression of safety. That steadiness was bewitching when her world kept tilting the way it had over the past week. It made her wish she hadn't promised to annul their marriage.

He repeated his vows in his resonant voice, his eyes as steady as his hands, and she hoped he couldn't feel how her fingers were trembling. What if he thought she was having second thoughts? He'd probably be offended seeing as he was only here at her behest to begin with.

When he produced a ring her breath caught in her throat. Had he purchased it here? Had he brought it from London? It was such a sweet thing for him to have thought of for a fake wedding he had been opposed to. What did it mean? The cool band of gold sliding onto her finger sent a shock through her system. She felt weak from an odd mix of exhilaration and anxiety as her eyes stung from tears. It made everything real.

There was no way for her to deny the gravity of the step she was taking, however warranted it was. It made her think about other things that would be happening tonight if she were truly his bride. It made her heart ache when she remembered this was only a temporary means to an end. They were doing this to save her brother. No matter what Elodia and Regina said, no matter what the circle of metal on her finger signified, none of this was truly hers. He leaned down and brushed his soft lips against her cheek, the shadow of his slight beard scraping across her tender skin. By the time she'd recovered from the shivers racing all over her body, he'd already pulled away.

It was done.

Chapter Five

It had been decided by Elodia and Regina that they would take one room and the happily wedded couple would share the other. A fact they had elected to keep to themselves until Ada tried to go to bed and found her things in his room. Ada knew Basil well enough not to fear him engaging in unseemly behavior. He'd taken one look at her bags in the room and picked up his own travel case, moving it to the adjoining sitting room, leaving the bed to her. No awkward glances, no stilted conversation where she imposed herself even further.

She was grateful for his discretion but at the same time it left her feeling even more alone in that alien space. Even more aware of the liminal nature of her relationship with Basil. In the morning, they would take off on the road back to Cheshire before continuing to London. *Two days*, she told herself, three at most, and her brother would be back home where he belonged.

Her brother.

She'd forced herself not to think about him too much since she'd found out the truth of his circumstances. Now that the wedding was over, and she had nothing to do but wait until the morning, the thoughts came hard and fast. Debtors' prison wasn't something spoken about in polite society, which meant that gently bred ladies like her didn't know much about it. What little Ada knew, however, was enough to chill her blood. Men wasted away there from disease or despair, forgotten and alone, disgraced and dishonored. A fate worse than simple death.

Her handsome, brave, kind brother was in such a place because of the greed of another man. Greed and prejudice. The mischievous man who made their mother's longevity noodles for her birthday, congee when she was sick, and mooncakes for the mid-autumn festival, so she'd always remember the taste of their mother's cooking. The brother who snuck her books deemed unfit for ladies, and taught her the same self-defense techniques their mother had taught him. The brother who spoiled her with trinkets and jewelry and dresses at every opportunity. Would she ever see him again?

She replaced her shoes with her bedroom slippers and then began removing her jewelry. By the time she sat down at the dressing table to take down her hair, her eyes were burning with tears. Every time she caught her reflection in the mirror, she seemed to look more depressed. Her brother was missing. Some evil men had snatched him away from his friends and family for money with no thought to the people he depended on.

She watched in defeat as the tears rolled down her cheeks one after the other. There was no staving off the fearful thoughts and desolation at the idea of being the only one of her family left. The only one left with her strange eyes and pin-straight hair that defied the hottest curling tongs. Would there be no one left to call her by her name? No one to connect her to the home and people she'd never seen? Unable to keep looking, she buried her face in her hands, pressing her fingertips into her forehead.

"Gēgē," she whispered tearfully. She couldn't imagine how he must be feeling trapped in that place, betrayed twice over by someone they had all trusted. Someone she had only narrowly escaped herself. A chill raced through her, raising her pores, and sending her arms around her torso. If not for Basil, she could have ended up in Trent's clutches and at his mercy just as Zhenyi had been. She couldn't bear to think of how close she had come to danger, and how impossible it would have been for her to save herself let alone her brother.

"Ada?" She heard Basil's voice and looked up to see him standing in the doorway to the sitting room. His jacket was missing, and he was drying his hands on a small towel.

"I'm sorry," she muttered turning away from him and checking her face for tears. Not only were her eyes red but her hair was still half in pins. She looked deranged.

"Are you crying?" he asked, entering the room.

"I'm not crying." She started pulling out pins before she remembered he wasn't actually her husband. Not really. Should she have her hair down in front of him? Did it even matter at this point? If he was in his shirt sleeves, surely she could have loose hair.

He crouched down on the floor before her and took her hands in his, trapping the hairpins between her palms. "I'm sorry. I've not been taking care of you as I should have."

She shook her head and kept her eyes on her hands, their hands. She already wanted more of him than she had a right to. She didn't know what she'd do if she met his eyes when he was this close, when his voice was so soft and kind. "You've been wonderful, Basil."

"You've been so steady and composed until now. I didn't think about how you must be feeling. This last fortnight has been very trying for me, but you must be half out of your mind."

She let out a mirthless laugh and shook her head as she forced back more tears. "My head has been spinning. All I could do was think of a plan, of what to do, how to prepare. Now there's nothing left to do. I've only now had time to come to terms with what's happened." She chanced a glance up at him. His clear blue eyes were full of concern as he waited patiently, the firelight glinting off his light brown hair. He was so compassionate and still, so calm as he listened to her speak her mind and her heart. "We trusted Mr. Trent, Basil. My parents, my brother, and I trusted him with everything. And he saw us as something to be looted. Something to take advantage of. If you hadn't warned me against it, I'd have gone with him to Cheshire, and he could have forced me into anything. I would have had no protection at all."

He shook his head. "No, I would have found you, Ada. I wouldn't have stopped until I had you safe."

She wasn't proud of the way her pulse jolted at those words, or how her heart ached sweetly in her chest. "That's not really the point. He would never have done this if my father was alive."

"You can't know that."

"I can!" She pulled her hands away from his and rose to her feet, striding away a distance. "Because my father looked like him—a white Englishman. Trent may have stolen from him, but he would never think to hand Zhen—*Richard*—over to kidnappers and lie about his whereabouts if my father were here. He would never have been able to do this because my father looked like he could and should be prosperous in this country. My brother and I... Trent can spin any lie about us that he wishes. I can't help wondering what might happen if we fail."

"What do you mean?" he asked, rising to his feet.

Like a summer shower the gust of temper was gone leaving her with a building sense of dread in her stomach. "What if we never find him?" She hated how small her voice sounded, how weak. Trent had counted on her to be weak. Weak and foolish. She couldn't stop it.

"Ada." Basil walked over to her and took her by the arms.

The weight of those broad, long-fingered hands on her arms unraveled a knot of tension inside her and the tears rolled down her face fast and hot. She buried her face in her hands and fought desperately for composure. Fought the urge to hide against him until everything was over, just like a child would. "I can't stop thinking of him alone. The things being said to him, the indignities he's suffering. I can't stop thinking that they might punish him for having things they think he shouldn't have. And he doesn't know if I'm safe. He doesn't know if anyone will come for him. He must be in agony."

He pulled her close and wrapped his arms around her in a light but secure embrace. For a moment, she froze in shock, but then the warmth of him sank in. The safety of being enveloped in his arms and held against him took hold of her, and she relaxed, burying her face in his firm chest. He had initiated the embrace. She didn't have to feel guilty about accepting it. He smelt of cedar and musk, full of assurance and solace. His hands stroked her back and her hair in long firm strokes. Her arms came up to wrap around his trim waist. He felt solid and lean instead of skinny, his body wiry and deliciously firm. Was it normal to feel this sense of familiarity even though two days ago they had never touched? When he spoke again, the rumble of his deep voice seemed to vibrate into her bones.

"I cannot speak for your brother, and I cannot tell you that he is doing well. What I can tell you is that he is a strong, broad-minded, intelligent man. He isn't a weakling either; he can handle himself. Leo and I will do our utmost to locate him and get him justice. It is all we can do, Ada."

She lifted her head and met his eyes, her fingers curling absently into the material of his shirt. "Do you really think what we've done will make things worse for him? Do you think they'll hurt him because of this?"

"I shouldn't have said that," he said, his thumbs swiping gently at the tears on her cheeks.

"But do you think they'll take it out on him? I can't lose him, Basil. He's all the family I have left." What if they thrashed him or maimed him because she was trying to be clever? Perhaps she should have gone into hiding as Basil had suggested, but then she wouldn't be able to stand in his arms like this. She wouldn't have known the delicious torture of relishing the feel of a man she couldn't have. She wasn't sure it was something she'd want to give up.

He tucked her loose hair behind her ears and framed her face between his palms. "You aren't going to lose anyone. We have a plan, and it's a bloody good one."

She looked up at him in surprise. She wasn't used to men cursing around her on purpose. "You're not supposed to use language like that in front of a lady."

"How very uncouth of me. You are absolutely correct. I apologize," he replied with no remorse in his voice whatsoever.

She couldn't help but smile. "It is a good plan, isn't it?"

"The best plan. Trent will never see us coming," he replied, a small smile softening the lines of his face.

"And, incidentally, it was *my* plan."

"Yes, dear," he replied easily.

A glow filled her at the amused affection warming his voice and lighting his eyes, making her forget that she wasn't actually his wife. They weren't meant to be this close or physically familiar. She didn't want to move. She liked the way he looked at her as if she were a partner in crime or an old friend… or something else. The tenderness in his gaze was turning into something else, and his grip on her waist and shoulders was tightening ever so slightly. His hold shifted as if he was going to bring her close again, and his lips parted on a breath. Her eyes fell to his mouth, her mind running wild at the idea of touching them. She'd never been kissed before. The idea of it being Basil, of giving everything over to this man was thrilling and perfect. This gentleman of a man who wiped her tears and listened to her anxious thoughts without making her feel like a child. Who brought a ring for their wedding so it didn't feel like the sham it was.

She met his eyes again and wondered if his face was closer or if she was imagining things. She pressed her lips together, wetting them with the tip of her tongue and saw his gaze drop to them. His hands flexed on her back and she knew that he was going to kiss her. And when he did, she was going to kiss him back.

Basil seemed to realize this as well and thought better of it because in another head-spinning moment, he'd released her and taken a step back. "Are you all right now?" he asked, turning from her to face the doorway.

She nodded, locking her knees to keep from sinking to the floor. Her body was tingling everywhere his had made contact with it, still reliving and reacting to the fantasy she'd so nearly experienced. She missed his embrace with an intensity that made no sense. *Was this what desire felt like?*

"I'll sleep on the sofa," he said, walking towards the adjoining door and that delicious thrill in her veins iced over.

"What? Why?" she asked, before she could think about what she was asking.

He paused, his head dropping forward. "Because it would be best."

"I—" she froze and bit her lip. She didn't want to sleep by herself in a strange room with her fearful thoughts waiting to reemerge the moment she didn't have a distraction. She wanted him to come back and hold her to keep her fears at bay. "You don't have to."

"I think I do."

What are you doing? "It would hardly be improper anymore; you are my husband now."

"Am I?" he asked softly.

Her breath froze in her lungs as the meaning behind that question hung between them.

You could be. The words were on the tip of her tongue but she couldn't dare speak them.

Two signatures on a piece of paper could give her the protection of his name, but it didn't change the relationship between them. She'd set the line; it wouldn't be fair for her to move it now. He didn't deserve that.

"Never mind," his voice came again. "I will sleep in here; you take the bed. I'll see you in the morning." Then he disappeared through the adjoining door.

It was for the best. He was right. She would find a way to cope on her own. She turned away and reached up to her neck to begin unhooking the front of her gown and froze. This was one of the few that fastened in the back. *Damn.* She would need to call him back. "Basil," she called, and the movement in the other room stopped.

"Yes?"

"I need help with my dress. It buttons in the back." She turned her back to his room and waited with bated breath and burning cheeks until she heard his footsteps and then felt his fingertips graze the skin of her upper back. "I'm sorry, I didn't think I'd be traveling without a maid."

His fingers worked against her back as he began silently unfastening the row of small pearl buttons along her spine. His warm breath puffed across her skin as he worked on his task, and her eyes drifted closed as she allowed her mind to wander. In the penny novels she'd read, the knight would gently slide the garment off his lady's shoulders to catch a glimpse of her before deferring to chivalry and turning away. She wondered what Basil would do. Would he prove more a knight or a warlord? A shiver coursed through her, and he paused.

"Are you feeling well?" he murmured.

"Yes," she replied, willing her heart to stop racing.

"You're trembling. You must be freezing."

She couldn't respond to that convincingly. It was colder here than London, but she couldn't pretend the distance from the fireplace was the reason she couldn't seem to catch her breath. Her dress loosened gradually until she heard him take a step back, felt his hands fall away.

"Do you need help with anything else?" he asked.

She pressed her lips together against a scandalous suggestion and shook her head.

"I'll be in the other room then," he said before walking away again.

Ada waited until she heard the door shut firmly before lifting her eyes from the ground. She needed to get control of herself. She removed her gown, her crinoline, and her stays. Moving quickly, she slipped on her cotton nightgown and put out the few candles in the room before crawling into bed. Thankfully, it was comfortable enough with a soft mattress and smooth sheets.

It took her about five minutes to realize the bed was far too large for her to relax. She was plagued with ideas of her brother's situation. Was he cold? Was he hungry? Had he been beaten? If they didn't find him, would he die there, hungry and alone? Would they never be able to lay his body to rest? A series of unexplained creaks sounded from the window, the wooden panel walls, the floor by her bedroom door. She froze, her heart hammering in her chest. Footsteps sounded in the hallway, and she began counting in her mind. As a nightmare-prone child, she'd always run to her brother's room or her parents. In school, she'd shared a dorm with Regina and Elodia.

Now she was alone.

A shiver ran through her, and she squeezed her eyes shut, hoping for some of the images to go away. Trying to remind herself that she was a grown woman and not a child. That her friends were just on the other side of the door. That she wasn't actually alone. Something tapped on the wall and a gasp stuck in her throat.

That wasn't going to work either.

Swallowing her fear, she threw back the covers, slid her feet into her slippers, and walked through the connecting door.

He had retired to the sofa in front of the fireplace, which while warm enough, couldn't have been comfortable. But that wasn't what was drawing her attention. Basil was only wearing his trousers. The sight of his bare chest nearly sent her scrambling back to her room but the idea of having a nightmare in that big bed, in a strange place, left her frozen.

She hadn't expected him to be this muscular. The firelight danced over his skin and the dusting of dark hair over his chest, stomach, and lower... If he were her husband, she'd know what that bare skin would feel like against hers. She squeezed her eyes shut and turned away from the sinful image he presented. It didn't make any sense to dwell on that when everything about them was a favor. A duty.

"Basil," she whispered and waited for a response. Nothing. "Basil," she tried a little louder, and then she heard a rustle of movement.

"Ada?" More rustling. Lord, his voice had a new husky edge to it that she hadn't prepared herself for. "Ada, what are you doing here?"

"I can't sleep," she said turning towards him but keeping her eyes firmly fixed on her slippers. "It's cold and there are noises and I think someone is—"

"—Alright." She heard him sigh "What time is it?"

"I don't know." She squeezed her eyes shut and clenched her hands together. "Will you sleep in here please?"

"What?"

She had never felt more like a child. She was twenty years old and couldn't muster up enough courage for one night. "I can't sleep by myself. Will you come in there with me?"

"In the bed?"

"Just to sleep."

"Ada…"

She couldn't hear him say 'no'. "I won't touch you, I promise. I'm not asking because I'm wicked or sneaky, I just…I keep thinking of Richard and I don't sleep well alone or in strange places, you can ask anyone. I'm not lying."

"Right."

More silence. The mortification she felt at that quiet and stillness nearly had fresh tears springing to her eyes. *I shouldn't have come.* "I'm sorry," she whispered, "I shouldn't have asked. Goodnight." She turned and ran back to her room, wondering how it seemed darker and even more foreboding now that she knew she'd have to face it alone. She crawled back into the bed and pulled the covers up over her head. With every passing second, she could hear her heart beating louder and louder. She clenched her fists in the linens and fought to control her breathing as tears soaked into her pillow. All she needed was for Basil to hear her crying. She didn't want him to feel guilty for protecting himself.

Footsteps sounded across the floor, and her eyes flew open as her breath caught in her throat. There was a brief draft as he pulled back the covers, the bed depressed behind her, and she felt him lay down. The gratitude filling her chest nearly overwhelmed her.

She peeked over the edge of the blankets. In the dim light of the fireplace, she could see him sitting upright with his eyes closed, his arms crossed over his chest. He'd put back on his shirt. "Thank you," she whispered.

"It's no problem. I'll stay until you fall asleep," he said, and she nodded even though she was almost certain he couldn't see her. It took her a few minutes to realize her plan was flawed. His proximity had her mind racing and her skin prickling with awareness. Her thoughts veered towards his life. Had he wanted someone else before he decided to attach himself to her? How would his family view this latest turn of events?

"Basil?"

"Yes?" he replied.

"Was there another person, a woman, you wanted to marry?"

He let out a sharp breath. Was that a laugh? "You're asking me this now?"

She felt a stab of guilt and a sinking in her stomach. She'd been so focused on saving Zhenyi and romanticizing these new feelings that she hadn't wondered if she was derailing Basil's life with her plan. "I'm sorry."

"It's not your fault. I could have said no. Yes, to answer your question. My father was in negotiations on my behalf with Lord Ashwood. I was meant to marry his daughter."

Lord Ashwood was a viscount if she recalled correctly. She couldn't remember what his daughter looked like. "Oh. Did you like her?"

"I didn't dislike her," he replied. "I was meant to post the banns this week."

"I'm sorry."

"Stop apologizing. This isn't your fault."

"The only reason you're here is because of me."

"I'm here because an asshole kidnapped one of my oldest friends. I didn't have to marry you at all."

He really should mind his language around her, but she was too grateful for his presence to point it out. "I forced you."

"Ada, I am very tired, and I could be sleeping on the chaise in the other room. I would appreciate it if you would stop implying that I, a grown man, was kidnapped by three young women and forced into wedlock."

She choked on a sudden snicker at the image his words conjured. When he put it like that, it sounded ridiculous. "I'm sor—" a warning glance from him stopped her from saying it. "Noted. You are a gallant hero."

"I'm glad you're aware of the fact." His tone was even, but that small trademark smile was spreading across his face. She wondered what it would look like if he smiled fully. Would it reach his eyes? Would they sparkle?

"What is your Miss Ashwood like?"

"Nothing out of the ordinary. Sensible, pretty, kind. Amenable to country living."

"Dowried, no doubt."

He gave a wry chuckle and nodded. "Yes. She wouldn't have done otherwise for father. He's not the sentimental type. The penniless and unconnected need not apply for a place in the family of the Viscount Sterling."

"Your father is a viscount?" she asked.

"You didn't know?" he asked.

If she had at some point, she'd forgotten by now. It would have been in Debrett's. She was certain Zhenyi had mentioned it before. "Will he be very angry with you?"

"He will be apoplectic," he sighed.

"Because I'm Chinese?"

"Because I've made him look a fool who cannot manage his family. There will be a twofold scandal. First, because I asked him to find a wife for me and then abandoned my betrothed before the banns were read, and second, because I eloped with you, an unconnected daughter of the merchant class with mixed blood. The sky will fall."

Was that what his family was like? Basil was so kind and clearheaded, a man with the most beautiful heart she'd ever met. She couldn't imagine his family to hold such bigoted views. Basil calling off an engagement, however, was bad form. To make this choice on account of her, to throw over a viscount's daughter for her sake… yes, he wouldn't have an easy time coming back from that. Neither of them would. "Your father doesn't like Richard, does he?"

"He likes him well enough. But there's a difference between befriending someone and marrying them."

"Ah," Lord, what had she dragged them into? "I'm sorry. You said you didn't want to, and I forced you."

"Sweet suffering Jesus, Ada, you didn't force me."

"Yes, I did." He'd come to warn her, and she'd derailed his entire life, forcing him to betray his family. In the dark silence, his hand closed around hers, warm and firm. She glanced up at him and her breath caught in her chest at the earnest and somber gaze he'd fixed on her.

"I agreed to this because it was necessary, not because of you, but because of the circumstance. Richard has been like a brother to me. You are the dearest thing he has in this world. No matter what happens to him, and I do believe we will bring him back, he would want you safe. You have no idea how many times he's had to defend me at school. How many times he's stepped between me and disaster."

"Why would you need defending?" she asked.

"Why? Because I was a skinny boy who hated getting dirty and generally preferred books and music to people."

Ada pressed her lips together against a smile and nodded. He would no doubt imagine she was laughing at him. She remembered him from her childhood, but she would never have described him in such a way.

"The point is, I would never have allowed you to be harmed because it was inconvenient to me. Never."

"But your family."

"My family..." he sighed. "I love them, but I learned long ago that I must be able to face myself. No amount of family can make up for a lack of integrity. If I didn't do everything in my power to protect my friend and his interests, how would I be able to face myself?"

The words were bittersweet. With every moment in his presence she grew more assured that her husband was probably one of the best men she'd ever met. A man worth keeping, a gentleman worthy of the name. It also reminded her that, for him, she was no more than one of her brother's interests.

She had no right to ask for more from him even if it stung. It was silly. He would never have even thought to marry her in different circumstances and neither would she. In other circumstances she wouldn't have understood the true beauty of his nature. She would have been left in blessed ignorance of what she had missed in him. But now she knew. It had taken two days for her to understand that if she wasn't already in love with him, she very soon would be. This wasn't destiny, this was a means to an end. Even if he was kind, gentle, and forthright with the most beautiful blue eyes. Even if his voice sent tingles scuttling over her nerves and settled something deep inside her all at once in a way no other man had before.

"That is true," she whispered. "Thank you."

"You're welcome," he replied.

"I hope you can explain things to your Miss Ashwood," she said willing it to be true. She didn't want him to suffer for his choice. Not that her wishes would make a difference in the end.

"I think that ship has sailed."

"Perhaps it will serve to illustrate your character to her."

"Unreliable? Reckless? Undeserving?"

Was that how he saw himself? "Honorable. Compassionate. Loyal." *Beautiful. Wonderful.*

He didn't speak again, just squeezed her hand softly and she smiled in response, her eyes already drifting closed.

Within moments she was asleep.

Chapter Six

*S*HIT. THAT WAS Basil's first thought when he awoke the next morning. The sun had yet to fully rise, the bed was warm and comfortable, and he knew that he had slept well even though he'd gone against his habit of sleeping nude. He hadn't meant to fall asleep there. He'd had every intention of leaving once Ada was settled. But between her even breaths and the light weight of her hand in his, he'd drifted off. That wasn't the problem.

The problem was his earlier premonition that Ada would be able to make him do things he knew were a bad idea was proving to be worryingly accurate. He'd allowed the sight of Ada with loose silken hair, with tear-stained cheeks, and in a demure nightgown to distract him from what he'd realized on the journey to Scotland.

She never stayed put in her sleep.

To the contrary, she gravitated to the nearest warm body. He'd woken up to her thigh sliding across his and her small, slender hand furrowing under the hem of his shirt. His arm had found itself around her narrow shoulders, cradling her body as she rested against him, her head on his chest.

At first, he'd reveled in waking up to the feel of a woman in his arms, supple and deliciously warm with sleep. His hands had wandered around, caressing the long line of a slender back and arms, the rounded slope of a firm backside. Perfect. The woman in his bed was so welcoming and deliciously soft against him, and her scent was everywhere. It was precisely that scent which had jolted him into awareness. There was only one woman he knew who smelled like violets, and his hand had no business on her ass.

Even more problematic was the cock-stand making itself more apparent despite the realization that the woman in his arms was his best friend's sister. If anything, that insight was making things worse for him, because she wasn't the skinny twelve-year-old with bright eyes and a sly smile. She was a beautiful twenty-year-old siren. A fact that was growing ever more difficult to ignore. Ada stretched against him with a husky sigh, her thigh riding up even higher to brush against his swollen sex, her nose pressing against the skin of his neck.

Fucking hell, it was torture. He needed to get out of that bed.

He froze and closed his eyes tightly. Fuck it, he couldn't wait for her to wake up on her own. Slowly he inched his body away from hers, hoping to slide her head onto the pillow. She murmured as her hand slid over his chest and ribs. In a desperate bid for sanity, he grabbed her hand, arresting its agonizing descent. He heard a sharp intake of breath and shifted his head to glance down at her mussed hair.

"Are you awake then?" he asked in as neutral a tone as he could manage. Slowly, as if to avoid his detection, she pulled away incrementally, first her hand, then her leg, then her head, and the rest of her body.

"I'm sorry," she murmured once she had retreated to her side of the bed.

"It's alright." *More than alright really.* He wasn't only to linger in bed or otherwise but he had no objections to being fondled by her in the morning. Even if the inclination bordered on masochistic.

"I didn't realize—"

"It's fine, Ada. It's my own fault, I didn't mean to fall asleep."

"Still, I didn't intend to molest you."

She sat upright and pulled the blankets up to cover her. He wasn't sure what maidenly modesty she was still trying to protect, but he couldn't help but find it adorable. Especially with the bright flush spilling over her cheeks and the bashful way she refused to meet his eyes. She was such a confounding mix of timidity and assertiveness. A girl who would marry a man she knew by reputation alone in order to protect her family, but couldn't sleep alone. A woman who couldn't help reassuring him, when he was only beside her to fend off shadows in an unfamiliar room. A champion and a damsel all at once. He didn't know what to do with her, but the effect on him was inconvenient at best.

Her behavior the night before had been confusing, to say the least. Her distress over her brother was one thing, but the ease with which she allowed him to hold her was something he hadn't been prepared for. Her familiarity with him had his hands lingering on her shoulders, in her hair, at her waist when he should have let go. That was all before the fiasco this morning.

He knew she trusted him implicitly. She would never have asked him to share a bed with her otherwise. What he couldn't gauge was whether she saw him as a man or more as a brother. Were the moments he imagined a tension between them due to embarrassment or because she was as attracted to him as he was to her? It was just as likely that she was desperate enough to take on a little risk for a good night's sleep. He'd wondered if she was playing a game with him until he'd heard the broken note in her voice when she'd all but begged him to stay with her in the room.

He liked how she demanded comfort and affection and gave it in equal measure. He liked holding her far too much. Christ help him, he actually liked giving in to her. Was he turning into some kind of mentally deficient lecher? He had been perfectly content with Felicity Ashwood until he fell asleep holding Ada's soft slender hand in his. Was that correct or had it begun earlier? Had it begun the moment he'd put that ring on her finger? Why had he used *that* ring? He could have gotten a cheap one at the smithy. He hadn't even thought about it at the time, he had simply slid it on because it felt right.

A knock sounded on the door, and he slid from the bed facing the wall, wondering how long he'd have to wait before he could face her without having to answer embarrassing questions.

"Didn't you bring anything to sleep in?" she asked suddenly. He glanced at her, and she lowered her eyes again. He looked down at his rumpled trousers and shirt. There was no way to explain to her that he didn't sleep clothed in general, even when traveling.

"I didn't think I'd need them," he replied.

"But what will you travel back in?" she asked her hands folded in her lap, as demure as a nun. He'd almost believe it too if only he couldn't still remember what her hands felt like on his body.

He tilted his head. What did she think he meant to do? "Are you worried I'll embarrass you?"

"No!" she exclaimed. She looked up at him, her outrage causing her to forget her embarrassment for a moment. Then her eyes fell to the open neck of his shirt, and she lowered her gaze to the bed linens.

"I have a change of clothes, Ada," he said, taking pity on her. The poor thing was probably waiting for the floor to devour her.

"Oh, alright then."

He needed to return to his side of the room and get dressed, but he didn't want to leave. He wanted to stay in this room with Ada, half dressed and avoid London as long as he could.

The knock sounded again, and he responded instinctively. "Yes?"

There was an audible gasp from the other side of the door, and Ada's eyes widened comically as she shook her head.

Fuck... If the carriage ride back wasn't so damned long, he would have found this wildly amusing. He could imagine the shocked faces of Ada's friends on the other side of the door. They were so impressive that it was easy to forget how sheltered they actually were.

"Who is it?" Ada called.

"It's us," Regina replied, "Are you still abed?"

That was his cue to get moving. He'd almost forgotten that he wasn't actually on his honeymoon. This was the first stage of a rescue mission, not some romantic elopement. Basil trotted around the bed and through the adjoining door to the sitting room as Ada moved to open the door to her friends. He closed the door behind him and leaned against it, glancing down at the erection that still hadn't calmed all the way down. The journey back was certainly going to be interesting.

London, Twelve hours later

HE WASN'T DISAPPOINTED. The carriage ride to Cheshire had been easy enough, as he'd simply ridden with the footman, but the train ride had bordered on farcical. Ada still refused to meet his eyes, and he could barely stand to have her touch him at all. He knew too much to pretend he didn't see her as a woman. He knew what she looked like in bed, from the silken hair flowing down to her waist to the long lines and unexpected curves of her slender body so delicately framed in the firelight through her cotton nightgown. There were reasons men were never meant to have that image until after a woman was his wife. How on earth would he be able to stay in control of himself now?

Sharing a transport with her two best friends helped. From the carriage to the train the three girls kept exchanging meaningful glances between each other and then at him. Elodia was clearly amused by the entire situation, but the smugness was a little concerning. Regina seemed to vacillate between outrage and curiosity but who or what she was outraged about was a mystery to him. It was *their* clever plan to leave a room for him and Ada.

Somehow, they made him feel embarrassed. Which was utterly ridiculous because he had nothing to be embarrassed about. It was hardly shocking for a man to be in his wife's chambers after the wedding night. Even if the marriage was unconsummated and they weren't, strictly speaking, planning on staying married. A decision he was beginning to regret. Perhaps that was the issue. He was more embarrassed that it had taken one day and night alone with his best friend's sister for him to realize that everything he'd planned for his life was… unsatisfactory.

How had he missed that he wanted more from his wife than convenience? How could he have known that a demanding, affectionate thug of a woman who bullied him into changing tack was something he had needed all along? He'd had her stubborn sunshine in his life and now the idea of returning to that manicured silence felt like death.

He knew what her body felt like pressed against him, and her touch against his bare skin. How was he meant to go back to a time when he didn't know the shape of her body without her stays? How was he supposed to keep his mind from wondering whenever he smelled violets? Needless to say, when the train arrived in London, he was conflicted. He needed space to sort out his thoughts and determine a new course of action. Under the guise of finding a porter, he slipped out of the room and escaped to the platform. He took a deep breath and started his search for a free porter.

"Thompson."

Basil turned to see his friend Leo watching him with amusement.

He sighed and shook his head. "Kingston."

"I thought we planned to meet a few days ago."

"We did."

"My mother got a hastily scrawled note saying otherwise."

"Yes, there were some extenuating circumstances."

Leo's hazel-colored eyes flicked up over Basil's head and his eyes brows shot up. "So I see."

Basil turned around to see Ada emerging from the train. Her deep dark eyes met his, and somehow the image of her in her apricot-colored travel dress surrounded by smoke had him catching his breath. He didn't even realize he had moved until her hand was in his, helping her down the steps. She smiled softly at him, and his throat went bone dry.

"Ah," Leo murmured.

Basil turned to see Leo extending a hand to Regina who took it with marked interest. An interest that Leo seemed to share as he helped her down the stairs. Even after she'd reached the platform, their eyes had remained fixed on each other's. He could hardly fault the poor girl. Leo had always been a favorite with the fairer sex, from his chiseled features and deep, tawny complexion to his dimpled smile and his tall, broad frame. It was an embarrassment of riches really. Basil didn't think he was a fright to look at but standing next to Leopold had him feeling like the plain cousin.

A deep purple glove caught his attention and he turned to help Elodia disembark before moving them further away from the locomotive.

"Any luck with that porter, Mr. Thompson?" Elodia asked, her glittering brown eyes flicking down to where his fingers still grasped Ada's.

Who they hell did she imagine she was, his governess? "Not as yet, Miss Hawthorne," he replied.

She pursed her lips in amusement and nodded.

"No worries about that," Regina chimed in before daintily removing her glove and letting out a glass-shattering whistle that had the entire group wincing save for Leo. He seemed utterly fascinated with her. Basil would keep that small observation on hand for later, when Leo would no doubt rake him over the coals over this current turn of events. Within seconds another voice was heard.

"*Rajani Elizabeth Mason!*" a deep female voice thundered.

Regina's eyes went wide with fear, her shoulders hunching up to her ears, looking more like a cornered spaniel than the self-assured young woman he'd witnessed over the past few days. Slowly, she turned around to greet a furious South Asian woman in a stunning amber-colored gown and a gentleman with light brown hair and a medium build who was desperately trying not to smirk.

"Aai," she began but any attempt at platitudes was met with a torrent of angry, indecipherable words. Everyone got a taste of it as Mrs. Mason's furious eyes alighted on each of them in turn before she snatched her daughter's hand from Leo's arm, took hold of her arm, and dragged her away. The gentleman, who Basil assumed was her father, gave them all an affable look before tipping his hat.

"Good day to you, Miss Thornfield, Miss Hawthorne."

The two girls dipped into a curtsey, their eyes downcast and expressions subdued. *So they were capable of feeling shame.* He wasn't sure they knew the sensation based on their dealings with him.

Leo let out a low whistle and turned to Basil with raised eyebrows. "About those extenuating circumstances…"

"I need a drink and a blood oath of silence from you first," Basil grumbled, refusing to meet his curious and no doubt amused eyes. The last thing he needed was a debriefing with Leo when there were witnesses.

"Maybe we should check on her in a few days," Ada said.

"Or a few weeks," Leo responded. "Miss Mason's language was particularly spirited."

"How do you know what she said?" Elodia asked.

"I served in India before I became an inspector, which reminds me, Thompson…" He turned to Basil, all levity gone from his face. "You and I need a talk."

"Is it about my brother?" Ada asked.

Leo glanced at her. "It is."

"Then you need 'a talk' with me, not him. He's *my* family."

"He's family to both of you now from the look of things," Leo commented, nodding at the ring on her hand, and Ada flushed again but stood her ground.

"All the more reason," she said lifting her chin in defiance.

Leo glanced over at Elodia who was watching him expectantly. "I'm assuming you will demand a hearing as well."

"That would be a safe assumption, yes," she replied evenly before her eyes flicked over his shoulder. "Here, porter." Her voice rang out and the pale man froze and glanced over to her. "Go fetch us a carriage." He blinked in shock before nodding and scampering away.

She turned her attention back to Leo and opened her mouth to speak again but her eyes widened abruptly and her back straightened. Basil followed her gaze and saw a middle-aged man with a gold handled cane watching her with tightly folded arms and a steely gaze. Then the man strode forward with single-minded intent.

"Ellie," Ada whispered, and he watched her clutch Elodia's arm in alarm.

Who was he? Basil glanced at Leo who shook his head in response. Did he not recognize this man either? If anyone had told him there was a man who could turn Miss Hawthorne into a meek young woman, Basil wouldn't have believed them. The change from the audacious and spirited young woman into this meek and nervous creature would have been amusing if Basil wasn't concerned about Ada. It was clear from Ada's reaction that she knew who he was too. What was less clear was the reason for their obvious fear. Basil instinctively slid his arm around Ada's waist.

Elodia cleared her throat and yanked down on her jacket. "All will be well, Ada. He loves me too much to kill me."

Basil fought back a smile as realization set in. So this was the Viscount Melbroke, Elodia's formidable father. Clearly, he'd been alerted by Miss Mason's parents when they had all stolen the carriage and disappeared overnight. The gentleman paused at their group, his blue eyes fixed on his daughter. He then glanced at Ada who swallowed audibly.

"Miss Thornfield," he said, his tone icy cold.

"Thompson, actually," Elodia murmured, and his eyes

snapped back to her in an unmistakable warning before finding Basil's.

"Thompson. As in Viscount Sterling?" he asked. The speed with which the connection was made had Basil's hands sweating.

"Yes, my lord."

"I thought you were courting Miss Ashwood?" he asked.

Basil couldn't think of what to say to that. He'd courted her a bit but how much information had leaked out about their pending engagement? "I was."

He nodded and looked at Ada again. "Well, I imagine you are about to have your own troubles with your father, Thompson."

"Yes," Basil murmured.

Melbroke looked at Leo who was watching him with raised eyebrows. "And you are?"

"Leopold Kingston, formerly of Scotland Yard," he replied.

"Scotland Yard? I would have guessed military."

"That as well," Leo replied.

Melbroke nodded at him in acknowledgement before turning to Elodia again. "And you, dearest daughter."

"How did you know I was here?" she asked meekly.

"Captain Mason and his wife. I admit I was concerned about locating you when I arrived, but then I heard the ear-piercing whistle of a highwayman, so I simply followed that." The anger seemed to have faded to annoyance.

"I was coming straight home papa, I promise."

"Straight home from Brighton does not include a stop off at Gretna Green last time I checked," he replied, every word crisp with sarcasm.

"I can explain."

"You always can," he replied, a note of rueful amusement now coloring his ire. Elodia's eyes dropped again, and Melbroke's mouth twisted in irritation. "Come along, you. Good day gentlemen, Miss Thompson." He gave Ada a pointed look and left with a firm grip on Elodia's arm.

Leo turned back to Basil, clearly entertained. "And then there were three."

"What have you found, Leo?"

"I know where they are keeping Richard. Some old acquaintances at Scotland Yard and I took turns stopping by Giltspur Compter and making some vague inquiries as to new inmates. The man at the gate didn't like it. I believe he thought I was getting above myself."

"How curious and unexpected," Basil replied before they shared a grin.

"I've been tailing Trent the last couple days, and he has been looking for you, Mrs. Thompson. He is panicking."

"Where's my brother?" Ada asked.

"Based on Trent's movements, I think he's at the docks by the Thames. I saw them move someone night before last to a holding room there. He's visited there three times so far. But that panic is going to cost them."

"The docks aren't nearly as secure as a debtor's prison."

"Indeed, and he has fewer people to watch Richard. If there was ever a time to move, it is now. There is a shift change in roughly…" he paused to check his pocket watch, "three hours. The gap in time is around fifteen minutes."

"You mean to get him tonight?" Ada asked.

"Yes. The longer he is trapped there with Trent running out of options, the more likely he will begin taking out reprisals on Richard. The sooner we get him, the better."

"Perhaps I can stay with Ellie," Ada said turning to Basil. Something about the way she looked up at him with all that trust in her wide eyes had his heart clenching in his chest.

"No. Miss Hawthorne's house is being watched and likely so is Miss Mason's. You need to be somewhere Trent can't connect you to." He wasn't sure how he was going to manage it, but he didn't have any other options.

Leo looked at Basil askance, "You don't mean?"

His mother would scold him raw, but she wouldn't turn Ada away if Basil vouched for her. His father would pitch a fit, but he'd never counteract his mother in their home. "It's the only place he'd never think to look."

The porter Elodia had sent for ran up to them, looking around in obvious confusion. "Is it just you three, sir?"

"Two," Leo replied. "I have arrangements to make. I'll meet you there, Bas."

"Yes."

"Don't go in until I'm there," Leo instructed, laying a heavy hand on Basil's shoulder.

Basil nodded before tightening his grip on Ada's waist and pulling her along as they followed the porter to the carriage awaiting them.

"What are you talking about, where are you taking me?" Ada asked, glancing between Basil and Leo's departing figure with a puzzled frown.

Basil heaved a sigh. "I'm taking you to my parents."

Chapter Seven

Sterling House
London

To say that Ada was both anxious and annoyed with the current turn of events would be an understatement. While she trusted Basil entirely and was grateful to Mr. Kingston for his efforts in finding her brother, she was uncomfortably aware of the shift in her role. Now that the delicate flower had been secured, she was to be shunted off while the men sorted out the rest of the business.

She understood the logic of it, and she knew that she had no real ability to sleuth at all, but the highhandedness was galling. Basil and Mr. Kingston had determined what was to be done with nary a word and without a single reference to her, as though she were a mere child being transported. Or a piece of luggage. She knew it sounded ungrateful. They were, in fact, older by nearly a decade, but they could have at least pretended to consider her.

Now she was on her way to being deposited at his parent's London residence. His parents who were the Viscount and Viscountess of Sterling. The moment she met them would be the moment he told them he had shamed their family for a woman who was unworthy. For a friend. They would blame her. There was no way around it. She'd almost rather take her chances by herself. She could lock herself in her bedroom for the night. The prospect of Basil hiding her away in a tower somewhere suddenly seemed far more appealing.

"What are you thinking?" he asked suddenly.

"What?" She turned towards him, but he was looking out the window.

"You've sighed three times in as many minutes. What's wrong?"

She had not. Had she? She pressed her lips together and took a deep breath. "Nothing, it's only that you are a member of the nobility."

He shifted restlessly in his seat, as if the mention of that fact made him uncomfortable. "I didn't realize it mattered to you."

"Well, it wouldn't have. But now I'm about to meet your parents."

"Just my mother," he looked down at his hand resting on his knee, and one finger began tapping.

Did she have to come out and say it? "Basil. I'm half Chinese."

He glanced at her. "Are you worried that she'll throw you out and disown me because I polluted the family line or some such nonsense?"

Well, if he was going to put it that way. "Yes."

He scoffed lightly and shook his head. "Nothing so dramatic from her, I'm afraid. My father and brother, however, are another story. Either way, they can't do anything about it. I think the old girl will rather take it in her stride, I imagine."

"Really?"

"Yes. Although, I wouldn't mention the annulment to her," he said glancing at her.

"Why not? Wouldn't she prefer that?"

"My father would, my mother… she may take the long view. Marriage is marriage and I am only the second son after all. Don't let her bully you into doing anything you don't want to do, Ada. She comes across as empathetic, but she is a little tyrant."

"Right."

"They are my problem, not yours."

Were they truly so horrible? He was warning her about them as if they were adversaries instead of his own flesh and blood, and just as he was about to leave her on their doorstep without warning. How would she manage in a den of wolves on her own? She'd never had to face it alone. Now, it seemed, for the next few days at least, she wouldn't have a choice. "Every hour that passes, this marriage seems like less of a good idea," she grumbled unconsciously.

Her words fell into a thick silence that seemed to amplify them. With every passing second, they sounded harsher. She stole a glance at Basil and saw him still staring at his hand with a queer smile on his face. The angles of his face seemed harder all of a sudden, as if he'd become a different person. One who wouldn't comfort her when she cried or hold her hand while she slept in dark rooms.

"Cheer up. You won't have to live with it for much longer if all goes well. Not everyone can escape their mistakes so easily," he finally said, his voice perfectly civil, but lacking the affection she'd always associated with him even when he was annoyed.

She winced. *Bloody hell.* She couldn't fault his comprehension, but did he have to take it in the worst way possible? Did he really think she saw him as something to tolerate? Is that how he saw himself? The description didn't match what she knew him to be. "Basil, that's not what I meant."

Another silence and he met her eyes. "Then what did you mean?" There was a quiet defiance in his face masking a vulnerability she'd never noticed before now. She never imagined he would need her assurance.

"I never wanted to cause you any trouble with your family. This arrangement was meant to be the shortest path to achieving a goal we both wanted. Now I'm becoming some kind of recompense for a debt you had in a past life."

He smiled and the sardonic stranger melted away and he was her Basil again, taking her gloved hand in his. "You aren't as much trouble as you think, honestly."

Her Basil. When did she begin thinking of him as hers? She leaned her head against his broad shoulder, and tried not to think about how soon she would have to leave his company. She knew she didn't want him to let go of her hand. Her body warmed as she gazed into his blue eyes. It wasn't the first time she'd noticed how beautiful they were, but in this moment with her hand in his in the small space of the hired carriage, there was an overwhelming intimacy she hadn't prepared for. This was more dangerous than when he'd helped her with her dress and sharper than when he'd held her hand as he slept beside her in bed. She had to cut it somehow, had to stop herself from giving away something she couldn't afford to lose. "Because I take instruction so well?"

He watched her for a moment, as amused realization sank in. "Little liar. That's what you've been stewing over, is it?"

"No." She slid her hand out of his, and turned her body to face forward with the brattiest expression she could manage.

His expression was dubious, but he shook his head. "Either way, you're incorrect. It's because you are useful and level-headed."

"Not all the time," she griped but she couldn't help the pleased smile on her face.

"I don't want to frighten you, but my family isn't like yours was, Ada. My brother and I have never really been close. The closest relationships I have are with Leo and your brother."

"But your father. This will cause a rift, won't it?"

"It will. But I'm more concerned for you honestly. They won't be kind, Ada. They will assume the worst but frankly their bigotry is so generalized it would be a waste of energy to take it to heart."

She wasn't sure if he meant that to be comforting or not. *My family is wildly racist so don't take it personally when they inevitably hate you.* She supposed it made sense, but she was certain he didn't know what it was like for his entire existence to be seen as a problem. "Was that meant to be reassuring?"

"It's the best I can manage at the moment. Worst case scenario, my father keeps a bottle of brandy on the bottom shelf in the westernmost corner of the library. You're an old married woman now. Feel free to imbibe to your heart's content."

She looked at him askance. That was his advice? "Much obliged, I'm sure."

Ashford Hall, the London residence of the Viscount Sterling was off-putting, to say the least. The white and brown stone residence seemed enormous to Ada as they approached it in the carriage. If there were gardens, then they must have been in the back of the house because all she saw were the walls, the wrought iron gate, and what seemed like a forest of trees.

"How old is your family title?" she asked weakly.

"Same as your family business, about two hundred years give or take," he replied.

"Oh." She hadn't thought of it in quite that way. Did he really see his family title as equivalent to her family's business?

The carriage came to a halt and the driver came around to open the door. Basil gave her hand a squeeze of support before he exited. She heard him give the footman instructions to move her bag to the front door before he turned to her. She held out her hand for him to take but instead he grabbed her waist and deftly plucked her from the carriage, setting her on her feet on the ground. It took her a full minute to recover from that, which judging by the twitch in his mouth, he found terribly amusing.

"All right?" he asked.

She glared at him while her heart thumped away in her chest. How was she supposed to see him as her brother's friend when he kept doing things like that? Why was that smug gleam leaving her knees weak instead of stiffening her spine? It was annoying. She was only human after all. No woman would be immune to being snatched up as if she were a pastry or a leaf.

He tucked her hand into the crook of his elbow, covering it with his other hand, and started down the short driveway to the front door. As they reached the stairs, the door flew open to reveal a pretty, middle-aged woman in a light green day gown with the same medium brown hair and blue eyes as Basil.

"Darling!" she exclaimed, opening her arms to him. He smiled and went to her, dropping Ada's hand. She hugged him tightly before pulling away and cupping his lightly bearded face in her hands. "Are you finally becoming a pirate?" she teased.

"No mother," he replied, shaking his head with amused exasperation. "Is The Vicar here?"

She frowned lightly, her mouth pursing. "I do wish you'd stop calling your brother that."

"I'll do that when it stops being true. Is he home?"

"No, he's taken his family for a seaside holiday. They won't be back for at least a week."

"Perfect, and father?"

"Does this curiosity as to the location of our family members have anything to do with the young lady standing behind you that you have yet to introduce me to?"

He turned to Ada, who watched him with wide eyes at the foot of the stairs. Whatever warmth she had for Basil did not extend towards her, no matter how civil she was behaving. Ada had a suspicion she would have been nicer if she was a maid.

"I assume you haven't become so revolutionary as to bring a prospective maid to my front door."

"Not yet, mother."

"Well come in then; you weren't raised in a barn." She stepped to the side and allowed them in before shutting the door. She gestured to Ada. "Well?"

"Ada, I'd like to introduce you to Lady Euphemia Thompson, the Viscountess Sterling. Mother, I'd like to introduce you to Miss Adelaide Thornfield."

Ada glanced at him sharply. It was strange how rejected she felt over that slip of the tongue. She had to remember that she wasn't truly his wife. He certainly had not, for all his kindness.

"Thornfield?" his mother repeated carefully, her eyes fixed on Ada's hand.

Basil closed his eyes for a moment and gave his head a sharp shake, "Thompson, actually. Mrs. Adelaide Thompson."

Euphemia's eyebrows shot up and she took a deep, slow breath before releasing it. Ada braced herself for the worst as the viscountess turned to her with a carefully mild expression. "Delighted to meet you, Mrs. Thompson," she said.

"And I you, Lady Sterling." Ada sank into the expected curtsey in response. If that was what the viscountess's 'delighted' face looked like, Ada would drink a bottle of vinegar. That way at least they would appear equally 'delighted'.

"I'm curious as to how you are acquainted with my son, seeing as that's a family heirloom on your finger, Mrs. Thompson."

Ada choked on a gasp and glanced down at the gold band on her finger with roses etched onto the band. Had he given her a family heirloom for a fake wedding? What on earth did he mean by it?

"Based on my son's inability to remember your last name, I take it that this was a rather sudden turn of events?"

Basil cleared his throat and hid his hands behind his back looking like a naughty boy. "Yes, we've just come back from Gretna Green, Mother."

She stared at him silently for one humming moment. "How very interesting. So, is this a courtesy visit?"

"Not exactly. I… I have a rather urgent matter to see to. I need to leave Ada here for a while."

"Leave her?" his mother repeated.

"A while?" Ada interjected. If his mother hadn't been standing in front of her Ada would have slapped him. He made her sound like a parcel!

Basil, to his credit, seemed to notice their reactions and attempted to correct himself. "Rather I was hoping that you could host her for the night. My residence isn't necessarily up to the standard of care that Miss—I mean that Ada is used to."

"I think we need to have a talk."

"Mother, I do not have time for that now."

"Basil, I have never been in the habit of housing unexplained persons in my home. I shall not be commencing today. Make time," she replied coolly.

Ada saw, not for the first time, where the steel in Basil came from. Mother and son faced one another for a few tense moments. She was cool and indomitable, and he was stubborn and brimming with frustration. Ada had no interest in getting between them, but what they truly didn't have time for was a standoff.

With bated breath, Ada reached out and touched Basil's tense arm. When he glanced at her she squeezed. His jaw twitched, and the mutinous fire gave way to resignation.

"I can give you ten minutes," he said at last.

"Excellent."

HE DIDN'T HAVE time for this, and he resented being strong armed into an explanation because his mother was a nosey busybody. But Ada... Once again one look from her had him backing down. It was the smarter choice, he told himself, as he followed his mother into the sitting room with Ada's hand still on his arm. He was asking a favor, and Ada would have enough to cope with, staying here on her own with his parents. He hated leaving her here. Hated the fact that he didn't have any safer options for her.

Ada settled down beside him on the sofa facing his mother, and he waited for the first question. He had to leave Ada with at least one ally, even if it was a lukewarm one. His mother's eyes rested for a moment on Ada's hold on his arm before she met his stare.

"I imagine you've not forgotten that you were engaged to Miss Felicity Ashwood."

"I have not."

"And if I recall correctly, you sought out your father in search of a wife, did you not?"

"I did."

"Then please explain why you have eloped just as the banns have been posted."

"He posted them?"

"Your brother did."

Basil closed his eyes against a rising wave of helpless irritation. He'd specifically asked him to let him post the banns himself but trust his brother to step all over any plans Basil had made. "Those will need to be retracted."

"Yes, obviously. But you understand the effect this will have on not only Miss Ashwood's reputation but on ours. Especially yours."

"I do."

"Then what the hell were you thinking?"

He opened his mouth to reply, then paused at the last moment. Of anyone to know the truth, his mother was undoubtedly the best option, but it was a low bar to clear. Ada had wanted this kept a secret. She hadn't even allowed her closest friends to tell their parents, which would undoubtedly have simplified the trouble of keeping her from harm. Her uncle was a serious problem, however. The only way past him for certain was for Richard to be found quickly and quietly. Men like Mr. Simon Thornfield would always have people like Basil's father and brother on their side. Why would she be comfortable with his family knowing the truth? He didn't want to leave her here on her own. Perhaps this was a bad idea.

He should have taken her to Leo's mother. She was equally unknown by Trent, and she would have treated Ada like her own family once she knew her relation to Richard. *Stupid.* He'd been so focused on protecting Ada physically that he'd ignored her mental state. Now it was all he could think about and the look in his mother's eye wasn't filling him with confidence. Did he have time to run to the Kingston home now?

Tick tock, Thompson.

A firm compression on his arm drew his attention to Ada and her somber eyes. He'd always cared about her safety, but in such a short period of time she'd become vital to him. He wanted more than her safety; he wanted her smiling. He wanted that damned haunted look out of her eyes. He wanted her to never be afraid again. She squeezed his arm again and gave him a slight nod. It was all he needed.

"Richard Thornfield has been kidnapped."

"Your oriental friend from Cambridge."

Basil fought the urge to grind his teeth. "My *Chinese* friend, yes."

"Did I say something wrong?"

"Yes. He's not an object, he's a person." He couldn't keep the ire out of his voice, couldn't stop it from flashing in his eyes.

His mother's chin lifted in defiance, and he waited for her to dismiss him, to force him to leave. He wouldn't back down anymore. If he didn't take it seriously, his mother never would. Ada may only be his wife for a fortnight but as long as his ring was on her finger, he would protect her as if she was his life mate.

Then the viscountess let out a slow breath and nodded. "I beg your pardon, Mrs. Thompson. I did not mean any disrespect."

Ada nodded but stayed silent.

"So, he is missing?"

"Yes. The foreman had debts and decided to fix them through embezzlement and ransom demands."

"My goodness."

"I married Ada to ensure that her family business wasn't ruined on account of one bitter, greedy employee. The court might argue with an unmarried young woman but not the daughter-in-law of a viscount."

"Ah."

"Everything has happened so quickly. I didn't have time to warn you or father."

"And your friend?"

"I've only just found him. The foreman is entangled with some desperate and dangerous characters and the safest place for Ada was here. I don't expect your blessing or your recognition. I only ask that you allow her to stay here for a night or two so I can get her brother and return her to him safely."

"I see." His mother let out a small breath, then stood and walked over to the bell pull by the door. Within moments a maid opened the door and curtseyed. "Ah, Maria, see to it that the blue room is made up, we shall have a guest here for some time. You will attend her."

"Yes, mi 'lady," she replied, glancing into the room at Basil and Ada.

"And tell Cook to expect one more for dinner," his mother added, following her stare to where he sat.

The girl's eyes snapped back to her mistress and then down to the floor. "Yes, mi 'lady."

"Is Thomas nearby?"

She gave a jerky nod.

"Send him to me."

"At once, mi 'lady." She curtsied and scampered away, probably half terrified his mother would dismiss her for peering openly at a guest.

He didn't know how he felt about what had just happened. Part of him was grateful and a bit ashamed that he had doubted her. The other was wondering if it would be enough for Ada. "Thank you, Mama," he finally said.

"Nonsense. I would be delighted to host my new daughter-in-law. It will give me some time to get to know her since you elected to deny me the opportunity beforehand."

He opened his mouth to respond but, in the end, kept silent on that point. There was no way to save face without revealing what he hoped to keep from his mother.

"My lady," Thomas said with a bow.

"Thomas, my son shall need a carriage,"

"No," Basil stood and rushed over to where she stood.

She turned to pin him with a cool stare. "What do you mean 'no'?"

He took her hand in his. That coolness was masking something else, he knew. He had hurt her at some point today and there were a few guesses he could make at when and how. Later. "I appreciate the idea, Mama, but where I'm going a viscount's carriage will be too obvious. I'll hire a coach when I leave."

She nodded once. "Very good. Never mind, Thomas."

Thomas bowed and left the room. Euphemia turned to face Basil with a softer but still guarded expression, before glancing at Ada again. "I'll leave you to your farewells," she said and left the room, closing the door behind her.

Farewells. The time had come to leave her behind. After days and nights of near constant contact, he was reluctant to leave, even if he was leaving her in the safest place he could. He turned towards her, unsure of what to do with his hands now that they were alone, and she wasn't near. What on earth had happened to him? Ada stood and walked over to him, her face full of apprehension and without thinking, he reached out to her.

"Will it be very dangerous?" she asked as his fingers curled lightly around her upper arms. Her small hands rested on his chest, and he wondered if she could feel his heart hammering away behind his ribs.

"Not too much so. You heard the plan. It'll be in and out. Leo will be scoping out the area to verify where Richard is. I will meet him, and we will get your brother. I'll be careful, and I'll get your brother back to you. Don't worry."

She nodded, her eyes fixed on her fingers as they clutched at the fabric of his jacket. It wasn't enough. He knew that. "I think your mother is annoyed."

"She's extremely annoyed but not with you. I promise." He needed to stop touching her, but he couldn't bring himself to do it. Instead, he tucked a tendril of inky silken hair behind her ear, trying not to notice how soft her skin felt. Would he ever get to do it again?

She nodded again but said nothing more, lowering her eyes to where her hands lay between their bodies, lingering just as he was, needing to touch because words wouldn't come. He hooked his fingers under her sharp chin and lifted her head so he could see her face. He searched her rich dark eyes intently for a sign that she felt alright. That she knew she was safe, and he wouldn't leave her somewhere terrible for the sake of convenience. He knew he didn't have any words to reassure her. The only thing that would do that was Trent behind bars and her brother back in their home. "Ada," he murmured softly, and her eyes flooded with tears almost instantly. He couldn't stand it.

He folded her into his arms, his hand cradling her head against his chest. She settled against him as if she'd gone to him a million times. Her forehead rested heavily on his collarbone, and he felt her shoulders shudder silently as her fingers tightened on his coat. He rested his cheek against her hair and closed his eyes, rocking her from side to side, rubbed circles on the center of her back with one hand while the other pressed her closer. He knew what she felt like without her stays, and the difference now was frustrating. It made him want to pull her tighter so he could feel the shape of her under the steel, starch, and silk. "It's only for tonight," he murmured. "I promise. Whether I find him or not, I will come for you tomorrow."

He couldn't tell who he was reassuring anymore, her or himself. He drew her away carefully, leaned down, and pressed a kiss to her forehead in lieu of where he wanted to kiss her. His fingers brushed over her tear-stained freckled cheek as she gazed into his eyes. The utter trust in her eyes filled his chest with warmth until it ached, until his throat was burning. Everything about her, from her faith in him to how close her face was to his, was overwhelming. He had to break the tension somehow, had to take that look out of her eyes so he could get back in control of his body again.

"Don't forget the brandy," he said, and watched as surprise flashed across her face followed by the first genuine gleam of humor he'd seen light up her eyes as she laughed. It left him breathless.

"I won't. Thank you, Basil," she whispered.

"Ada, anything for you." Why had he said that? The words poured out of him without prompting, leaving him embarrassed at their truth but relieved to have them out. Her eyes widened in response and her lips parted to speak but then she looked away as a flush crept over her cheeks. Her full pink lips pressed together, and he'd never wanted anything more than to press his to them in that moment.

Had he made her uncomfortable or was she pleased to hear it? She wasn't pulling away from him, her body hadn't stiffened. He wished he had the time to know what it meant, but Leo was waiting and at this rate he would end up being late if he didn't leave.

Consciously he loosened his grip, lowering his arms and taking a step back from her warm body. "I'll see you later," he said, and she nodded in reply.

Not trusting himself to stay a moment longer, he turned and left through the open door where he saw his mother watching him with an odd expression on her face. Panic swept through him like a cold wind. What had she seen? What was she thinking?

"I thought you were leaving," she said, and he blinked as his brain fought to process it.

"I am. I'll see you tomorrow." He turned and walked to the front door, knowing that he would have to clear the air with her later when there was time. Perhaps when his skin wasn't aching from the loss of Ada's touch.

"Basil," his mother's voice came from over his shoulder, and he paused. "Have a care with my child."

He smiled. It was what she'd always said when he was a boy. He hadn't heard her say that phrase in such a long time. He glanced over his shoulder at her and wondered if he was imagining the glint in her eyes. "Always," he replied, giving her the response he knew she was waiting for.

Chapter Eight

Ada would never admit to anyone that after Basil left, she'd stayed by the window with her nose pressed to the glass, watching him stride across the street. To say she was uneasy about staying with his parents under the circumstances would be a hideous understatement.

"Well then, Mrs. Thompson. I think it is high time we had a talk."

Ada spun around to see Basil's mother standing near the chair.

"You do take tea, I imagine?"

Ada stared at her for a moment, considering the absurdity of the question. Why wouldn't she take tea? "I do. Thank you, my lady."

"Have a seat, please."

Ada walked back over to the sofa which now seemed too large without Basil. This entire house seemed to be too large without him taking up space beside her. A maid wheeled in a tea service and Ada braced herself for the inquest that was coming.

"When did you become acquainted with my son, Mrs. Thompson?"

"You may call me Ada, my lady."

"Is that short for something?"

"Adelaide."

"Then I shall call you that. I dislike nicknames. I find them too common."

"I've known Basil since childhood, but it was always through my brother, Richard."

"I remember your brother. I only met him a few times, but I suppose the unique is intrinsically memorable."

Unique. It was a kinder way to refer to her than 'alien' or 'strange' but there was an unmistakable meaning there and it wasn't altogether positive. "Yes."

"If your brother attended Cambridge, then I take it you are accomplished yourself. Do you draw?"

"I do."

"Watercolors?"

"Yes. And embroidery."

"What about music? Which instruments do you play?"

"Piano and the guqin."

"The what?"

Ada paused. Perhaps that was better left unsaid. "It's a stringed instrument. It used to belong to my mother."

"Ah. I don't believe I've ever heard it played before," she paused. "Have you ever been to China, Ada? Your mother hailed from there, but that doesn't necessarily mean you've been there."

"No, I've never been. My brother has a few times."

"Goodness, that must be an arduous journey."

"It is, from what he's told me."

"Have you ever wanted to go?"

"Yes. I'd want to meet my grandparents, my cousins."

The viscountess paused and took a deep breath before she spoke again. "Family is important."

"Yes." *Finally*, Ada thought, *some common ground*.

"I imagine your brother is as dear to you as my child is to me."

"He is." *More so*.

"So, I will not begrudge the cost of this ... escapade to my son or my family."

How very kind of you. Ada didn't speak, but her grip on her fingers tightened.

"Basil's father will be less understanding. For your own sake, I suggest you take dinner in your room, I will speak to him tonight. He should be back around eight tonight for supper."

"Agreed."

Thames holding yards
London

BASIL HAD NEVER had great affection for London, but the smell of the Thames, especially at the Blackwell shipyard holding yards, was enough to make him want to set the whole city on fire. It was acrid and pungent all at once from the waste matter of a thousand-year-old city. He already knew that every stitch of clothing on his body would need to be burned. His stomach was roiling, and his body had long broken out into a queasy sweat, but he wasn't about to leave before he had Richard. Ada's eyes were constantly on his mind since he'd left her with his mother. The idea of going back to her empty-handed and seeing the worry and disappointment in her eyes was even more sickening.

Basil forced himself to breathe out of his mouth and stayed low as he moved across the muddy ground. Night had fallen hard in the time it took him to get from Ada to the rendezvous point with Leo. He wasn't a sleuth by nature, but he'd hidden to avoid enough fights when he was a small, skinny child to know the basic rules: stay low, quiet, and as small as possible. Most of all, stay alert. It had also taught him patience. The moonlight and torch lamps cast shadows everywhere, and his dark clothing made it easier for him to stay hidden from any unfriendly watchful eyes.

He crouched by a fence and scanned the area. There were workers further down unloading barges but only a few on his side. This had to be where they were keeping Richard, but just because Basil couldn't see the men didn't mean they weren't there. He needed to wait for Leo. His eyes strained in the dim lighting for a glimpse of the mark to indicate where they would meet. He had said it would be small and red. In retrospect, perhaps Basil should have sought more information. Red like a mark? Or a red ribbon? He could barely see anything as it was. A breeze floated by and something flickered up ahead near a wooden wall. *Was that?* Basil squinted, *yes*. Not flickering but fluttering. A red strip of cloth, barely visible near the dim light of a lamp. That was the mark. Only a few hundred yards away.

With a sigh of relief, he checked once more for people, then moved quickly and as quietly as he could manage. Once he reached the structure, he pressed his back against the side of the wooden building, keeping in the shadow it cast and making his way around to the tie. Now all he needed to do was wait for Leo. He didn't know how long he stood there, it could have been minutes or hours, but every tick of his pocket watch seemed to set his nerves on edge.

Was he early? Was there a different mark he should have seen? What if Leo needed to hold off on the rescue and he'd missed the message? What if he was too late because his mother had forced him to stay back that extra fifteen minutes? He wasn't sure what would happen if they ended up in a real altercation with a large group of kidnapping thugs. Their window for grabbing Richard was slim. While Basil could handle himself well enough in a fight provided it was quick and he threw the first punch, he wasn't the largest of men, not to mention a notoriously poor shot. He did know how to take a hit and land a punch well enough provided it was one-on-one. What time was it? He pulled out his pocket watch and angled it towards the light, but before he could read the time, he saw the glint it set off. *Fuck.*

"Oy!"

He shoved the offending accessory into his pocket and backed away, crouching down in an attempt to remain hidden. A dark figure emerged from the shadows and came towards him.

Fuck. Fuck.

"You don't work 'ere, what are you up to?" the gruff voice came.

Basil clenched his hand into a fist and straightened his legs, moving his feet shoulder width apart. One solid punch was all he needed to get away. He just needed to keep his head and pay attention to his opponent. Just as he was about to lunge at him, the man let out a grunt and hit the ground. Someone was behind the would-be assailant. Someone who had taken him out in one blow. Basil planted his feet and waited for what was likely to be the fight of his mostly sheltered life. The light shifted and he caught sight of hazel-brown eyes. The relief he felt was visceral.

"Kingston," he murmured, fighting to stay standing on now gelatinous legs.

"All right, Bas?"

He heard the humor in his voice before he saw the corner of his mouth twitching. He'd be annoyed with that later, when his heart wasn't trying to climb out of his chest. "Were you late or am I early?"

"Neither. I came ahead to get the lay of things. He's in the third hall down; they left a few minutes ago."

"Was Trent with them?"

"No, but they are coming back within the hour. We need to move." Leo started to walk away but Basil grabbed his arm, stopping him.

"How is he?" He wasn't sure why it mattered right now. They needed to move but he couldn't get his legs to work.

"You know Richard," Leo said rolling his eyes.

Basil smiled, relief flooding his chest. "Indeed." No doubt their friend was giving those bastards an earful and a fistful at every opportunity. He wasn't a man to surrender his dignity at any price, regardless of the circumstances. "Lead the way then."

He followed Leo down to the hall in question, staying low and close by. Leo paused at the third door and shot the lock off before pushing the door open. A man lunged at them almost immediately. Or at least that's how it seemed to Basil, who was on edge ready to strike out at the first person he couldn't recognize. In truth, the unfortunate gentleman had simply fallen onto the ground. A quick peek revealed Richard standing in the middle of the room, impatiently removing a set of iron manacles from his wrists.

There were no fewer than three men strewn about the room on the earthen floor in varying states of injury. One was bleeding from the head, another from the nose, but both were unconscious. The third was groaning and trying to push himself to his feet until Richard walked over and swung the restraints down onto his head with ferocious accuracy. The sound of iron cracking against bone echoed throughout the room and the man went limp.

Richard straightened to his full height, his face set in a granite mask. The quiet fire in his brown eyes when he glanced at the door was enough to assure Basil that his friend wasn't the worse for wear, despite the blood and bruises around his eyes.

"Good afternoon, Basil, Leo," he said, his voice low and deceptively calm.

Leo chuckled and shook his head while Basil let out a sigh of relief. Ada would be overjoyed.

"Did you know we were coming?" Basil asked.

"No, but this idiot with the keys likes to drink." Richard nodded at the head bleeder against a crate. "It was a matter of time really."

"What was your plan for getting past the men outside?" Leo asked.

"I hadn't gotten that far yet," Richard replied evenly, "but it was probably going to be messy."

"That's one word for it," Leo replied.

"Are you quite finished here?" Basil asked. Richard walked towards them, filthy, certainly fragrant, but full of vim and vigor. And stone-cold rage.

He aimed one vicious kick at the ribs of the man on the

ground in the doorway, his face a mask of fierce satisfaction.

"Quite."

RICHARD DIDN'T SPEAK again until they were in a hired carriage on the way back to his home. Richard's anger was a palpable thing filling the enclosure, despite the open windows. Basil and Leo watched him carefully from their seats, unwilling to move, waiting for the explosion. Basil had shared a room with him, but he'd never seen him in such a state. His dark hair was greasy and untidy, his sharp jaw was covered in a beard. It hadn't taken long for Basil to understand that Richard wasn't someone to trifle with, even when he was fifteen, but the man sitting across from him was almost terrifying. His stillness as he stared out the carriage window made it even more ominous.

"Where is Ada?" he finally asked. Basil saw Leo looking over at him with interest, but he refused to even glance his way. This conversation was bound to be awkward enough.

"She is safe."

"I asked where," Richard repeated, a tense edge to his voice.

"She is with my mother," Basil replied, hoping he wouldn't ask anything further.

Richard closed his eyes and let out a long breath, his hand clenching into a tight fist on his thigh before releasing it. "Why with your mother?"

"Because it was the last place anyone would look for her." *And because she's my wife.* Basil saw Leo raise his eyebrows and bit back a curse. Ada's face floated into his mind, heart-achingly sweet and sad, desperate for hope, and terrified of being left alone.

When he glanced at Richard, his dark eyes were fixed on him expectantly, as if he was awaiting the full explanation. The heaviness of that stare had Basil's palms sweating. In Richard's current mood, there was no certainty he wouldn't throw him out of the carriage once he knew. But there was still a slight chance he was either too distracted or too relieved to do it. In the end, he wouldn't appreciate Basil playing games.

"There's another reason. Ada and I... I married Ada a few days ago."

"You what?"

"I haven't done anything untoward."

The stillness of Richard's face was alarming. "You marry my sister without my permission and say you haven't done anything untoward?"

"She didn't really give him a choice," Leo murmured.

"Shut up," Basil hissed, and Leo covered the smile spreading across his face and looked away.

Richard frowned, "What?"

"Nothing. It is a marriage in name only. It was for her safety. She was concerned about your uncle being her guardian if we couldn't find you. She seemed to think he would have less than honorable intentions towards both of you. It would be easier for her as a married woman to take control of things and ensure your safe return."

Richard nodded again and turned away to look out the window, his gaze fixed intently on the passing streets and people. The silence stretched out for a few humming minutes before he took a deep breath. "Good. That's good. Thank you, Basil."

"You had to know I wouldn't let anything happen to her." At least he wasn't in trouble for now.

"And you, Leo, thank you both for looking for me."

"Don't annoy me. It's no more than you would do for either of us," Leo replied easily, turning to face his window.

The answering smile from Richard was small but heartfelt. "True enough."

"I've reported Trent to Scotland Yard. I have former colleagues on standby to take him in. What do you want to do, Richard?" Leo asked.

His answer would determine how soon the night would end. If Richard was content to see justice done, then Leo would see to it on his own. But judging by Richard's mood, he would want to get a few kicks in first before allowing the law to do its work. Richard didn't respond visibly at first. For a moment Basil wondered if Richard had heard Leo's question, but then he saw one grimy finger with a ragged fingernail tapping a slow methodical cadence on his knee. The wheels in his head were churning away.

"I want a bath and a meal. In that order," he said finally.

"And then?" Basil asked.

"I'm going to take that slimy little fucker apart."

Chapter Nine

Sterling House
London

THE HALL CLOCK was right outside Ada's bedroom. She could hear it ticking down the minutes and hours that she had been waiting. She was glad to be allowed to eat in her room. Between Basil and his mother she had no intention of meeting his father ever if she could avoid it. All the man would have to do is set eyes on her and the evening would go from trying to insupportable.

The room itself was beautiful, and airy, from the high ceilings and the delicate Rococo roses painted on the walls. The bed was plush and the chairs were comfortable. Perhaps it was the almost eerie silence, or perhaps it was simply the unfamiliarity putting her on edge. But she hadn't considered the reality of being alone for hours on end within earshot of a mechanical device marking the passing moments with incessant unbearable precision. She needed a diversion. Like a book.

Thanks to the blasted clock she knew it was around seven. Basil's father wouldn't be home for another hour if the viscountess was correct. She would have more than enough time to run down to the library and get something to occupy herself for the next five to six hours until her brain gave up and sleep took over.

Ada left the room and walked to the stairs. The bedrooms

were on the third floor so the common areas would be on the second. All she had to do was check each room she hadn't accounted for yet. As quietly as possible she descended the white marble stairs and began checking each room. On the fourth try she found the library. A push on the white door gave way to a room paneled with dark wood and towering shelves of books. It was a decent sized library, although a little smaller than the one she had at Thornfield House.

She walked along the wall searching for some indication of how it was organized. Was it by name of the author or title? By time period in which it was written? By the nationality of the author? Did she even have time to decipher it? Maybe she should simply go with the first book she recognized. She climbed up onto the ladder and peered closely at each of the titles.

Finally, she spied a volume by Moliere. *Candide*. Dark and humorous, she'd take it. She glanced down a few shelves and saw Alexandre Dumas. *The Count of Monte Cristo*. That was enough. With her two conquests, she carefully climbed back down.

"Who are you?"

Ada spun around and stared with wide eyes at the man staring at her in the doorway. He was an older gentleman, closer to sixty than fifty with silver threaded dark hair and a stocky build. He crossed the room in moments and took hold of her arm in a grip that was almost painful.

"Let go of me." She struggled to get her arm free but he jerked her forward, his blue eyes menacing.

"What are you doing in my house?" His house. Damn. How long had she been looking? Wasn't he meant to be back later?

Ada cleared her throat and prepared to answer the man she was certain was Basil's father. "I… my name is Adelaide Thor—" she paused "Thompson. Adelaide Thompson."

"Nonsense, girl. You are no relation of mine."

"Not of yours, no. I'm married to your son, Basil."

"Hogwash, Basil is spoken for. The banns were posted. Even if it is true, there is no way you could have gotten legally married so quickly. An English girl would know that."

"We weren't married in England."

He stared at her unblinkingly and the color leeched from his face. "Euphemia!" he bellowed, his voice setting her ears ringing.

In a blessed few moments Basil's mother was there, "What is it, Gerald?" her eyes fell on Ada and the grip he had on her arm. "Oh."

The woman was a bitch but she was the only person Ada had at the moment. "I'm sorry. I was getting a book and—"

"It's alright, Adelaide."

"Adelaide? Who is this person?"

His grasp loosened slightly as he stared at his wife in shock, and Ada took the opportunity to yank her arm out of his hold and move as far away from him as possible.

"Gerald, darling, why don't you follow me?"

"No. She said she and Basil are married. Is it true?"

Euphemia walked over to him, no doubt ready to retrain him if needed. "Yes, at Gretna Green a day or so past. The banns Hamilton posted will need to be recalled."

Basil's father closed his eyes as the implications settled in his mind. Whatever came out of his mouth next wasn't going to be something Ada wanted to hear. She had her books. She didn't need to be here to witness his fit of temper. While his attention wasn't on her, Ada began to move along the wall towards the door.

"It's incredible," he finally murmured.

"Gerald, please."

"Absolutely incomprehensible. When I think of the effort I spent on that idiotic child, when I think of the time and the money just so he can—" His ice blue eyes fixed on Ada suddenly. "Don't you dare try to scuttle away, you little harlot."

"Gerald!"

"No, enough. I want her to explain how she managed to marry my son in a matter of days. I want to know what tricks she used to ensnare my child and make him forget what he owes to his family."

"There were extenuating circumstances," Euphemia began.

"Has he gotten you pregnant?" The viscount looked at Ada.

"I beg your pardon?" Ada could feel her free hand curling into a fist. How many ways could the man think to insult her?

"That fool of a boy," he hissed.

"I am not pregnant. The very suggestion is an insult."

"You have—"

"My brother was taken captive by a person of desperate character." She refused to listen to any more of his half-concocted assertions. "To protect us both from further machinations, Basil agreed to marry me."

"And who exactly is your brother?"

"His name is Mr. Richard Thornfield."

He turned to his wife. "The manufacturer?"

"Yes." Euphemia replied.

"Are you trying to tell me that my son disgraced his family for a half-breed merchant's son?"

"I am telling you that your son is a man of integrity and loyalty and doesn't deserve your condemnation," Ada retorted.

"Not from where I'm standing,"

"Then *move.*"

He glared at her for a single terrifying moment. "You are very loyal, very quickly. That may be a sign of deep feeling or stupidity. But I will decide what my son deserves in this house, not you."

"Either way, it was clearly a matter of some urgency, Gerald," Euphemia said clearly attempting to calm him down. "He assured me he'll be back tomorrow."

"And you still have faith in his assurances?"

"He has no reason to lie."

"He had no reason to ask me to hunt down a bride for him if he was going to elope to Gretna Green with this—" he stopped short when he caught Ada's gaze, and she felt her lip curl in contempt as her hands curled into fists at her side. It was all she could do to stay where she stood and not strike him across his hateful face. "But if you are precious enough for him to betray his family, then I suppose he'll come back for you." Without another word, he turned and stormed out of the room, sending the door slamming into the wall.

Ada closed her eyes and tried to breathe through the worst of her anger. Dining alone had never been such a delightful prospect. The idea of sitting across a table from that man filled her with so much dread her skin was crawling. This man was Basil's father. She didn't understand how that was possible. Suddenly the idea of annulment didn't seem like the worst thing in the world. She felt a pressure on her arm and opened her eyes to see the viscountess watching her.

"I apologize for his behavior."

"You said he wouldn't be back until eight. I thought I had time."

"Either way, he knows now. There's no reason for you to stay above stairs, but you may still dine in your room if you wish."

"Thank you." Ada turned and left, her stomach in her throat.

TWO HOURS LATER, Basil was almost certain that Richard was no longer simply angry but had migrated into a new level of rage that bordered on irrationality. No sooner had Richard bathed, dressed, and choked down a meal of kidney pies and ale, then he had Leo rounding up some constables and Basil back in a carriage. Watching his friend as he stared at the passing scenery outside the carriage window, Basil was reminded of how dangerous Richard could be when he was in a temper. After fifteen years they had argued and sniped at each other more times than he could count.

He'd seen Richard vexed at the prejudice he'd endured from classmates and teachers or even in society. He'd seen him petty and full of righteous anger. He'd seen him stone-faced and uncompromising in the face of persecution, never showing the depth of his feelings to anyone. Not even to Basil. Perhaps he was beginning to understand that he had never truly seen Richard angry. Not like this.

Richard had always been lively and good-humored with energy to spare. He had always possessed a natural intensity even when he was fifteen, which made him engaging even when he was silent. But Basil had never witnessed that anger focused so clearly with single-minded intensity. The stillness seemed almost predatory even though Trent was nowhere to be seen. Like a wolf moving in on its prey, or a snake coiling itself ever tighter to strike, its eyes fixed on a threat.

"When did you marry Ada?" Richard asked suddenly.

Lord, were they back to that topic again? Basil had hoped they had passed that sticky subject. "Only a day ago. Once we found you, we meant to have it annulled. With you free, she wouldn't need my protection anymore."

Richard slowly turned his head to stare at Basil. "You're going to annul your marriage to my sister?"

"It was her idea."

"And you agreed to it?"

"It's her life, and you know what my family is like. She deserves more than I can give her," Basil replied softly.

Richard muttered something in Mandarin under his breath and shook his head. Basil couldn't claim any fluency, but he was sure he heard something about a 'stubborn idiot'.

He'd never felt smaller and more wretched in his life. He remembered the way Ada had clung to him, trusted him, confided in him over the last few days. They had worked well together and seeing someone so capable and composed view him as a source of comfort had affected him deeply. She had seen him in a way that no one had before, as someone vital to her happiness. He wanted that in his life. He wanted her, but he didn't have a right to her if she didn't care for him.

He couldn't be so selfish as to ask her to stay in a family that would treat her like a shameful aberration. She was so young. He couldn't take advantage of her naïvety and allow her to stay with him. A night with his parents would likely cure her of that idea.

The carriage came to a stop, drawing his attention from his musings. Richard disembarked immediately. Basil followed, looking at the establishment and the surrounding area. The pub they stopped at was in a more colorful part of town. Not rough exactly but geared towards the working class. Groups of both men and women stood and sat around eating and drinking, smoking, or laughing. A merry fiddle played while a group sang along. The street lighting was dim, and the roads were unpaved, but the general goodwill brightened the atmosphere. Within moments upon entering, he saw the reason Richard had been so insistent on this pub at this time. At the bar with two other men sat Trent.

"How on earth?" Basil wondered aloud.

"People have loose tongues when they think you're asleep," Richard replied before walking towards the unsuspecting man. "Donald. Fancy seeing you here."

Trent's back stiffened before he turned around and took in Richard with wide eyes and a pale face. "Mr. Thornfield."

"It's been a while. How have you been?"

"I—"

"Surprised to see me?"

The man's mouth opened and closed wordlessly as he grappled with the reality of his situation.

"Perhaps disappointed is more accurate."

"I don't know what you mean."

Richard's smile was almost feral. "I have to say I underestimated you. Such a cunning and resourceful mind. Such a felicity with numbers. Stealing money was one thing but arranging to have me kidnapped for a ransom… that takes a bit more than you would be capable of."

"I've never stolen anything in my life."

"I'm sure you believe that, but I have a couple of ledgers at home that disagree with you."

"You can't prove that was me."

"Oh, but I can. You are coming with me."

"And who's gonna make me? You and your toffee-nosed friend?" he sneered nodding towards Basil.

"We could, but you aren't going to give me that much trouble because I'm not the only one after you, am I, Donald?" Richard folded his hands behind his back and leaned forward slightly. "You're at a loose end."

A burly man rose to his feet with a concerned expression on his face but one look from Basil had him pausing.

"Alrigh', Trent?"

Trent held Richard's gaze for a moment while he thought over his options. There was no sympathy in Richard's face, but one thing was very certain. He wasn't a killer. Basil was sure that Trent wasn't likely to take his chances with murderers over one angry former employer.

"Alright, Bill," Trent replied. He threw back the last of his beer and then rose to his feet, squaring off with Richard.

"After you," Richard said stepping out of his way.

Trent lunged suddenly, but Richard was too fast for him. He darted to the side and used Trent's momentum to slam his face into the top of a nearby table. The impact reverberated throughout the room as Trent slumped to the floor.

Richard stared down at him with a ferocious expression and growled a phrase that Basil definitely recognized. "Bù zhīdào nǐ de jíxiàn."

Not knowing your limits

Basil fought back a smile as he watched the shocked expressions on the faces of the onlookers. The silence as they reevaluated the average-sized man in the middle of the room was too amusing.

The door opened again, and Leo entered with three policemen. He took one look where Trent was on the floor and let out a whistle. "Is he alive?"

"For now," Richard replied, "I'll leave him with you, Kingston." He turned and walked away.

Chapter Ten

Ashford House
London

ADA SPENT A sleepless night waiting for news. Despite the lush bedding and warm room, it was impossible for her to relax long enough to fall asleep. After that encounter with the Viscount Sterling, it took hours for her to calm down. Even now, the thought of him filled her with rage. How was it possible that such a man had raised someone like Basil Thompson? He was a perfect example of the worst parts of English society. Ada had never struck anyone in her life, but she had very nearly punched the man and to hell with the consequences. As it was, she could hardly wait until she was out of this house and with people who didn't make her into someone she didn't recognize.

She trusted Basil and because she trusted him, she trusted Mr. Kingston and his abilities. There was growing anxiety in her that she had been foolish to allow herself to invest in him so deeply. After all, she'd trusted Mr. Trent too, hadn't she? It wasn't until Basil appeared and showed her the truth that she even understood the extent to which she had been played.

Concern washed over her. Anything could have gone wrong with the plan, and they had no idea the scale of Mr. Trent's enterprise. What if they had gone in alone and become overpowered? What if they had brought the police force and triggered a desperate response that ended with all three of them dead? With every tick of the clock, her mind manufactured a new terror in the dark room. That age-old fear was rising within her, of being the one left behind. The last survivor.

Then there was Basil himself. She had always known that finding a husband would be a challenge. She was an oddity in English society. She had money to be sure but no arranged marriage to a nobleman like Regina or a titled father like Elodia. Finding a man who didn't covet her sizeable dowry and ultimately plan to squander it would be difficult. Finding a man who didn't see her Chinese heritage as something to overlook or, conversely, as something to show off at parties like an exotic pet would be almost impossible.

Basil had been an unexpected gift, despite the disagreeable circumstances. He was everything a gentleman should be, everything she could want. Dependable, loyal, honorable, clever, and compassionate. Beautiful. She kept thinking of his forget-me-not eyes, his full mouth, his body, his scent of cloves and lavender. Every time she closed her eyes, she kept remembering how soft his mouth had felt on her skin, how reassuring his hands were on her body. All she wanted was to stay in his arms until this entire nightmare was over. Part of her was beginning to think that was the only way she'd feel safe again.

Did he want her for his wife? She kept thinking of how they parted earlier. Reflecting on the tender kiss he'd left on her forehead, the overwhelming gentleness in his eyes. How could something so innocent feel so wildly intimate at the same time? She'd felt it down to her bones. For one breathless moment, she'd sworn he was going to kiss her, and she'd wanted it with a ferocity that almost frightened her.

His mother was cold comfort indeed. She had been civil, even kind, but there was no doubt in Ada's mind that it was all for Basil's sake. If she stayed married to Basil, she would always treat Ada as Basil's wife and not her daughter-in-law. And she was by far the better option. The very thought of his father made her blood boil, and she hadn't even met his brother yet. She knew it was unlikely she'd find another man who would treat her with so much respect, give her so much reassurance, and set her body on fire at the same time. Was that enough?

The worst outcome would cost her Zhenyi and leave her in a family that from all accounts despised her. The best would cost her Basil but leave her with a brother who loved her and would no doubt secure her future. Both options left her with a hole in her life.

The morning found Ada an exhausted raw nerved wreck. She stayed silent as the maid helped her dress for breakfast and styled her hair, not trusting herself to speak. She didn't really want to be around anyone who wasn't Basil or her brother. Should she ask for a tray to be brought up? They would likely think her stuck up but in her current mood she wasn't inclined to care. It was likely too late to request that. What if the staff had already set up in the breakfast buffet in anticipation of her? She would be wasting their efforts for the sake of a tantrum. Better to go down. Whatever it was, she wouldn't have to put up with it for very long.

While she walked down to the breakfast room, she weighed the odds of the likelihood the Viscountess Sterling didn't take breakfast in bed. It was likely low, wasn't it? It's not as if the woman wanted her here, and she certainly wouldn't expect any kind of company while she waited for her son to return. The scent of eggs and pork reached Ada's nose as she entered the breakfast room, lifting her low spirits. It was a pretty room, painted in light blue with elegant fixtures and heavy dove grey curtains at the windows. The very picture of elegance and refined taste associated with nobility.

"Good morning, Adelaide." The viscountess was seated at the round breakfast table.

"Good morning, Lady Sterling," she replied.

"I hope you slept well."

So calm and civil. As if her husband hadn't behaved like a brigand. A husband who was notably missing.

"As well as I could manage, my lady," Ada replied, picking up a plate from the sideboard and filling it with coddled eggs, fried ham, and tomatoes. She could feel annoyance pricking at her brain.

"Come sit beside me, dear."

Dear? Perhaps she was trying to make up for it herself. It only annoyed Ada further. She didn't have the energy to pretend or play games for the sake of appearances. However, turning down the attempt would be seen as churlish and immature, so Ada obeyed and sat beside her hostess. A glance at the viscountess's plate told her the woman had already been there for at least an hour. She could have simply left the room but it seemed ungrateful to point it out, even if the idea of making small talk was assassinating her appetite with every passing second.

She'd learned to eat regardless of her mood long ago at school. There would always be some kind of unpleasantness whenever she moved in society. She couldn't afford to fast whenever she was upset. Harming herself because of the actions of others only served their agenda instead of helping her. The Viscount Sterling might have been only too glad to see her hungry and pale-faced in a corner, but she wasn't about to give him any satisfaction at all. With one deft motion, she laid her napkin across her lap and prepared to eat another meal that she wasn't sure she'd enjoy.

"I take it the viscount will not be joining us for breakfast," she commented.

"No. He is not disposed for company this morning."

She imagined their subsequent talk hadn't gone well after Ada had returned to her room. "I could have eaten in my bedroom."

She waved her off. "No need for that. He's not avoiding you, I'm afraid." She gave her a wry smile and sipped her tea.

"Ah. I suppose he thinks you should have made me leave."

The viscountess didn't say anything, but she developed a sudden interest in her plate that lasted a few minutes while Ada cut her sausage into six equal parts.

"I hope you can understand the situation we are all finding

ourselves in," she finally said.

"Likewise."

Euphemia sighed, her fingers tightened on her knife and fork. "Yes, I suppose you are right. We are all doing our best to cope."

It was exhausting watching her struggle to compensate for the shortcomings of a man who didn't acknowledge he had any. "Lady Sterling—"

"I apologize again for my husband."

Ada looked up at her. "Lady Sterling, I do not need you to apologize on behalf of the viscount. He is more than capable of doing so himself when he is so inclined. I am also aware of how unlikely he is to apologize properly or at all. I have no interest in insincerity."

She didn't seem to know how to respond to that. She put down her knife and fork and rubbed her forehead with her fingers. "I would not like you to think badly of us."

"I don't. Basil prepared me. I wasn't sure how accurate he was being at the time but now I see hyperbole is not in his nature." Ada started on her now lukewarm eggs.

"I cannot imagine what he has told you about us for you to have been prepared for my husband's behavior." Lady Sterling scooped raspberry preserves on a golden-brown crumpet.

"Only the truth," Ada replied. "But your husband is not unique in his beliefs or his language. I've been facing him all my life. If it is any comfort to you, you are no better or worse than most."

"I'm not sure that it is. Basil's elder brother is a bit of a cross, admittedly. Those two have never gotten along. He takes more after his father."

"And Basil takes after you?" Ada asked, methodically scraping butter on toast.

"Well," the older woman seemed flustered for a moment. "I suppose he did in a way. But I don't fully understand him either."

"But comprehension isn't a requirement for respect or basic civility." Ada couldn't keep the snap of irritation out of her voice.

"Well, no," she blinked. "I assume that is where he and I are alike?"

Ada let out the breath she'd been holding and reminded herself that this woman was the closest thing to an ally she had in this house. "Yes."

"I suppose I could take that as a compliment, but it's not the only reason."

"Oh?" Ada glanced at the older woman to see her eyes fixed on her.

"I'll admit I wasn't pleased when I found out about this, and if I'm entirely honest, I'm still not. But I learned a long time ago that one must deal in facts before feelings. The simple fact is that you are my daughter-in-law. That particular ring on your finger was given to me by my mother. I gave it to Basil when he determined he would ask Felicity Ashwood to be his wife."

Ada looked down at the ring on her finger and lowered her hands to her lap unconsciously. She didn't know why. It wasn't as if she could hide it from her. Part of her felt as though she was offending the woman by flaunting it around.

"Another fact is Basil has never been one to act rashly. He likes plans, stratagems, and order. For him to have done this, it would have taken a considerable amount of feeling. Enough to overpower that hard head of his."

What was she trying to say? Was she trying to trick her into saying she and Basil were in love? Did she suspect them of planning this regardless of Richard's abduction? "Richard is very dear to both of us."

"I imagine he is. And I would have left it at simple loyalty if not for how careful he is with you, how attentive."

She wouldn't take the bait. She refused to entertain the idea that he wanted her. It would only get her hurt in the end. "He's a considerate person."

"Yes, he is. It's in his very nature, but not like that. He can seem very rigid, but he needs sentiment to shake him up a bit. Even as a child, he was serious, but he likes affection from the right people. He looks at you the way I've been waiting for him to look at Miss Ashwood."

Rigid wasn't a word Ada would have used to describe Basil at all, but affectionate certainly was. She'd lost track of how often he'd touched her arms and her back, how often he'd taken her hand knowing she needed the contact. How he'd comforted her with words and with his body, holding her tightly when she could hold back her fears no longer. She wouldn't have known that it wasn't typical for him to be so physically demonstrative, and now she wasn't sure what it meant.

"And I've noticed you, Miss Thornfield, are not immune to him either. You are appropriately appreciative, to your credit. Last night, however, I was worried you might strike my husband. At first, I thought it was his behavior towards you. Reason enough, I concluded, but then I realized it was something more. You didn't like how he spoke of Basil."

"I only conveyed my thoughts." And apparently, she had been all too candid in the presence of a peer of the realm.

"Yes, to his father, who is not easy to deal with. The only person I've ever seen stand up to him like that outside of myself is... well, Basil."

Would her behavior become an issue for him after she was gone? "Lady Sterling, I apologize if—"

"Oh hush, I appreciate your efforts on my son's behalf. That is my point. It was a novel feeling, not being the only one to speak for him. All things considered, you didn't have to do it. No one would have judged you for staying silent."

"He's protecting me. Repaying loyalty with cowardice is not in my blood." She met the older woman's eyes and saw something almost like humor.

"Indeed. It's a strange position I find myself in. I'm not quite pleased, but I'm not disappointed either."

What did that mean? Was that her way of saying she had passed muster? What an unnecessarily convoluted way to phrase it. "I suppose that was a compliment?" Ada inquired, annoyed again but at a lower level this time.

"I suppose it must be," the viscountess replied with arched eyebrows before continuing with her breakfast.

They ate the remainder of their breakfast in silence for which Ada was grateful. When the viscountess finished her tea, she sat back in her chair and turned to Ada with a quizzical expression. "I know you married for an immediate solution to a potential issue, but I trust that you will stay married, once your brother is found."

The one question Basil hadn't wanted her to answer. "I will do whatever he wants. You can rest assured I will not take advantage of him after he's helped me so much."

"You think he'll want an annulment?"

"I cannot speak for him," Ada replied as tears stung her eyes. She really didn't want to think about giving Basil up. Somehow, in that short space of time, she'd made a place for him in her heart. The idea of that space remaining vacant and aching for the rest of her life was unbearable.

"Let's change the subject then. Do you and your brother live mostly in the country or town?"

"What?" Ada blinked in confusion, "I suppose we are mostly in the country like everyone else."

"Do you attend the theatre?"

"Yes. My brother takes me whenever he has time, although he prefers the more serious ones."

"You tend towards comedy and romance?"

"Yes."

"He is a good brother then?"

"He is the best of brothers. The very best. There is no one like him in this world." And she wanted more than anything to know that he was out of danger.

"I feel somehow I ought to thank him. He must have done a great deal for my son over the years for him to care so much about his wellbeing."

It was the first thing the woman had said that morning that didn't annoy her. There was a sadness on her face, or perhaps wistfulness that her son had needed to go outside of their family for a fraternal bond. "God willing, you will be able to thank him in person," Ada replied softly.

Their eyes met for a moment and a knot in Ada's chest loosened just enough for her to give the older woman a small but genuine smile.

They both heard the footman say, "Good morning, sir. They are in the breakfast room."

Before Ada knew what she was doing, she'd flown to her feet and bolted across the room to the door and down the hallway to the landing. She caught Basil's eye from where he stood at the staircase and waited for an indication of how things had gone.

The smile spread across his face slowly and he nodded once.

Without a single thought, she ran down the stairs into his arms, hugging him around his neck. He caught her midair, staggering backwards a step, and spun them in a circle. Their laughter rang out in the corridor. When he placed her down on her feet, their eyes met for an instant, then, while she was still out of breath, he leaned in and kissed her. She gasped softly into his mouth but then her eyelids fluttered shut as she leaned into him.

She hadn't expected a kiss but the moment his mouth touched hers, she wanted it with a ferocity that would be alarming if his tongue didn't feel so decadent tracing her lips. Her fingers curled into his shoulders on instinct as she tried to meet him kiss for kiss. His hands slid from her waist to her back and shoulders, before curling around the base of her skull and pulling her closer.

His mouth was so soft despite the roughness of his beard as it moved tenderly against hers. He kept pulling her closer, his hand wandering over her restlessly as if he couldn't get enough. She released his shoulders to curl her hands around his neck as he adjusted the angle of his head to kiss her deeper. It was a dream, it had to be. But how could she have imagined what coffee would taste like on his lips, or how his tongue would feel against hers? How could she know how her entire body would come alive with the most exquisite heat and sensitivity?

No amount of Regina's novels could have prepared her for the reality of being kissed by Basil. The whimper she let out when he pulled away would have been embarrassing if he hadn't been out of breath himself. He pressed his rough cheek against hers and panted softly as he held her close. "Ada, I—"

"How is he?" she interrupted. If he apologized for that kiss she would dissolve into the floor and never recover.

"He's at your house, clean and safe."

"Is he faring well?" she asked.

"He's more vexed than anything, already plotting. You know how he is." He pulled away just enough to meet her eyes.

She laughed and nodded. Rubbing her nose against his. "I know. But he isn't hurt?"

"He has some bruises, but I imagine he hurt them worse."

She laughed again in relief, pressing her face into his neck. Maybe she wouldn't have to give him up after all. Maybe it was as his mother said, he cared for her as something other than Zhenyi's sister. He wanted her as much as she had grown to want him.

"You!" A voice bellowed from the landing above.

Ada stiffened and looked up to see Basil staring over her shoulder with a stony expression.

"Father."

Oh God. She tried to step away from him, but he wouldn't let her. As if he wanted her near him, especially with his father nearby. As if he wanted his father to know he wasn't ashamed.

"You reckless, disrespectful little ingrate." His father began and Ada could feel her temper spiking again. *Who the hell was he to speak to anyone in that manner?* She turned to look at him and her mouth opened to issue a scathing retort, but Basil spoke first.

"I can explain."

"I have heard it, but I will admit to a modicum of curiosity as to what you think would excuse this behavior, or what could have possessed you to bring this girl into our family."

Ada felt Basil's grip on her waist tighten, as if he was trying to protect her. "Would you like to do this in the foyer or in your study?"

With one fiery look, the viscount turned on his heel and stalked down the hall to what Ada imagined was his study. Basil looked down at her and brushed his fingers over her cheek. "Do you want to hear this?" he asked.

She could have cursed herself for being a coward but the last thing she wanted was to be in the same room with that man again. If she could avoid it for the rest of her life she would. She shook her head, and he nodded before releasing her and trotting up the stairs to face off with his father.

WHEN BASIL HAD seen Ada earlier, the first thing he'd noticed were the dark circles under her eyes. He'd wondered what kind of night she had passed in his family's house. Now, sitting in his father's study while the man paced back and forth like an irate bear, he had his answer. The thing he'd feared most had happened, his father had met Ada and, as expected, it hadn't gone well at all.

"Why, why would you do this? To me, to our family, to Miss Ashwood?" his father griped, and Basil marshalled every ounce of his patience to embark upon what he was certain would be another fruitless combative interaction with the man who sired him.

"It was never my intention to go against you, father."

"Ever since you were a child you've been disobedient—"

"If that is true, then your shock seems a bit overdone," he replied fighting the urge to roll his eyes.

"—but typically, your disobedience always had a benefit to you. What on earth did you get from *this*?"

Ada. The answer was on his tongue where her taste still lingered with a speed that unnerved him. It was as instinctive as it was incorrect. He didn't have Ada. A moment of madness didn't give him anything. "As I said before, my intention was not to act against you. You said you knew why already. I assume you were told about Richard?"

"Yes, she spun that tale," his father replied with a dismissive wave of his hand.

"It's not a tale. It's true." Did he really think they had lied, or did he think Ada was the liar?

"Is it?"

"Yes. Beyond the fact that I only just got him back home last night, I was the one who told her. The overseer at their main factory was holding him for ransom to settle his debts. Rather than allow that man to succeed in ruining him and his family business through Ada, I married her to keep her and their money out of his reach. I worked with a mutual friend to find Richard and bring him home to the family he has left."

"Thornfield has an uncle, does he not? Family of his own outside of that girl?"

"None worthy of the name," Basil murmured thinking of both Richard and Ada's reactions to their uncle. He'd never met the man and already he didn't like him.

"And what of our family? Is your friend more important than us?"

"Is there an answer that would satisfy you?"

"How am I supposed to face Lord Ashwood when you've jilted his daughter? Especially with you flaunting your Oriental adventure around London?"

Basil's hand tightened on the armchair as his neck flushed. *Oriental adventure?* "Ada is not an adventure."

"She is not your wife; I can tell you that much."

"The law would disagree with you."

"I will not have it. To jilt a fine upstanding girl of good breeding like Miss Ashwood who is better than you deserve, for *that*. I will fix this."

He didn't want to think of what his father meant by that. Fix it? "I am sorry to have harmed Miss Ashwood. She didn't deserve this."

"No, she did not."

"But neither did Ada or Richard." He met his father's steely blue eyes and not for the first time felt himself detach emotionally like an unmoored boat. "I know my explanation seems insufficient to you, but it was to help my friend in a way that only I could have. I would do it again."

His father stared at him, eyes widening and nostrils flaring in growing outrage. "You dare to say that to me, when I have your mess to clean?"

A mess to clean. It seemed like his whole life had been a mess for his father to clean. It was bizarre, really, how every conversation they'd ever had in this room went like this one. He could speak to Felicity. He could explain everything to her as Ada had suggested. Perhaps she could even forgive him enough to pick back up their engagement. It was hardly common knowledge at the moment. The cursed problem was that he wasn't sure he wanted to. He didn't want to marry Felicity Ashwood and spend his life clinging to the coattails of this man, or men like him. He knew that life and the idea of it left him inexplicably drained, not physically but mentally. As if his brain could no longer cope with the idea of it. He didn't want to be there anymore, didn't want to look at those cold blue eyes, didn't want to hear him say anything else about Ada or Richard.

He wanted to leave. "I don't need you to clean anything. I can account for my actions to Miss Ashwood myself." He rose to his feet.

"Put your ass back in that seat."

"No," he pushed in the chair and rubbed his forehead. He hated fighting with his father. It always left him feeling hollow and flat, as if he'd lost something in the process.

"I am not finished with you yet, boy," he growled, stalking towards Basil.

"I am finished with this conversation. Unless there is another topic you wish to discuss, I need to get Ada back to her brother. Thank you for your... hospitality."

"Don't you dare!"

"Good day, my lord." He turned and plodded towards the door. Even the air in the room seemed heavy. As he flung the door open, he took a deep breath and focused on Ada and his mother standing outside in the hall. How long had they been there? What had they heard?

"Basil," his father spoke coolly now. "If you step outside that door, don't you ever think of returning to this house again. Do you understand me?"

He hesitated at the threshold. The horrible finality of those words rang out into the hall, settling on his shoulders. He noticed as Ada shook her head slightly. She didn't want him to leave. Bless her bones, she was worried about him. Only she could manage to care about his feelings at a moment like this. Even now, facing her own disgrace, knowing what his father thought of her, her first worry was his isolation. Reaching for her would be an unspeakable relief, even if he couldn't hold onto her hands the rest of his life.

In that moment, he made his choice. "Understood," he replied and strode forward, stopping only to pick up Ada's bag and grab her hand before heading down the stairs and out the door to the waiting carriage.

He loaded her bag onto the back and climbed in behind Ada, settling down beside her. His eyes didn't start burning until she slid her arms around his waist and nestled her head into his chest. Her comfort felt like home, but he didn't like that he needed it. He should be the one comforting her after what, he was certain, was a horrible night with a man who most likely insulted her in every way possible.

Basil loved his father, but he hadn't liked him since he was old enough to truly understand him. His father was a good enough husband, but he was just short of being a good person. Even the family he claimed to love came second to his reputation. There was nothing worth risking that.

Perhaps cutting ties was the best way to make it up to him. Then, at the very least, he'd be able to say he'd punished his son with ostracism. What had Basil gotten in return? The young woman holding him tightly. Basil knew that he'd had no business kissing her at all, let alone like that. Their arrangement was always meant to be temporary. Now she was resting against him, her arms wrapped around his waist, and he couldn't bring himself to let her go.

Just the thought of walking away from her had his arms tightening their grip on her slight frame. She let out a contented sigh, and his heart clenched in his chest. He'd never expected to feel this much for her, never intended to rely so heavily on her honest compassion so quickly. He'd never expected her to fit in his arms as if she was made to be there or look at him as if he were the solution to every problem. It made him agree to crazy things like a marriage in Gretna Green, sleeping next to a woman whom he couldn't make love to, and sneaking around a dockyard at night.

Leo would have managed alone, but Basil felt a personal need to be there. He wanted to be the one who protected her and gave her everything. He wanted to be the reason her eyes lit up with laughter or clouded over with desire, but he couldn't. He was meant to keep her safe until her brother was able to protect her again. He wasn't supposed to trick her into giving up her chance at a good match. As sheltered as she was, it would be easy for her to believe she felt more for him than she did.

An annulment wouldn't be as easy as she expected, especially without his father's help. He would get it done for her though, and he would do it on his own. He wouldn't ask him for anything again, wouldn't acknowledge him in public again. If he wanted to issue ultimatums, then he could deal with the consequences. Basil would survive on his own terms even if he had to leave England to do it. And Ada...in time she would be able to marry someone else with better prospects and a future as bright as her eyes. He would treasure these last stolen moments with her before he walked away. Before they became distant acquaintances again.

His fingertips brushed against her temple, savoring her smooth skin as he peered down at her. There were faint circles under her eyes. "Did you not sleep well?"

"I was worried about you all," she replied, pressing her face against him. And she didn't sleep well left alone in unfamiliar spaces. Nothing could have been more unfamiliar or uncomfortable than a house where his father was raging, he knew that well enough.

"I can only imagine what it was like for you. I'm sorry I left you there."

"There wasn't another place. You said so yourself."

"Technically there was, but it was clear across town, and I thought of it too late. I wouldn't have been able to take you there and meet Leo in time."

"It's already in the past. My brother is home now. I have you to thank for that."

"And Leo."

"Yes, give him my thanks, will you? I don't know when I'll see him again."

He nodded. His fingers lingered on her face, trailing from her temple, over her soft cheek, down to her graceful jaw. He couldn't stop touching her, not when she was pressed against him like this. Her eyes were full of eager acceptance, and her mouth dared him to take more with every fluttering breath he felt against his neck. His fingers hooked under her chin, and he leaned down to kiss her once more. One more couldn't hurt, could it? It wouldn't change anything, that was for sure. Her eyes fluttered closed in anticipation. His nose brushed hers, then the carriage stopped.

Damn. So that kiss in the foyer was the first and last kiss.

Basil moved her away from him and leaned back against the seat, closing his eyes as his entire body rebelled against the action.

He wasn't satisfied. He wasn't satisfied with what he'd had. There was a growing awareness that in less than a week she had very likely ruined him for any other woman. That in less than five days he'd fallen in love with his wife. What in the hell was he meant to do with that knowledge now? *No good deed goes unpunished*. He could feel her eyes on him, could hear the questions she wasn't asking. *What's wrong? Why won't you look at me?*

Should he speak up? Should he stay silent?

How long did it take to open a damn door?

"Basil," she began, and the carriage door opened. He rushed to step out, the half-polluted air of the city a welcome change to the stifling longing of a closed carriage. His feet firmly on the solid pavement outside Richard's fashionable London home, he held out a hand to help her out of the carriage. He kept his eyes on the white columns, the ebony door with its polished brass knocker. Well beyond what he had to offer. Richard would make her understand that. No, he had no business confessing anything. How could he dare take her from this place to his shabby home? What had passed between them would remain a tale with which to shock her grandchildren. An interlude relegated to memory, where it belonged. Whatever small disappointment she felt wouldn't last for very long.

When her gloved hand tightened on his, he chanced a short glance to see her watching him with that small frown of concern. He was behaving like a cad. He gave her a small smile and nodded towards the door. "Go on, he's waiting for you."

She hesitated for a moment, before her excitement caught up with her. She nodded with a grin and spun around gathering up her skirts. He watched as she flew up the stairs to the front door, knocking on it rapidly. The butler answered, and she ran inside while he pulled down her bag and handed it to a footman to take it into the house.

Basil stared as Ada's figure disappeared into the entrance hall. Gone. Once she saw her brother again, she would remember what all this had really been for.

"Sir?" Basil blinked hard and focused on the footman who was staring at him expectedly.

Had he asked him something? Christ, had he seen him staring at her like a lovelorn puppy? "What is it?"

"I asked if you were coming in, sir?" the footman asked.

"No," Basil replied, before walking down the street.

Chapter Eleven

Ada handed her gloves, bonnet, and cloak to the butler, "Where is he, Lewis?" she asked.

"I believe Mr. Thornfield is in his study, Miss Ada."

"How did you find Brighton, Miss?" he asked.

"What?" Ada turned to him.

"Brighton, you went with your companions."

Lord, that was right. The last time she had seen Lewis, her only concern had been begging to go to Brighton with Regina and Elodia. Too much had transpired in such a short period of time, so much had changed. But now Zhenyi was back home. All was right with the world. She was more than half sure Basil was as in love with her as she was with him.

"Brighton was absolutely spectacular," she replied before running up the stairs and down the hallway at the first landing, half anxious and half excited. She knew that Basil wouldn't have lied but the nightmares that had plagued her since she knew her brother had been taken still haunted her. She didn't know what he would look like or if he had been seriously injured or not. For a moment she paused by the door, then she walked through.

There he was standing at his desk without his jacket, facing the window. The light streaming in cast a silhouette around his lean, strong frame. For a moment it seemed that nothing was different at all. His dark hair was a few inches too long, as usual. Perhaps his waistcoat was a trifle looser, but no limbs were missing, and she couldn't see any bandages. Then he looked up and she saw the colorful bruises marring his usually flawless tawny skin. The dark circles under his eyes. The harsher angles on his face left by hunger. He had suffered no doubt, but he was here. Her Gēgē.

Unconsciously, she took a step forward and the floor creaked, signaling her arrival, and he turned around. Upon seeing her, he smiled fondly and put his hands on his hips. "So, you still know to come back?" he teased.

All her trepidation and relief came bursting forth in a torrent of tears. He walked towards her with his arms outstretched, and she ran into them, flinging her arms around his neck as he lifted her off her feet.

"Brother," she sobbed in Mandarin, desperate to speak it with the one person who would understand it. The one person she'd nearly lost forever. His hold on her tightened further. "I missed you."

He let out a sharp breath before pressing a kiss to her temple. "I missed you too, A'Wei."

A'Wei. The name she thought she'd never be called once more. "I was so scared I'd never see you again."

"Silly girl, you know I'm too willful for that."

She breathed him in deeply. She had missed that scent and the comfort it brought, sandalwood and cloves. "That's true. You are too mean-spirited to make anything easy for anyone."

"Mean-spirited?" he replied with feigned outrage as he pulled her away from him. "And what about you? I heard you got married, insolent girl," he teased.

She laughed and wiped her face.

"I always knew you were an impudent little sprite but who knew you were so wanton? I haven't been gone a fortnight."

"You aren't cross with Basil, are you, brother? He was only trying to protect me."

He tilted his head to the side, his eyebrows raised in interest. "Are you worried about him now? Instead of your brother?"

"I didn't mean that. He was worried about your reaction."

"He was right to be worried," he replied, sliding an arm around her shoulders and walking her over to sit on the chaise near the fireplace.

She frowned. Was he being serious? Somehow, she'd never imagined that he'd be truly cross by what they'd done. There hadn't been a better choice.

"I'm not pleased, A'Wei. I understand why you both did it and I am glad that you are safe, but I'm not happy that you got married without my presence and without my blessing."

"I'm sorry, Brother."

"And Basil…it's not his fault but right now I can't help but see him as another white man who took something else from me."

Something else? Was she a pocket watch? Was that how he saw Basil? A thief? Then another word caught her attention. "What do you mean 'something else'?"

He glanced at her in surprise and then shook his head ruefully, as if he'd spoken unintentionally. "Father's pocket watch, I can't find it. I had it at the debtor's prison, but when they moved me…" he trailed off, his mind lost in a memory that made his jaw clench. She couldn't remember a time when Zhenyi didn't have that pocket watch. He'd received it on his eighteenth birthday, but to Ada it had always been there. Passed from one Thornfield to another, always meant for her brother. The idea of such a thing being stolen and likely pawned was painful. "It's just another thing I can't get back."

She didn't know what to say. She couldn't recognize the bitter and exhausted man beside her. She wrapped her arms around his and leaned her head on his shoulder, hoping to offer him as much comfort as he would accept. He covered one of her hands with his and leaned his head against hers.

"I'm sorry, Mèimei. I'm not truly angry with you or him. I'm just angry. I'm angry I didn't know what Trent was before it was too late. I'm angry at myself."

"You could still see me married you know. Basil and I were

planning to get it annulled as soon as you were back."

"Is he that intolerable to you?"

"No. But it was always a means to an end." Then she remembered the kiss they'd shared, the way he'd looked at her in the carriage. Perhaps not.

"Why, did you seduce him?"

Maybe. "Brother!" she slapped his arm and he laughed, "What are you saying?"

"You keep defending him. I'm getting suspicious."

"Well, *we* didn't really take no for an answer, but we technically didn't force him."

"We?"

"Gigi, Ellie, and I."

Richard blinked slowly and raised his eyebrows again. "You mean to say you three ladies whisked him away to Gretna Green?"

"He wouldn't appreciate you phrasing it like that."

"But I can feel my anger abating, it's better for him if I see it that way. He was already engaged."

"He didn't tell me that until after."

Richard chuckled and shook his head. "Mèimei, I've been worried about getting you married for no reason. Turns out you'll abduct any man who takes your fancy. I'm raising a highwayman," he said, nudging her playfully with his shoulder.

"Brother!" She slapped his chest and moved to stand up. He pulled on her hand, sending her tumbling back into the seat, and wrapped his arm around her shoulders, pinching her cheek with his other.

"If his father wants to defend his honor, I'll make sure he challenges you to a duel instead of me. I'm still recovering. How's that?"

Ada rolled her eyes in response and dislodged his hand from her cheek. He was so annoying. She was too happy to have him back to take much issue with it. The more he joked, the more guilty she felt about what she'd done. Basil had mentioned that his father would be angry, but she couldn't have imagined he would break ties with his flesh and blood over it. Basil had stood his ground, but Ada had seen the look on his face when he made eye contact with his mother before he left his parents' house.

"He wasn't happy."

"Do I need to teach you to shoot?"

"Probably not."

"Whatever he said, you cannot consider it the opinion of everyone."

"It's the opinion of many. But it's only an opinion, even if it is shared." She tilted her head to the side and glanced up at him. "Isn't that so?"

His answering smile was slow but genuine. "Exactly so," he replied before kissing her temple. "Didn't he bring you here?"

"I thought he came in behind me," she said, walking back out to the hallway. Two footmen were carrying her trunk up the stairs, but her husband was missing. "Lewis," she called out and the butler came out of the parlor.

"Yes, Miss?"

"Where has Mr. Thompson gone?"

"He left directly, Miss; said he had some business to take care of."

Business? Ada turned to look at her brother who was watching her very carefully. "I didn't know he wasn't staying."

"It's probably nothing, Mèimei. He'll be back for dinner. He only has bachelor lodgings in London after all, and we have a cook."

But Basil didn't return.

FIVE DAYS. IT had been five days since Basil had left Ada at her home and walked off. Three days since her first letter arrived. It seemed his body was rebelling against it. He had no appetite to speak of, he could hardly focus on one task at a time, and his head was pounding. Every nerve in his body felt raw. He'd gone to see Miss Ashwood, to offer her an explanation before he went to have the banns retracted at their local parishes. If she hadn't heard the news by now, she certainly would soon enough. He didn't want her to discover she was no longer engaged while gawping spectators openly speculated. She had been gracious enough. Her parents were less so.

Her father was loud and red-faced. Her mother was cold and rigid but pale with anger. There hadn't been an acceptable explanation for them, he knew that well enough. In the end, he'd simply sat there and allowed them to vent their anger until they ran out of words. Then he'd apologized once more and left. It seemed Basil was destined to disappoint and vex parents all his life.

Through it all, Miss Ashwood was the only one who didn't seem angry or even disappointed. She'd sat in the chair with her hands in her lap, somber and wary of her parents, but there was no accusation in her eyes. In fact, Basil suspected she might have been a little relieved. Not the best thing for his ego but it was a balm for his conscience at the very least. Yet another woman spared from the prospect of being his wife.

After that, he hadn't wanted to return to his half-finished home with admonitions ringing in his ears. As a last resort, he'd taken a walk, hoping that the fresh air would do something for his nerves, but then he'd seen Ada with Richard. In that moment, his heart ached so much he feared something was physically wrong with it. She was the picture of elegance in her dark green walking costume. All that dark hair was hidden under her bonnet and his fingers itched to touch it.

She'd written him three letters so far. Two sent by post and one sent by a footman. He'd devoured each of them but responded to none. He saw rather than heard her laugh at something her brother said, his ears straining for a shard of that joyful tinkling sound. Was she as happy as she seemed? Did she even need him anymore? His throat tightened.

God, he needed to go home. He wasn't fit for the public if the sight of her sent him to pieces. And if she saw him, if she walked towards him, he would run home. He didn't care who saw or if it made him a coward. It was better than sobbing in public.

Once Basil managed to find his way home without disgracing himself, the one thing he wanted was silence and the better part of a bottle of brandy. What he got was his part-time housekeeper, Mrs. Crouch, and her husband pacing anxiously by the front door.

"Still here?" Basil asked. He came every day serving part time as Basil's butler and footman but she only came twice a week to stock the larder and clean the few rooms Basil used. Normally, on those days he left at four o'clock to walk her home and have dinner, before returning for the rest of the night.

"Aye sir, we were leaving but then," she paused to glance in the direction of the sitting room before continuing in her Irish lilt, "The gentleman arrived and we didn't think it would be proper to leave him here unsupervised."

"What gentleman? What's going on?" Basil asked. Was it Leo? It couldn't be. Crouch was familiar enough with him to leave him here until Basil returned.

"Is that him?" A familiar voice sounded from the next room. Basil's shoulders tensed so abruptly it felt like a spasm. Only one person had that unique effect, his brother, Hamilton.

This bitch of a day was only going to get better, it seemed. Basil took a deep breath and turned to the Crouches with a smile he barely felt. "I think you'd better leave now. I'll see you later on this week."

"Do ye need me to stay here, Lad?" Mr. Crouch asked, laying a heavy hand on his shoulder.

Basil shook his head and looked away from the Irishman's worried brown eyes. It was strange how the ones closest to him were invariably unrelated to him. "No, please. Go. He is *my* problem," he replied.

The Crouches shared a disbelieving glance but allowed him

to usher them out the door.

When Basil turned back around, his brother stood there in all his snobby, sneering glory. Stocky, mousey haired, and spoiling for a fight. The heir to their father's title, or as Basil called him, *The Vicar*.

"You took your bloody time, didn't you?"

Basil walked past him to the sitting room. "I'm sorry to have kept you waiting. I was entirely ignorant of your intention to visit me today." He didn't have the energy to keep his tone civil.

"I'm surprised you have the balls to show your face in public after this last stunt you pulled."

"What's life without its little surprises?" He sat on the sofa and waited for his brother to return with his ridiculous gold handled cane.

"Are you trying to be funny?" Hamilton asked, squinting at him in disbelief.

"Not especially. Before we begin, do you have anything to say that father hasn't covered already?"

"I'm here to speak some sense into you. To prevent you from throwing away your life for the sake of someone who is beneath you."

Heat crept up Basil's neck as his blood began to simmer. "Who are you referring to?"

"That little slut you married to shame us."

Fuck civility. If he wanted a fight, he was going to get one. "Watch your mouth."

"Don't you dare lie to me. It's all over town that you eloped with that little half-breed—"

Basil interrupted, refusing to listen to any more slurs. He was fighting to keep his hands to himself as it was. "I did marry. But she is not a slut nor a cross-breed as you claim."

"You are saying mama and papa have been deceived? That you didn't throw over Miss Felicity Ashwood to save an incompetent oriental merchant and his conniving little sister?"

"I'm saying my wife is a woman of impeccable character and

morality. She is also fully human. So, when you accuse me of marrying a 'cross-breed' and a 'slut', I truly have no idea what the fuck you are talking about."

"Don't play word games with me."

"It is no game, brother. As a proud Englishman of above average education, you should understand your own language enough to use the correct words." Basil leaned forward, balancing his elbows on his knees, rubbing the knuckles of his hand. "If, however, you are unequal to the task, I'm more than willing to offer you assistance." *With my foot up your ass, if needed.*

"You think I'm going to mind my words for that—"

"And if you refer to her by either of those terms or indeed anything close to them in my presence again, I will break that jaw our mother gave you. Am I understood?" It would be messy. Hamilton was shorter but he was broader and heavier. But Basil had a barrel's worth of frustration to expend, and he wasn't looking for a quick fight. He wanted to tear something apart. If his brother didn't mind his words, he'd pound his face through the floor and apologize to his sister-in-law later.

"You think father is going to let that girl be part of our family? You think I will?"

"What can you do about it?"

"You are a disgrace."

"That is your opinion." And a popular one lately.

"You are no longer my brother."

"That is your choice. Since we are strangers now, please leave. I don't have the habit of inviting unfamiliar persons into my house."

"What, this palace?" he sneered, glancing around at the unfinished walls, faded rugs, and the furniture in desperate need of reupholstering. "Perhaps it's best you left Miss Ashwood to your betters."

He didn't have a response to that but he certainly had no intention of allowing Hamilton to know how deeply those words cut today. This was all Basil had to offer. Faded, half-finished, and thoroughly second rate but at least it was his. He would build himself up in his own time and find a reasonable facsimile of what he'd tasted briefly with someone else.

"What are you doing, Basil? There isn't a person alive who can survive without family or their connections. Do you think you're any different? Who do you think you are? What do you expect to accomplish on your own?" Under the condescension was genuine bafflement. He probably couldn't fathom anything worth risking his position or his reputation. It was pitiful, but Basil was too tired to think about it too much now.

Perhaps there was an unexpected gift in not being an heir. When nothing was predetermined, more was possible. "I expect I will find out."

"I will be watching to see what a second born son can manage without his father's name or his mother's connections. You are nothing without them, without us. I am curious as to when you will finally understand that."

Basil stood. He wanted him gone, and from the looks of things, he wouldn't move unless he was physically thrown out. "I'd be flattered by your interest, but I rather suspect it's because you have nothing better to do."

"I hope it's worth it. I hope they were worth it."

"Who? Richard? He's worth ten of you," Basil scoffed. "I have work to do. I believe I asked you to leave. See yourself out."

"Enjoy her for now. We'll see how long it lasts," he called over Basil's shoulder as he walked the few feet to his office, shutting the door behind him.

Basil leaned against the wall, willing his heart to stop racing. The pit in his stomach was yawning ever wider. *Enjoy her for now. I will fix this.* The words from his father and brother kept circling in his mind. What did it mean? Would they actually harm Ada to keep her out of their family? Would they truly do something like that? She'd married him to escape her uncle, but her uncle had never threatened to harm her, had he? If he held onto her only for them to strike out, was that keeping her safe?

Richard was back, Trent was put away. If all of this was to keep her safe, then he couldn't falter at the last second for his own greed. It was time for him to fulfill his final part of the bargain. His stomach churning, he sat down behind his desk, pushed her opened letters to the side and pulled out a sheet of paper and began to write.

Dear Richard,

Chapter Twelve

ADA WOULDN'T CALL herself an anxious person by nature, but at this point she was certain none of the London staff agreed with her. Ada had waited three days and nights for word from her husband before sneaking into Zhenyi's study to find his address. Clearly the man needed reminding that she was still waiting for him to make her his wife. But it had been two days since then and nothing had come.

In that time, she sketched and watercolored a vase of hothouse flowers, learned and successfully executed two new strategies against her brother at 'Go' (much to his annoyance), and watched the post like a hawk. Lewis didn't even bother setting letters on the table anymore. He just brought them directly to her. Richard hadn't commented on it but today he'd asked her to join him for a walk in the park.

The moment she returned home, she'd headed for the foyer table, nearly upending the vase of flowers on it in her haste. There were several letters addressed to her brother, but none for her. Her heart sank in her chest as doubt began to gnaw at her. She'd believed that after the kiss they had shared he returned her feelings. But if he had, then what was the reason for not only his absence but his silence? Had she been wrong all this time? Was he avoiding her because he didn't care about her in the same way?

"Everything all right?" Richard asked in their mother's tongue.

She nodded and plastered what she hoped was a cheerful smile on her face, turning to face him with the letters in her hand. "Yes, these are for you, brother."

Richard stared at her for a long moment. His face was inscrutable and his eyes sharp. He let out a short sigh and walked past her, pausing to snatch the letters from her hand. "Follow," he called out, and she obeyed, terrified of what he was about to tell her. Had he already spoken to Basil? Did he know something she didn't?

When they reached his office, he gestured for her to sit on the chaise. He set the letters on his desk, removed his jacket, and sat beside her, taking one of her tightly clenched hands into his. She felt ill. "I've given you enough time to manage this on your own. I assume breaking into my office didn't yield you the results you wanted seeing as he hasn't written to you as of yet."

A cold rush of shock rippled through her body. "How did you—"

He gave her a pitying look, "Silly girl, did you think no one saw you? You think I didn't notice half my papers were miraculously disturbed? Only you would be so bold as to touch anything on my desk."

"Oh," she looked down at her hand clenched in her lap. She'd been so focused on finding the address, she hadn't thought about the state she'd left his desk. He hadn't said a word about it either.

"Now that we've established that you'd make a terrible spy, I believe it is time we discussed your marriage."

"What do you mean, brother?"

"I was trying to be delicate, but if you insist on being obtuse..." His tone was frank but loving. "Are you quite certain you understand the relationship between you and Basil?"

"I—" she stopped herself. She thought she had. Every passing day chipped away at that certainty like a chisel on flint.

"Tell me exactly what the agreement was."

"I already told you." She tried to pull her hand out of his, but his grip tightened.

"Tell me again."

Ada looked away from him as her eyes began to burn. Somehow, she wondered if the repetition was for Zhenyi's benefit or for hers. "I asked him to marry me in order to secure my fortune and ownership of the mills until we found you and brought you back, dead or alive."

"Go on."

"If you were alive, then we would annul the marriage as soon as you were safe."

"Did he at any point tell you that he was changing his mind?"

Had he? He'd held her close. He'd taken her hand. He'd kissed the breath out of her in his mother's foyer. But he'd never actually told her he wasn't planning to annul their marriage as they'd planned a fortnight ago. Did any of it count if she'd never heard the words? "No," she whispered.

"What did he do to make you think he had?"

She glanced over at Zhenyi and immediately looked away. His face was serious but there was a quiet, patient threat in his eyes she was growing used to. This wasn't her sweet, mischievous brother anymore. This was the domineering guardian with something to prove. If she told him the truth he would act and possibly leave her a widow. "Nothing."

He let out a slow exhale, released her hand and shifted his weight until he leaned back against the seat, casually crossing his legs. She stole a quick glance at him to see one arm laying on the arm rest, the other hand dormant on his leg. "A'Wei, I'm not going to ask you again, but you are not leaving this room until you answer."

So, he was comfortable, but he wasn't willing to let anything go as yet. "Promise you won't get angry."

"No. Talk." Two words, sharp and curt slashed through the air. He was running out of patience, and she was running out of time. They were both stubborn, but Zhenyi had nearly a decade of a head start on her when it came to holding his ground. Capitulation was only a matter of time. The question was, how annoyed did she want him to be when he eventually faced Basil? Maybe if she gave in sooner, it would give him a fighting chance.

"We...kissed. Once."

"Only once?"

"Yes, brother, when he came to bring me to you. He has been nothing but a perfect gentleman.

"Except for kissing you in his parents' home."

"Well, yes, but I wouldn't consider that a mark against him. I wasn't exactly unwilling." She could have spent the entire day kissing him. Or the rest of her life. She knew her unwillingness to let go was due to the memory of what Basil's kisses felt like. She didn't want to consign them to the past.

The answering silence stretched out until she looked up to meet Zhenyi's wide-eyed incredulous stare. As if he knew what she'd been thinking of. She pressed her lips together against a giggle, and he shook his head slowly.

"I thought it meant his feelings were the same. But it's possible it was something else. If it is, then..."

"Then?"

"Then I suppose you'll get to see me marry one day after all," she said, with trepidation and what felt like hot coal sitting in her gut.

Chapter Thirteen

It had taken roughly two days for Basil to get himself together after sending that note to Richard. He'd spent hours wearing himself into a nasty frazzle at the impending confrontation, then more time marshalling his feelings into some sort of acceptance. Ada had never been his no matter what the blacksmith at Gretna Green said. He'd done his duty to his friend and now it was time to move forward.

He washed and changed his clothes, went to his club for a round of fencing and luncheon, then returned home to work on the plans for the country estate. His mother had left him a letter and an invitation to dinner. The letter informed him of the developments with respect to the Ashwoods, not that he was overly concerned about them. The banns had never had a chance to be read before Basil retracted them, so the engagement had never truly been announced. Felicity was already newly engaged to a barrister whom she'd been secretly in love with. Now that Basil was married to Ada, Felicity was free to marry the barrister with her parents' blessing. In the interest of quieting scandal, the Ashwoods had opted for civility instead of rancor.

Considering such a happy result, Felicity had gone out of her way to invite not only his parents but Basil and Ada to her wedding and her engagement party. So now he supposed he could inform his mother of the upcoming annulment. She hadn't been as intractable as he'd expected with respect to Ada, but he imagined she would be secretly relieved. The invitation to dinner had nearly been thrown into the fire. He wasn't interested in dining with his parents or pretending for the sake of appearances that everything was all right. He didn't want to compromise, even if it meant starting over.

Instead of burning it, he shoved it to the side and picked up the blueprints for his partially finished home in the country. He'd gotten it at a bargain due to the extensive work needed but few things had given Basil more pleasure than renovating it. Now there was no wife to prepare it for, and he would settle for someone he liked rather than the one he loved. The true price of knowledge. He would never have known how much he was losing if it hadn't been for Ada. He didn't know how he felt about that fact.

The doorbell rang. "I'm not here," Basil called out, waiting for Mr. Crouch to answer the door and convey his apologies. But there were no footsteps, and the bell rang again. He bit back a curse before rising to his feet and striding towards the front door. Mr. Crouch wasn't back yet from dropping off his wife. He hoped whoever it was knew how to take 'no' for an answer, otherwise he couldn't be held accountable for his actions.

He jerked open the door and came face to face with the one person he knew for a fact didn't meet that description.

"Basil."

"Richard," Basil sighed.

Richard held up an envelope with a seal Basil recognized.

His seal.

And from the look on Richard's face, Basil was about to lose two hours of his life.

He gave a tight smile and stepped back to allow his friend to enter. "I see you got my note."

Richard went directly to the sitting room and sat down in a chair, crossing one leg over the other. "Would you care to explain this to me?"

Basil blinked in confusion and sat in the opposite chair.

"Which part?"

"The part where you are expecting to annul my sister, but she is preparing to move into your home."

Basil's mind froze. Ada was thinking of keeping their marriage? "She what?"

"You see my confusion." Richard smiled widely but without humor.

"Why would she think that?"

"Something to do with an unexplained kiss you reportedly shared with my innocent baby sister." He tilted his head to the side with a deceptively curious frown.

Basil's mouth went dry. "Ah." It was all he could manage. "Um, would you care for a drink, Richard?"

"Not particularly. Start talking."

Full disclosure was best at this point. Quick and relatively bloodless. Basil clasped his hands together and leaned forward in the chair, braced for a quick exit in case his dear friend lunged in his direction. "I... there was a kiss when I went to get her from my parents' home. I will take responsibility for it. She was relieved that you were safe, and I perhaps let it go too far."

"You will 'take responsibility'?" Richard repeated.

"Yes. It shouldn't have happened, and she is too young to understand that."

Richard nodded and glanced down at his hands and their perfectly manicured nails. "Can you understand why she might think there was more to it than a misunderstood release of emotions?"

Basil's shoulders shifted in discomfort as his ears began to burn. Something about the way he said it made it sound pedantic and ridiculous. "Why are you saying it like that?"

"Like what?"

"Like you think I'm an idiot."

Richard smiled in response, but it was enough for Basil to know he agreed with his assessment. "Are you in the habit of being accosted by women?"

"Not as a rule, no."

"But you seem to have allowed Ada a few liberties, have you not?"

Liberties? What the fuck had she told him? "I don't—"

Richard interrupted. "Allowing yourself to be whisked away to Gretna Green when you knew you were engaged, for example."

"That was different. It was for your benefit and her safety."

"Perhaps it was, but can you honestly say every single action you have taken since then has been with only me in mind?"

He couldn't get a read on what he was trying to say. Was he upset? He seemed more smug than angry. "Why are you asking me this? You didn't want her married to me anyway."

"I came here ready to thrash you bloody, but from the state of you I rather suspect you might have fallen in love with my sister."

Basil shook his head and stood, unable to have Richard's eyes boring into him any longer. In love with her? So what if he was? As if that was the most important thing to consider. As if love was some kind of magical protection against everything else that would surely come for her as his wife. Would it protect her from his father and brother? Had it protected Richard? What if their determination extended to his and Ada's children, what then?

"And I know she is in love with you."

So that was his game. He wanted them to stay married. Basil walked over to the window and stared at the dull grey sidewalk. His chest was so tight he could barely breathe. "That doesn't matter. I am not a good match for Ada."

"Enlighten me."

Basil couldn't remember the last time he'd won a debate against Richard, but there was a first time for everything. "My family would never welcome her which would only make her miserable. The only thing I have to recommend me is my relation to a viscount and viscountess. If I break with them, there is no advantage socially or otherwise to being my wife. I'm not rich.

Without her dowry, I can't actually provide for her to the same level as others."

"I'd forgotten about your family," Richard said with a small sigh.

Was that it? Had that done it? "So, you agree?"

"I do not."

Fuck.

"I'll let you in on a little secret," Richard continued, "I was upset when I found out you'd snatched my baby sister out from under my nose when I couldn't stop you."

Not this again. "For fuck's sake, Richard, you were *missing*. You could have been dead for all we knew—"

"True. And the more I thought about it, do you know what I felt at the thought of you being her husband?"

Basil shook his head.

"Relief."

"What?" He turned and saw that his friend was watching him with an expression he'd never seen before.

"As Ada's brother and now her guardian, I have essentially two duties to her: securing her dowry and finding her a suitable match. It has been a terrifying prospect because the men in this country by and large don't see my sister for who she is, just like they don't see me. They see her as an exotic, conveniently biddable doll at best and a corruption of English blood at worst."

Basil looked away, embarrassed at the accuracy of that statement. How closely it echoed the words of his father and brother. *I will fix this. Enjoy her while you can.*

"Some of that sounded familiar, did it?"

"Some of it, yes," he replied keeping his eyes on the unpolished floor. The rest sounded eerily close to something Trent might say. Trent who was now in Newgate for kidnapping and lord knew what else. Intention to murder? Did he ever mean to give Richard back once he had the money? Would his brother do something like that to Ada? Could he count on his mother's tepid support to protect his family?

"I can't change that. I can't protect her from all of it. But *you* see her. She wants to stay your wife, and you are not indifferent to her, no matter what you say. If you tell me that you don't want the trouble of marrying someone like her, I will not argue. But if your feelings echo hers, then I'll tell you frankly there isn't another man alive whom I'd trust with my sister more. You are her best option."

As if she would be better off in a nunnery if Basil didn't stay married to her. As if it was so simple as just the two of them. He couldn't stop seeing the possible cost. "You make it sound as though I'm her only option."

"From where I'm standing, you are. And she agrees."

Basil shook his head wordlessly, unable to accept it. "That sounds like rashness born of desperation. She is young yet, there is no reason for her to settle for me when there are options elsewhere. What about China?"

Richard scoffed, "You think they want a western girl marrying into their families?"

"But you have family ther—" Basil fell silent when Richard shook his head. The certainty and resignation in his eyes was unnerving. How long had he known this?

"Women are meant to uphold and continue the traditions of the family. They would never allow Ada to marry into their families when she wasn't fully raised in that culture or tradition. Ada looks like them, but they would never mistake her for one of them. We look too different to belong here and act too different to belong there. We are both of us caught in the middle."

It was something he never had to consider when it came to himself. There were so many different points of privilege between them. Basil had to marry well financially to support himself, but he had both his parents and the protection of his race. Richard had neither but was far wealthier and in control of his life and livelihood. Basil had never needed to question where he belonged, whereas Richard knew he didn't belong anywhere. "You never told me about this."

"Because it's none of your fucking business."

Basil choked on a laugh and nodded, fighting to clear his throat. "Fair enough."

"Joking aside, Basil. I don't trust you because you are my friend. You are my friend because I trust you. You've earned it day by day, year by year. This last escapade has only vindicated that trust."

The words should have filled him with warmth, but they only made the twisting in his stomach worse. Trust was one thing, but what would happen when she realized her fantasy had an ugly cost? How could he possibly be enough to make up for it? "She wouldn't be happy in a family that doesn't respect her." *That wanted her erased.*

"No, she wouldn't be happy married to a man who didn't respect her. If you value her and you care for her—"

"I can't, Richard. Let her find someone else. There must be someone else."

"I won't force you. But if you think you are doing this for her sake, you're wrong. This isn't about her, it's about you."

"That's—"

"I won't say anything more about this. I'll leave you to your idiocy." He stood and walked out the door.

Basil stood there, fighting the urge to throw a book at him. Smug bastard, telling him his own business. He wasn't the right person. He couldn't protect her from anything, couldn't give her anything she didn't already have alone.

THE NEXT DAY Ada elected to pay a visit to Elodia after receiving an invitation to tea. It wasn't expected. Ada hadn't heard from Elodia or Regina since that day at the train station, but she had enough sense to understand why. What they had done was necessary but would have absolutely tested, if not broken, any semblance of trust between her friends and their parents. Eager to see her friend, Ada dressed in her favorite hunter green calling gown and took a carriage to Elodia's London home.

The look she received from the butler when he answered the door was pointed but a little amused.

"Good afternoon," Ada said, wondering what he'd overheard in the past days.

"Good afternoon, Miss Thornfield. Miss Hawthorne and his Lordship are awaiting you in the front sitting room."

Clearly, he hadn't heard much if he was still calling her Miss Thornfield. Another piece of information filtered through. The viscount was joining them? That couldn't bode well. Ada kept her gloves on in case she was about to be officially banned from the premises but followed the butler to the sitting room. Elodia sat in a white muslin day dress glaring at someone beyond the door frame who Ada imagined was the viscount.

"Miss Adelaide Thornfield," the butler announced, and Elodia's head snapped to the left before a grin spread across her face. Within moments she had run over to catch Ada in a breath-defying hug that allayed the worst of her fears.

"I missed you."

Ada giggled and hugged her back, "And I you. How have you been?" she asked, drawing back to take her in.

Elodia rolled her dark brown eyes, "In a word? Secure. Father refuses to let me leave the house without his supervision." She took Ada's hand and drew her over to the sofa.

"Because the last time I did you went to Scotland without so much as a 'by your leave', came the viscount's voice. "Good evening, Miss Thornfield."

Ada spun around and dropped into a curtsey. "Good afternoon, My Lord," she said, and he nodded in her direction before shifting his attention to his scowling daughter. He was a handsome man, with bright blue eyes, a strong yet elegant figure, and grey creeping in at the temples of his light brown hair.

"That was different, papa. Mr. Thornfield—"

"I'm aware of the particulars of your latest adventure, Miss

Elodia Hawthorne. But you seem to have a talent for finding 'extreme situations'." He met her annoyed stare over his reading glasses before pursing his lips and returning to his newspaper.

Ada shuffled over to sit beside Elodia on the sofa and removed her gloves. The viscount normally took Elodia's exploits in stride, meeting each with a certain mix of humor and admiration, but this last venture had been one test too many.

"May we have the room, papa?"

"Not a chance. I stay or Miss Thornfield leaves." His tone was even but there was no mistaking the steely resolve in it.

Ada unfastened her bonnet and set it beside her before meeting Elodia's eye and shaking her head. He was within his rights. Elodia sighed. "Have you heard anything from Gigi?"

"Not a peep, but I'm reasonably certain she's alive."

She took Ada's hand. "How have you been, Ada? How is your brother?"

"He is well. He's been sticking very close to me."

"With good reason. Is he—well, was he hurt?"

"Not much, all things considered. Basil said he was angrier than anything else."

"It must be such a relief to have him home safe." Elodia's gaze dropped down to their hands and a strange look flitted across her face. Wistful and relieved at the same time.

"It is," Ada said, wondering for a moment whom Elodia had been concerned for most all this time. Was it possible? Did Elodia have feelings for Zhenyi?

Elodia looked up when a maid wheeled in the tea service and that singular expression was erased by an overly bright smile. She added tea leaves to the hot water in the silver teapot. "And I suppose we can finally enjoy our seasons next year."

That gave Ada pause as Elodia picked out a small selection of finger sandwiches and placed them on the side table near her father. It was a sudden turn considering how Regina and Elodia had been encouraging Ada to forego an annulment from the beginning. "What do you mean?"

Elodia blinked in confusion, her smile faltering as she returned to her seat. "The annulment. Has it not been obtained?" she murmured. She glanced down at Ada's hand. "Is that why you are still wearing that?"

"It isn't certain that we will annul as yet," Ada replied, covering her ring with her other hand. A sickening feeling was taking root in her stomach as a cold sweat sprouted all over her body. She could hear her brother's voice in the back of her mind. *Did he at any point tell you that he was changing his mind?*

"Did you decide to stay married then?" Elodia asked carefully.

"Well... there were certain developments lately," Ada said but even to her ears the words sounded pathetic, dripping with delusion. Development implied progression and she had no reason to think anything had truly changed between her and Basil. Except for that damned kiss that she couldn't get out of her mind.

Elodia stopped pouring a cup of tea and glanced at Ada, dread all over her face. "I suppose it's my turn to ask now. What do *you* mean?"

What was happening? Ada couldn't help but feel like she had missed a crucial piece of information. She glanced at the viscount to see him watching her with something like sympathy. Then he stood and left the room, closing the door softly behind him. He'd been so adamant about staying with them, why would he leave so suddenly? What did he know? "Have you heard something, Ellie?" Ada asked, her throat tightening until the words were barely audible.

"Well, no which was, quite frankly, the point."

"I... I don't understand."

Elodia let out a terse breath and laid a dark slender hand over Ada's. "There hasn't been any gossip about a jilted socialite or anything about the engagement being called off. I saw Miss Ashwood out at the theatre with the Viscountess Sterling a few days ago when papa took me to see *Lucia di Lammermoor*. As there didn't seem to be any bad blood between them, I could only assume that Mr. Thompson's engagement to Miss Ashwood had resumed because you and he had resolved your own connection quickly, as planned."

Ada shook her head slowly as her brain struggled to comprehend what she was hearing. She sat back and jerked her hand out of Elodia's grip, clasping her fingers together in her lap. What did it mean? Was it truly already over without her even knowing it? "He must have come to an agreement with Miss Ashwood. Richard went out yesterday, I thought he went to speak to him. I thought…" She'd thought Zhenyi would talk him around.

She thought she had meant more to him in the end, that he had seen her as more than a duty to be discharged. She'd thought Basil wasn't the sort of man to kiss a woman for no reason. She'd gotten carried away in such a small amount of time, caught up in the idea of him as a literal white knight, a hero out of a fairytale: chivalrous, honorable, kind, and handsome. Even heroes had feet of clay. Had it been that easy for him to let her go? Had she been so unmemorable? Had her own inexperience turned their kiss into something else? Something he had never felt or promised?

"I'm sorry, Ada," Elodia whispered, and Ada forced a chuckle past her viselike throat and shook her head.

"Why are you sorry? I have my freedom, my dowry, and my brother. I have everything I wanted." *And so it seemed did Mr. Thompson.* Not Basil. Not anymore. She was going to break her own fingers if she gripped them any tighter, but she couldn't let go now. Not when it felt like that clasp was the only thing keeping her heart together in her chest. "I suppose we will have the rest of this season, Ellie. It's not over yet."

"Oh, Ada," Elodia shifted closer, and Ada turned away, terrified of meeting her eyes and finding pity there. She had made an utter fool of herself, it seemed. The kiss that had filled her with so much anticipation now served as a source of humiliation. How uncomfortable he must have felt with her staring at him as if he'd hung the stars, when all he'd wanted to do was deliver her to her brother and move on with the rest of his life.

"There are so many diversions in London, and plenty of suitors to entertain us."

"Very true," Elodia replied, clearly attempting to placate her. It seemed she knew the truth that only Ada had missed. Her marriage was already over. Zhenyi knew it, the viscount knew it, and so did Miss Ashwood.

Her eyes fell on the engraved golden band she still wore on her right hand. Did she even have the right to wear it anymore? Why on earth hadn't he taken it back? Why would he give it to her in the first place? The humiliation was unbearable. "I…I have to go now, I have to—" she'd meant to think of an excuse, but nothing was coming to mind.

I have to go crawl into a hole. I have to go to my room and scream into a pillow. I have to put all this behind me the way he did. The way he'd put *her* behind him.

She met Elodia's eyes and the sympathy there nearly finished her.

"Go," she whispered.

Ada gave a jerky nod, stood without any further encouragement and fled, refusing to meet the eyes of another soul or stop walking until she was in her room with the door securely closed.

Safe within the privacy of her bedchamber, she sank onto the floor by the door and pressed her forehead into her knees. Numb hands clasped tightly around her legs. She breathed slowly and unevenly until the worst of the waves of humiliation had passed, leaving her clammy and weak but her eyes dry. She'd always hated crying in public. Hated the idea of surrendering her dignity under the scornful gaze of the London ton.

She'd feared crying on the way home with the way her throat ached so sharply. But now she was safe, nothing was coming, as if her mind still hadn't processed what had happened. Why hadn't Basil said anything if he was still intending to leave her? Why would he leave that cursed ring on her hand, a family heirloom that his parents had clearly meant for Miss Ashwood? What did he mean by it?

How could she face Zhenyi like this?

What would she tell her brother?

She stayed on the floor until it was time to get ready for dinner. By that time, she'd decided one very important thing. She was not going to give in to self-pity no matter how much her heart ached.

So what if Basil didn't share the same feelings she had for him? So what if he had seen fit to dispose of her as quickly as possible? He and his family had done her a very great favor. The impending trouble she'd anticipated had never surfaced. Whatever words his father had spoken, Basil had managed to keep his connection with Miss Ashwood. They would marry, he would be safe.

What did it matter if he'd kissed her like she was the only oxygen in the room for no reason than to sate some latent curiosity? His lapse had given her an enviable entrée into the world of womanly pleasure. Few women could claim such an exemplary experience for their first kiss. His discretion meant that she would be able to begin anew and find a new husband with the world none the wiser. It was a blessing in disguise, and she would never allow herself to see it as anything else.

Her eyes were burning again but this time she wasn't afraid of the tears, only unwilling to give into them. After all, there was nothing to cry about and more importantly, nothing to be embarrassed about. *So stop crying you ninny! It's already over.*

When her maid arrived to dress Ada for dinner, she was sitting by the bay window looking out over the garden, having won the temporary skirmish against tears. She was determined to maintain that track record. Zhenyi would take one look at her and know that she was all right. Everyone would know she was excited about her future, not mourning a ruptured illusion.

She donned her favorite evening dress (a sumptuous, coral-colored, brocade silk that set off her complexion perfectly) and spent extra time on her toilette that night, daring to darken her eyes with charcoal and using a touch of lip rouge. She'd even had her maid use curling tongs to add ringlets to her coiffure which was an exercise in futility, honestly, because she knew full well they wouldn't last longer than an hour. Possibly two.

She went down to the sitting room with her embroidery to wait for her brother to arrive. He hadn't been home when she left for tea with Elodia, and she'd hidden in her room the rest of the day, so she didn't know if he'd arrived yet. The longer she sat pulling needle and thread through silk to bring a vase of peonies to colorful life, the more it occurred to her that Basil's behavior had crossed from odd into downright discourtesy. There was no excuse for the silence from him over the past week. Not after that kiss.

Even if he intended to break off the marriage, he could have spoken to her, written to her, faced her like a grown man instead of hiding away. She knew their relationship was objectively nowhere near as familiar as his with Zhenyi, but they had gone through enough to warrant more than this cold, hard absence. Why was he treating her as some kind of a threat, or worse, as a stranger?

The door opened and the sound of low voices caught her ear. One was Zhenyi, who she recognized instantly but the other... Was it him? Had he come at last?

Irrational, ungovernable hope burst in her chest, and she sprang to her feet, throwing her embroidery onto the seat and running out the door. The disappointment when she reached the foyer to see only her brother was crushing. Zhenyi glanced over at her from his conversation with a footman and stared for a moment before finishing his instructions. Her dissatisfaction must have shown on her face because he shook his head with a sad expression and sighed.

"Are you unhappy with me already?" he asked her in their native tongue. "It's a bitter pill to swallow, A'Wei, but I shall endure it with all my might."

She frowned at him in confusion, "What are you talking about?"

"Your face. Only a week I've been home safely and already you've grown sick of me."

Recognizing his playful mood, she rolled her eyes in annoyance "That's not true." She bit her lip, embarrassed to admit the truth to him. He was right. For all her convictions, there was nothing she wanted more than for Basil to claim her as his wife. "I thought you were—"

"Ah, you thought I was speaking to your husband?"

"Yes," she murmured, keeping her eyes on the floor.

"I hope you can bear the disappointment long enough to enjoy this meal with me, Sister."

"Of course," she replied, finding a smile for him, and hooking her arm through his as they headed back to the dining room.

Basil was being a misery but that didn't mean she couldn't enjoy her brother's company. His evening jacket was made of a rich, dark ochre and his waistcoat was a deep crimson and umber brocade silk which complemented his dark eyes and warm skin tone perfectly. It wouldn't take long before the shadows on his face cleared and he was his handsome self again.

"What are we having?" he asked.

"Turtle soup and a haunch of beef, I believe. I left the other particulars to cook's discretion."

"How delicious," he commented, patting her hand affectionately and then taking his seat across from her. They never sat at the end of the table unless there was company. Zhenyi was in a good mood this evening despite their conversation about Basil which had ended with him reading a missive and leaving her in his office. He hadn't brought it up again, and the constable hadn't come looking for him which meant that Basil was likely still alive. Outside of that, she had no further information.

"You are looking very beautiful tonight, Sister," he commented, as his soup was served.

"Thank you."

"Your best dress, that double strand of pearls, and someone's taken a pair of curling tongs to your head."

"What about it?" she asked, resisting the instinct to touch her hair in embarrassment.

"As unflattering as it is to admit, I feel none of that was for my benefit."

She placed down her spoon and took a sip of water as he tasted his turtle soup. "It was for mine. I've been so anxious for this last while, I haven't had time to pamper myself properly. I thought tonight was as good a time as any."

"How very true."

"I had tea with Ellie today," she said watching him for a reaction.

There was an infinitesimal pause as he ate his soup, but she caught it. "How did you manage that?"

"Well, her father refused to leave the room."

"I cannot blame the man. The three of you are enough to turn anyone stone grey."

"After that meeting, I believe that Basil is planning to annul me after all. And that he will be marrying Miss Ashwood."

Zhenyi's hand rested on the table with his spoon caught between his fingers. Slowly, his head raised until he was meeting her stare. There was a strange look on his face. His eyes were piercing but his expression was forced. "Is that a fact?" he said finally.

"Yes, so if you could make those arrangements as soon as possible, I would appreciate it."

He smiled slowly and nodded but somehow it felt as if he was laughing at her. "I will, of course, if that is your wish."

He was being far too agreeable. No tension in his voice, no ire in his eyes, nothing. A man had kissed her and was planning on leaving her behind and he had nothing to say about it? He was building up to something. She could feel it.

"I have to say, A'Wei, I'm surprised at you."

"How so?"

He shrugged. "I never expected you to accept this sort of indignity with such equanimity."

"What?" She felt as though she should be insulted by that comment, but she wasn't sure.

"A full week has gone by. He's had time to renew his engagement without bothering to finalize his business with you."

"Evidently he's had business to attend to." *With Miss Ashwood.* "His parents weren't pleased with what he did. It's a miracle they were able to smooth things over so quickly."

She hated how meek and tired her voice sounded. She hated that she felt the need to defend his neglect as if she were fine with it. How could he kiss her like that, look at her with those eyes, and still set her aside as if she were nothing but a puppy he'd returned to its owner? Was that how he saw her in the end? Had it all truly been mere kindness? How could he leave her twisting in the wind with so many questions left unanswered and respond to none of her letters?

"One could say that as his wife, you, his most important business, have been sitting here waiting patiently for days."

"I'm not his wife. Not really." It was obvious he didn't see her as his wife anymore if he ever had.

Her brother hummed doubtfully and pulled a face but said nothing else.

"Maybe he thought he was giving us time together," she suggested. Zhenyi gave her a look of disbelief and almost pity.

"Don't defend him, that's Miss Ashwood's job now."

"I'm not defending him," she lied, as her temper spiked. Was he actually scolding her? How dare he bring up Basil's fiancée. "Don't presume you are more angered by this than I am. I am the wife in question after all." If he pointed out how quickly she'd taken back up that title, she would throw her dinner roll at his head.

"So you are. For the time being anyway. However, if he believes that he can treat you this way without consequences, perhaps it is better that it ended now."

"You think he is looking down on me?" she asked.

Again the pitying look. "Sister, it is no longer a matter of what I think or not, it is a statement of fact."

"You're right," she agreed.

"I'm always right," he replied easily. "But it's good of you to bow out gracefully and avoid causing him and Miss Ashwood further disruption. Especially after all he's done for us."

Further disruption? Is that all she was to him in the end? Something to get past? Something pretty but ultimately unwanted to dispose of so that he could have the life he wanted. Angry, humiliated tears burned her eyes. She would step aside if that was what he wanted, but not without an explanation first. He had no right to treat her like this, and she wouldn't allow him to do it without hearing from her first.

Her eyes fell on the stupid ring on her finger. If he wanted to cut ties, he could do it face to face like a man. If he was too much of a coward to come to her, then she would go to him.

She pushed herself to her feet and her brother looked up at her with wide eyes that she would probably question at a later date.

"Lost your appetite?" he asked.

"Not exactly. I'm taking a carriage," she said walking out of the dining room.

"Where are you going?" Zhenyi asked, strolling out behind her.

"I'm going to speak to your stupid friend and return this… this *blasted* ring to him so he can give it to its proper owner."

"Now?"

"No time like the present," she said, snatching up her cloak from the coat stand and throwing it around her shoulders.

"It's rather late, sister. Don't you think you should wait until tomorrow?"

"I've waited for him long enough," she snapped. Zhenyi jumped back from her, his eyes wide and wary. She closed her eyes and forced herself to calm down. It wasn't his fault. None of this was his fault. "I'm sorry, Brother. I waited for him to bring you to me, I waited for him to return to take me home with him,

I waited for him to tell me what we were to each other. I waited and I got this, gossip from a friend and a ring that isn't even mine. I want answers and I'm not going to stop until I get them."

She flinched instinctively when his hands touched her cheeks but instead of squeezing them to tease her, he simply held them, a gentle smile on his face. "My little sister has grown up."

"Do you think I'm being unreasonable?" she asked, her fingers curling around his wrists.

"Not at all. No sister of mine will be put aside like an unwanted kitten." He said with a frown and her eyes widened as his words sank in.

"You," she slapped his chest, and he grinned before taking her hands in his.

"But it's too late to let you go alone, so your big brother will drive you there."

"Thank you," she said rolling her eyes. He was definitely up to something, but at the moment, she was far too grateful to care.

Chapter Fourteen

Trent couldn't believe that he was in the clink. Couldn't understand how everything had gone wrong so quickly. He'd had a plan. It was meticulous and well thought out. The one factor he hadn't accounted for was that sly-faced heathen girl. How? How had he missed that she would be the one to cause his trouble? Thornfield had known. His sly little smile in the storeroom made perfect sense now.

He'd known his brat of a sister would ruin everything. Sneaking off to Gretna Green with a viscount's son to get married like the opportunistic little slut she was. That weakling husband of hers arranging to have Thornfield snatched out from under him. That nosey, jumped-up little darkie setting the entire police force on his scent.

Now he'd have the police and those loan sharks after him once he got out. Little did that negro know, this was his town. He had people everywhere, even in places as high and mighty as Thornfield himself. The sound of boots on the floor made Trent look up. He sneered and shook his head when he caught sight of the guard.

"You took ya time," Trent said, as his cousin Ian unlocked the door to his cell.

"You've got yourself in a right mess this time, Donnie."

"Don't give me a sermon, just get me outta here."

"Keep your voice down for the love of Christ," he hissed as

he led Trent through the maze of cells and down a dark stinking corridor. "I ain't doing this for you. Some toff tipped me to get you out. Says you have a job to finish."

Trent grinned. That's right. A good Englishman always took care of his own. No way that gent was gonna let him hang for this. "He say anything else?"

"He said he'll meet you by the two trees."

"Good."

"Whatever it is you are doing leave me out of it. I got a wedding comin' up, I can't lose this position."

Trent groused. "So much for blood being thicker than water."

"Don't even go there. I've covered for you hundreds a times. But they's saying you kidnapped a toff. What the hell's you doin' kidnapping a toff for?" He pushed open a metal gate and past a copse of trees, staying far from the torches.

"He owed me," Trent snapped as they approached a lone wagon.

"Everybody always owes you," Ian grumbled before flipping up a tarp on the back of a wagon. A dark figure sat facing away from them in the driver's seat. "Get in and stay quiet." He gave a sharp whistle, and the horse began to move, taking him to freedom. A second chance was what he was getting and he'd make sure it went exactly how he needed it to.

Chapter Fifteen

26 Grosvenor Square
London

Basil stared at the small, deep brown glove on his cluttered desk. He wasn't exactly proud of stealing his wife's glove but in his defense, it hadn't been intentional. Somehow during the journey from his parents' home to her brother's, her glove had ended up in his pocket and her bare hand was in his. He had been in such a state of confusion that day, elation that his feelings were shared and despair at the prospect of letting her go. Richard thought him an idiot, but there was no doubt in his mind that if Ada knew she could walk away, she would. It would be a scandal, of course, but not one from which she couldn't recover. Not with all her virtues and the dowry that Richard would no doubt secure for her. The thought of a life without her produced a dull ache in his chest that he didn't dare to examine. How had she managed to sink herself into his skin the way she had?

It was ridiculous how much he missed her. There was no logical reason for it. He'd spent the last fifteen years of his life emotionally self-sufficient. It had never been a hardship to be alone. One of his favorite aspects of his friendships with Leo and Richard was their ability to entertain themselves without encroaching on his mental and emotional space. All of them knew how to share a space while working independently. It had taken less than a week to destroy all of that. His mental discipline was in tatters.

All it had taken was one twenty-year-old girl. He'd made the judgment and a promise but staying away from Ada was taking every ounce of his energy and control. He wanted her to fall asleep against him, wrap her arms around him. He wanted to smell that scent of violets. Christ above, he wanted to kiss her again. It had been days since that kiss in his parents' London home, and he still couldn't shake the sensation of her in his arms, her slender hands in his hair, and her mouth moving eagerly against his.

Even now, sitting in the self-appointed office in his modest terrace house, he couldn't bring himself to focus on the figures in his ledger. Every time he tried, Ada floated into his mind. Either a siren clad in only a nightgown bathed in moonlight and firelight, or asleep against his chest, or with desire clouded eyes and a kiss-swollen mouth. Just the thought of it had his trousers tightening and his breath deepening. He could still feel the cool silk of her dark hair in his hands and the solid weight of her slender body against him. Had he only married her two weeks ago? Sighing in frustration, he scraped his hands over his face, roughly pulled on his hair. He needed time, that was all. Time to purge her from his system and get used to his own company again. The thought was thoroughly unappealing.

The tinny pitch of the doorbell manically ringing jolted him from his ruminations. He glanced in its direction before checking his pocket watch. Nine at night? Who the hell was coming for him at nine o' clock? At first, he decided to ignore it. Then the thudding began, or rather the pounding. On his front door. At nine o' clock. As if his life wasn't in enough shambles. If this went on, the neighbors would notice, and then he'd never get a moment's peace.

Cursing under his breath, he stood and stalked over to the front door with every intention of beating the idiot on the other side senseless. He yanked the door open, words hot on his tongue, and saw his darling, beautiful… livid wife. It was as if he'd manifested her out of his own yearning. Although it had to be said that if he had dreamt her up, she would have looked more loving, and less like a fire breathing harpy.

"Have a good talk," Richard called, and Basil looked up to see his friend drive off in a phaeton, leaving him alone with Ada who was glaring at him in a way he'd never experienced before. He'd never really associated Ada with having a temper, but he certainly knew better now.

"I'd like a word with you, Husband," she said, her even tone at odds with the ferocity in her eyes, before pushing past him to enter his home. He closed the door without thinking, leaving them in the dimly lit atrium, utterly alone. A rustle of fabric and the gleam of white skin told him that Ada had removed her cloak.

"Is something wrong?" he managed to choke out as his palms began to sweat.

"That is exactly what I came to ask. Why did you leave me at my brother's house without a word?"

Shit. "Ada…"

"Why haven't I heard from or seen you since then? I've been waiting for you for over a week."

Hadn't her brother spoken to her? He didn't have a ready response to that.

"Shall we, um, go to my office?"

"Fine."

He led her back to his cluttered office with the books and papers scattered over every piece of furniture. When he turned to face her, however, he immediately regretted not staying in the dark hallway. She had always been beautiful, but the image of her in that confection of a dress, her slender shoulders on display, and her full breasts peeping out the top of the neckline with fire in her eyes and a passionate flush on her cheeks had his breath caught in his throat. Under any other circumstances, he would have crossed the room in seconds to devour her. However, as it was…

"I'll clear a place for you to sit down." Anything to keep his hands occupied.

"There's no need. I'm not in the mood to sit," she snapped, folding her arms, her head tilting to the side expectantly.

Don't look down, don't look down. "You seem upset about something."

"Do I?"

"I don't know why exactly." That wasn't entirely true, but he'd hoped she wouldn't have decided to push the issue.

"You don't know why? You kissed me, dropped me off at my brother's without a word, and you can't understand why I would be upset?"

"That's not quite true."

"I wrote to you. I wrote to you constantly, and you never responded to any of my letters. Did you not receive them?"

"I... I received them."

"Then what the hell are you doing?" she replied, prowling over to him with a glint in her eye that made him a little nervous. "Do you look down on me so much that you think you can treat me like a piece of baggage to be picked up and put aside at your leisure?"

"Of course not," he replied, hoping to calm her down. Clearly, he had miscalculated.

"Then what?"

"I've been speaking to a solicitor," he said.

"About what?" Her confusion was disconcerting.

"About the annulment?"

"So, you are annulling me?" Her entire expression changed then to dull outrage. If he'd thought himself in danger before, he'd been mistaken. It was now. He was in danger now.

"I agreed that we would annul our marriage after—"

"We did agree. But then you kissed me in the middle of your parents' house, so I naturally assumed that perhaps you were no longer considering that course of action."

"That was a mistake." A mistake he had been paying for every night. He still couldn't get the taste of her out of his mouth or forget the feel of her body under his hands.

"A mistake?"

This wasn't going well. "Perhaps that isn't the right word. Ill-advised."

"Yes, that sounds much better," she sniped, her eyes narrowing slightly.

He swallowed past his dry throat and took the long way around his desk. He needed to maintain distance between them, partly because she looked capable of anything, and partly for his sanity. She was truly dazzling in a temper, even when her ire was directed at him.

"What I mean is that I shouldn't have done it. You deserve better than what I can offer, Ada. With your temperament, your accomplishments—"

"My dowry," she interjected, closing in on him.

"That as well, yes. You don't need to settle for me. We agreed to an annulment, and you shouldn't be cheated out of what you deserve because of a momentary indiscretion on my part."

"A—" she stared at him in bafflement, her brow furrowing, and her mouth slightly parting.

"You would regret such a mistake."

She let out a short, mirthless laugh and shook her head. "Regret…Basil, you never claimed to be the cleverest of men, but I didn't actually think you were a fool."

That froze him. A fool? How was he a fool for thinking of her happiness and wellbeing? "I beg your—"

"Settle? You think I am throwing myself at the first decent man available because I'm too simple to know better. Do you have any idea how insulting your words are?"

"I didn't—"

"I know exactly who I am and what I'm worth, and I have no intention of compromising my prospects for anything or anyone."

"I just want you to be happy. My family… you wouldn't be happy with them."

"But Felicity Ashwood would be, is that right?"

His brain seemed to stop dead in its tracks. "Miss Ashwood?" He hadn't thought of her in so long, it took him a moment to remember what she had been to him.

"I know that you've taken back up with her."

Taken back up? What the hell had Richard told her? "I have—what are you saying?" He took a step forward.

"Stop lying!" she cried desperately. The tears in her eyes sliced into his heart.

Never in a thousand years had he ever imagined being the one who made her cry, who put that look in her eyes. He stepped closer and carefully reached out, laying his hands on her bare shoulders. He tried not to focus on the silken texture of her skin "Ada, I am not lying. What are you talking about?"

"I know your mother has been attending the opera with her and Lady Ashwood, making sure she is seen with her future daughter-in-law."

"That is—" *Nothing to do with me.*

She shook off his hold and clasped her hands at her waist lifting her head to meet his stare. "I wouldn't have argued if you wanted to annul me and patch things up with your fiancée. I gave you my word, and I would have kept it no matter how much it pained me. But you had no right to ignore me like this. To take up an alliance without having the decency to look me in the eye and end this first is so unlike what a man ought to be."

"Ada." He wanted to say more but her words kept sucking the air right out of his lungs. He could see in those depths how much he had hurt her, how badly he had miscalculated the effect his actions would have.

"I know you never wanted or intended to marry me. I know I am not what you wanted or what your family wanted. I knew when you came to me you were doing it for Richard, that you were acting as a friend to him more than anything else. But I thought... I thought that your feelings had grown past that. When you stayed with me that night, when you held my hand, I thought you were doing it for me, because you cared for me."

"I have. I do." The words sounded feeble and insipid to his ears. They couldn't come close to expressing the fathomless depths of what he felt for her.

"When you kissed me, I thought it was because you wanted me. I didn't see it as a mistake, and I didn't realize you did. I haven't come here to stop you. If Miss Ashwood is what will make you happy, then..." *Then?*

She looked down at her hands and gnawed at her bottom lip as he stood there watching, terrified to touch her and incapable of turning away. She wouldn't say it. Perhaps she couldn't wish him well with someone else. Then she lifted her head and those dazzling dark eyes met his with determination and made his heart ache.

"I just wanted to tell you that a man should fulfill or end his commitments on his own. No one can do it for him." She pulled on her finger and then opened her palm to reveal her wedding ring. The ring he'd put on her hand only a fortnight ago. "This belongs to you."

He stared at the circle of gold in her small white palm and couldn't bring himself to take it back. It was what he'd claimed to want. He didn't trust himself to take care of her, didn't believe he had what it took to protect her from his father and brother. But if he didn't take it back, wouldn't it be another misdirection? Another unintentional way to hurt her? How could he explain that in his heart that ring was hers? That the moment he'd put it on her finger, he'd never thought of taking it back. "I don't want it," he whispered past his constricted throat.

"I cannot keep it, Basil. It was meant for your wife, for Miss Ashwood."

"I'm not marrying Miss Ashwood," he said.

She blinked in incomprehension. "What did you say?"

"Miss Ashwood is engaged to someone else. I am not marrying her."

She watched him with an indecipherable expression for one long moment and then lunged forward. He had just enough time to take a breath before her hands linked behind his neck and dragged his mouth down to hers. The shock of the contact left him frozen as her lips moved innocently against his. Her words reverberated in his chest. She drew away, her eyes unfocused and a little anxious.

What was his excuse now? There was no overpouring of emotion as he'd claimed, nothing to distract from the truth of what was before him. Ada standing here, setting him free with her words and begging him with her eyes to never let her go. *A man should fulfill or end his commitments on his own. No one can do it for him.* Whatever his reasons, he had married her. His heart had accepted her as his wife the moment he'd put that ring on her finger. He'd made a commitment to her with his deeds even if he'd been too much of a coward to admit it. *No one can do it for him.*

It was what Richard had tried to tell him. No one else could be Ada's husband but him. No one.

He took in her flushed face for one more moment and then yanked her up onto her toes and kissed her.

ADA WAS CERTAIN of one thing. She wasn't leaving this room until she was dead certain she would remain Mrs. Thompson. Nothing was beneath her. She would call on her brother, his mother, and the House of Lords to ensure it. Fortunately, however, her first resort of kissing him still seemed to be working out well. She pulled at his cravat, the buttons on his waistcoat, the hem of his shirt all the while kissing him as if her life depended on it. She couldn't move fast enough, couldn't decide what she wanted to focus on more. She couldn't think about what she was doing. If she allowed herself to consider her actions, she would sink into mortification. All she knew was she had to make sure he understood what she wanted. She had to make sure he couldn't leave her behind again.

"Ada," he murmured against her mouth, and she panicked instantly, kissing him harder, clinging to his shoulders as she fought to stay on her toes. Over and over, he attempted to calm her frenzied actions until finally his arms came around her, trapping her arms against her squirming body. "It's all right, Ada," he whispered into her hair, as he held her against him.

She squeezed her burning eyes shut and pressed her face into his shoulder, waiting for him to push her away. After a moment he adjusted his hold and drew her back before tilting her face up to his. Still, she kept her eyes shut, afraid of what she'd see. Then his mouth was on hers, kissing her slow and deep, leaving no more doubts in her mind or strength in her legs. He was going to take what was his. Finally.

His lips left hers to taste the skin of her jaw, her neck, and shoulders while his hands wandered everywhere, tangling in her hair, running over her breasts, and waist. She pulled open his waistcoat and cravat, pressing her mouth against his bare throat.

His groan reverberated against her as his hands tightened convulsively on her body. "Let me take you upstairs."

"No, no. Take me now."

"Darling."

She pressed her brow against his and held his face in her hands as she strained upwards to kiss him. "Don't stop. Please don't stop."

He moaned against her lips, his tongue pushing past them to taste her mouth. She shivered at the sensation, her fingertips pressing into his short beard. Her hair gave way to his hands as pins clattered onto the floor. His fingers worked along her back, unhooking her bodice and pulling it away from her. Next came the skirt of her gown, followed by petticoats and her crinoline until she stood before him in her chemise, stockings, and pantalettes. She helped him remove his waistcoat, shirt, and trousers, leaving him in his linen drawers. His body was so entrancing she didn't have time to be bashful about her own scantily clad form. She'd seen his bare chest before, but never this close. And she certainly hadn't touched him like she was doing now, taking in smooth skin and the slight roughness of the dusting of hair on his chest.

When she met his eyes again, they were fixed on her with an electrifying level of intensity. He pulled her against him, drugging her with deep and languid kisses while she slid her arms around his neck in total acceptance of whatever he chose to do. She loved his kisses, she loved the feel of his body, his scent, the low noises he made in the back of his throat. He hoisted her up into his arms, and she wrapped her legs around his waist as he carried her over to the sofa. He dropped to his knees, setting her down on the cushions before removing her evening slippers, sliding his hands up her legs to remove her pantalettes and her cotton stockings. The first time his slightly roughened fingertips touched the bare flesh of her legs, her breath caught in her throat. How could she have known it would feel so wonderful to have a man's hands on her skin like that? How could she have known how sensitive the insides of her thighs could be?

His mouth raced over whatever bare skin was available, pausing to kiss her breasts and tease her nipples over her linen chemise. She gasped, arching into his mouth, and running her hands over his bare shoulders. She wanted him to stay exactly where he was but more than that, she wanted him to keep going. His mouth traced over her stomach before reaching her calf, the inside of her knee. His tongue flicked against the inside of her thigh, and she collapsed against the back of the sofa, her hands still clinging lightly to his hair. The further his mouth climbed, pushing her chemise out of the way, the harder her breath came until he finally reached her sex. When his tongue flicked against a spot of incredible sensitivity, the sensation exploded throughout her body. A loud cry burst from her panting mouth, and her eyes squeezed shut against the intensity.

He groaned in response, sliding her leg over his shoulder, and putting his hands under her bottom to hold her writhing body in place while he sucked and licked and swirled his tongue all over the epicenter of all sensation in her body, building a delicious tension in her limbs. He slid a finger inside her and the shock of the fullness had her fingers curling into a fist in his hair. A second finger slid in beside the first and the chord within her snapped, sending her body into spasms as she churned her hips against his mouth and onto his fingers, chasing every ounce of sensation. When she came back to herself, she could feel his beard still against her thigh, his breath on her sensitive flesh.

She drew his face up to hers, and he complied eagerly, kissing her with growing hunger as he pulled her closer. He drew her down to straddle his lap, bending his head to devour her neck and shoulders as she curled herself around him. He petted her between her legs, his fingers probing and stroking that wonderful ache back to life. It wasn't until he pressed something blunt and wide against her entrance that she realized he was naked under her. That her bare bottom was resting on his naked thighs. He sank into her slowly, his teeth clenching onto her skin as his clever fingers kept their attentions between her legs. Even with all those wonderful sensations, it was impossible not to notice the discomfort of his thick flesh stretching her beyond what she thought she could bear. There was a sharp pinch that made her wince in near pain as he progressed within her until he was fully seated. She struggled to catch her breath as her body acclimated to the impossible fullness.

"Are you all right?"

"I don't know," she gritted out. "It's not hurting really but it burns, almost like there's too much in there."

He let out a short, weak burst of laughter, before capturing her mouth in a quick, hard kiss. "Not too much. Just give it a moment, darling."

"What should I do?"

"Let me distract you for a bit," he said pulling her chemise up over her head and leaving her as exposed as he was.

She opened her mouth to ask another question, but then he was kissing her neck, his hand fisted in the hair at the base of her skull. He suckled on the spot where her neck met her shoulder, and every thought went clean out of her head. It was like being devoured by a famished beast or a sailor on leave if Regina's books were to be believed. His mouth, teeth, and tongue moved over her skin with a steady urgency that left her breathless and tingling all over. Her skin seemed alive with sensitivity, magnifying the contrast of his soft mouth and the scrape of his beard. He took the tip of one of her breasts into his warm mouth, and she nearly choked. When he began to suck, her core clenched down hard on him. She winced at the discomfort, but it didn't last long. The more she clenched down on him, the less painful he felt inside her. It was as if she were melting around him, from her muscles to her bones until she felt the first stirrings of pleasure between her legs since he'd entered her.

Curious, she began to shift her hips experimentally to see if she was ready for more. He groaned loudly into her shoulder, and she felt his sex flex inside her. He nipped at her skin, his breath coming in deep gusts as his hands shifted to her hips. For a few moments, he guided her movements, showing her how to tilt her hips to hit that elusive spot within her that always made her breath catch in her throat.

"Do you like that?" he whispered into her ear, sending shivers throughout her body. She nodded weakly, her eyes clenched shut, and her hand tightened convulsively on his shoulders. "What about this?" He moved underneath her, the angle setting every nerve ending in her core alight.

She gave a sharp gasp before a guttural groan left her mouth. Delicious heat raced through her as they moved together. She rocked against him with single-minded purpose, her head falling back weakly as bursts of pleasure detonated between her legs where he ground into her. Without warning, a starburst of sensation sent her reeling, and she cried out, her entire body going rigid in his arms while she struggled to catch her breath. As it faded, she collapsed against him, kissing him ravenously.

He fell backward, drawing her down on top of him as he

caressed her naked flesh. Her midnight hair fell around them as she braced one hand on his chest over his thundering heartbeat and the other on the plush carpet beside his head. She ground down onto him and his head fell back as he arched into her with a shout. That made her eager for more as much as the ghost of her previous climax lingering in her body. Between what felt good for her and the sounds he made, she found her rhythm, rocking and swirling her hips. His hands moved up her torso, glancing over her stomach and her ribs to tease her sensitive nipples as he watched her with glittering eyes.

Her throat was raw with her cries, her mouth dry and chapped from her panting breaths and biting her lips. Her eyes fluttered closed for a moment as the wave of pleasure built again with even more force, threatening to leave her hollowed out and bruised in its wake. She searched blindly for his hands on her breasts, clinging to them in an attempt to stay grounded, and then she heard him call her name.

"Ada."

A shiver raced through her at the rough desperate tenor of his voice.

"Ada, look at me. I want to see you."

Her heavy eyelids lifted just as the wave crested and she called out again, riding him hard and fast, desperate for the torturous pleasure to fade, desperate for her body to stop seizing so she could catch her breath. Basil bucked up into her body and she heard his cries of ecstasy before he spilled inside her, hot and thick. She fell forward onto him, sweat-slicked and trembling. His hands came up to her face, pushing her hair back as she tasted his mouth again, unwilling to give up such a treat even for air.

A thought rose up within her, unbidden and unanticipated. What happened now? Was she supposed to go back to her brother's house to wait? She wasn't ready for this to be over. She wanted him to stay just like this against her, inside her. Her eyes stung with tears as his wonderful mouth raced over her forehead to her cheek and jaw, kissing and tasting her skin.

"Don't let go," she begged as she pressed her face into his neck, panting for breath and desperate for comfort after that delicious ordeal.

"Never," he growled against her skin. "Never. You're mine now."

Chapter Sixteen

His marriage was going to be an interesting one, that was for certain. There was no way he could pretend that his wife was anything but a woman who would demand no less than what she had decided on. In some miraculous twist of fate, she had decided on him. Until the day he died, he would never forget the way she looked, charging into his house with a face like thunder. The image of her above him, dark, lustrous hair spilling over her naked body, and her eyes full of lust and impatience would stay with him the rest of his life.

Her appearance now was a variation on a theme. His fiery sweetheart lay curled up beside him, skin to skin, half covered by the blanket he always kept in his study in case he forgot to tend the fire. Her dear head was resting against his stomach, her arm was wrapped tightly around his waist. Those soft, perfectly sized breasts were pressed against his hip. He'd spent the last hour playing with her hair, easing every pin from the strands, allowing himself to enjoy every texture of her the way he'd wanted to for days. She sighed softly, her breath wafting over his stomach in a faint caress. It was enough to remind him that it had been four hours since he'd made love to her, which was an hour longer than he'd wanted.

He'd glanced at her shadowed face and decided against waking her just yet. She'd barely slept at all, and he was a gentleman despite his determination to roger his wife rigid on the floor of his study. He couldn't get enough of her, or the way she made love to him like she was determined to pour herself into him, to bind herself to him body and soul. Her eyelids fluttered against his skin as her eyes opened, and she stretched her body along the length of his.

"Is it morning?" she grumbled.

"I'll be frank, I have no idea."

"Mmm, you make a lovely pillow."

"Thank you, darling."

"Did you sleep at all?"

"Are you nagging me already?"

"How long have you been awake?"

"Yes, I slept. And I've been awake an hour at most." He had no idea of that either. He was watching her face. not the clock.

"Why didn't you wake me?"

"I wanted to watch you sleep when I didn't feel guilty for once."

She pushed herself up to peer at him, and he watched her breasts pop free from their prison between their two bodies and hang free. He hadn't touched those beauties in too long. Maybe he could convince her to take him for one more ride before they had to leave this room and return to the world.

"Guilty? When were you feeling guilty?"

"You have a habit of attaching yourself to people while you sleep, and I've been the person beside you most of that time."

"But why guilty?"

"Because I wanted to be the one you attached yourself to. Because I wanted you."

She looked at him in askance. "You had a funny way of showing it. I had to throw aside all my dignity and hunt you down."

"I didn't realize you knew where I lived."

"Richard brought me."

Of course, he had... That was another thing he'd have to speak to his dear friend about. "Ada."

"Hmm?"

"Why did you think I was still engaged to Felicity Ashwood?"

"Well, Ellie—Miss Hawthorne—had seen her with your mother. They hadn't heard anything about it being called off, there wasn't any scandal about our elopement or bad blood between the families, so she thought we had already dissolved it."

"Ah."

"When I mentioned it to Richard, he didn't say anything to refute it, and I knew he'd come to see you earlier so it confirmed it for me."

Basil rolled his eyes. That little shit. "He knew I wasn't engaged."

"What?"

Basil gave her a wry look. "Your brother knew I wasn't engaged. He sent you here to ambush me." And it had worked. He didn't like that he was so easy to read but he couldn't argue with the results. He was a simple man in the end.

"Ambush you?"

"He wanted me to stay married to you, but I didn't think it was a good idea. He tried debate and when that failed, he got you all fired up and sent you to my door."

"What if you had turned me away?"

"I don't have a reliable track record of saying 'no' to you."

"You were doing well these past weeks. Why didn't you want to stay with me?"

"I was worried about you, worried about what you would have to face as my wife. My family is…" he shook his head. "You know what they are like. When it comes to marriage, they were always the selling point, a connection to the nobility."

"I just wanted you."

"I know, but without them I'm not much."

"I disagree. I don't need you to protect me from them, I need you to love me."

"You expect me to love you without trying to protect you from harm? Is that reasonable?"

"You were going to make us both miserable because you

didn't respect me enough to trust my judgement?"

"That… seems overly harsh."

"The realization was difficult to accept as well," she replied, pinning him down with her stare. How did she manage to be sweet and terrifying all at once?

"I respect you, Ada."

"In some things yes, but not in that. I will not be put behind glass because you need to play master. I don't need you in front of me, I need you at my side."

"Understood."

"Don't do that again." She tangled her fingers in his hair, holding his head in place as she pressed her forehead to his. "Promise me."

"I promise. I won't underestimate you again," he said.

The door opened and Mr. Crouch entered with wood for the fire. Both he and Ada seemed to realize the situation at the same time because they both let out a shriek. Crouch spun around to face the door and Ada tried to burrow between Basil's back and the armchair.

"I'm sorry, sir, I didn't realize you were still in here."

"No, it's my fault, Crouch. Maybe return in half an hour if it's not too much trouble?"

"Yes, sir," he replied before flying out the door and shutting it with a resounding thud.

"Well, I guess that answers your question."

Ada peeked up at him, her cheeks flushed bright red. "My question?"

"Good morning, Wife." He winked at her, and she giggled before burying her burning face against his side.

"Oh. Good morning."

🔥

ADA HAD DECIDED that she quite enjoyed being married. She and

Basil had moved to his bedroom after the inopportune interruption from the scullery maid, but once they were there, the lovemaking had continued. She didn't know what it meant that she didn't mind the seemingly insatiable appetite of her husband. He didn't seem to ever fully tire or hunger for anything other than her, which suited her just fine so far. She'd already grown used to his soft mouth and the scrape of his beard against her as he woke her. She'd grown used to being kissed awake by a lusty man with sparkling blue eyes and a low, smooth voice.

Now she sat in his lap in the dining room wrapped in his house robe, eating a late breakfast from his plate. Her delightful husband was wearing his shirt and trousers from the night before, thoroughly disheveled and debauched. He was full of surprises. She expected breakfast to consist of cold items like cheese, ham, and bread. Never would she have imagined seeing him standing over the stove in his kitchen frying eggs and bacon.

"You know, Ada, I don't typically share my food with anyone."

"Well, I have a bit of paperwork that says you have to share everything with me."

"Do you?"

"Mmm and seeing as how much I have surrendered to you from a legal and societal perspective, let alone the physical, I think the least you could do is share your eggs and bacon."

"It's the coffee I'm concerned about."

She pulled a face and snapped her teeth at him, triggering a chuckle in response. The doorbell rang and Ada heard Crouch answer it.

"Who on earth could that be?" Ada asked, sitting up straight. She was covered but hardly appropriately dressed for visitors.

"I'm willing to venture a guess," Basil said.

"Sir, I don't believe that they are taking callers at the moment."

Basil and Ada tensed in alarm.

"Nonsense, I'm family," they heard Zhenyi say. "Do I smell

breakfast?"

"Sir."

Ada began to crawl off Basil's lap but his grip tightened and he gave her a look. He wanted her to stay there? Wouldn't it be embarrassing for Zhenyi to see her like this?

Zhenyi burst through the door before pausing at the sight before him.

"Thornfield," Basil said.

Zhenyi blinked in shock for a moment before a sly smile spread across his face. "Good morning, Mr. and Mrs. Thompson."

"Good morning, Gēgē."

"Is that bacon?" he asked, stepping forward with an eager look.

"No, it isn't," Basil replied, grabbing the plate and sliding it away from him. "You two are like locusts. Go get your own food!"

"I suppose based on your current state of undress you two managed to sort out your differences?"

"Yes," Basil replied, still eyeing him warily.

Zhenyi turned to Ada. "And you've managed to talk my good friend here out of the truly idiotic notion of having an annulment?"

"Yes," Ada replied, giggling at the glare Basil was giving her brother.

"Excellent. I'll just show myself out then," he ducked out of the room, and just as Ada was about to relax, his head appeared again around the door. "I'll guess I won't be seeing you later on today Basil?"

"Get out!" Basil cried, grabbing a fork and throwing it in his direction, as he retreated with a laugh that they could hear until he left the premises.

Thornfield House
London

WHEN BASIL ARRIVED the next day to help Richard with the business ledgers, he grew immediately suspicious at the lack of commentary from his old friend. The longer Richard made no mention of what he'd seen the previous day, the more Basil dreaded the moment that discretion ran out. He'd never met a man more naturally kind with such a profane sense of humor.

When Basil looked up from the ledger on the desk and saw Richard smirking at him, he knew his time had run out.

"I'm glad that you and Ada have managed to sort yourselves out," Richard commented innocently.

"Due to your meddling," Basil replied evenly. "Thanks for that by the way."

"You are welcome." Richard sipped his tea.

Basil waited a few moments before plunging in. There was no point in avoiding the conversation now. "You could have given me some warning before sending her over."

"That is true."

"And you could have told her that I wasn't engaged instead of goading her into a temper."

A small, smug smile made an appearance. "That is also true."

"But I suppose the idea of me being trounced by your little sister was too appealing."

"It truly was."

Basil shook his head in rueful amusement. "Why are you like this?"

"Who knew how long you would have been stupid if I didn't send her?" Richard replied flippantly before his face grew solemn. "She was so sad, Basil. I would have torn your hide myself if I didn't know you were as miserable as she was. She kept waiting for you and dressing up for you and you never came. She broke into my office for your address so she could write you letters. She was stalking the footman for the post."

"I'm sorry."

"I don't need you sorry. You are my oldest, dearest friend and as that, I wish you the very best in your marriage. But she is my little sister."

Basil wasn't looking at his friend anymore. This was Ada's elder brother, the head of their family, her "Gēgē", as she called him. This man wasn't concerned with anything but the little girl he'd comforted during thunderstorms and protected from bad dreams.

"She is my only family in this country, and I've loved her and watched over her since before she was born," Richard continued. "She is dearer to me than the blood in my veins and if you ever put that look on her face again, I will kill you."

"You'll never get the chance. She's stuck with me now."

"I'm glad to hear it. Good friends are so hard to find, it would take me another fifteen years to replace you." He winced and shuddered as if the thought itself was traumatic.

Basil looked away and shook his head, calling on every ounce of his self-control to stop himself from laughing. It would only encourage the man. There was truly no one more endearing or impudent than him. "As your friend, I suppose it would be unmannerly to inconvenience you in that way."

"I knew you would understand. There's another matter I want to discuss with you."

Of course there was, Basil thought. "Go on."

"I'm settling on Ada's dowry, and there is one request I have of you."

"Am I going to like this request?"

"Likely not, but listen anyway. Your properties, the one in the country and the one in town. I want to finish them."

There was a prickling at the back of Basil's neck, as if his body was preparing for a feeling he wasn't sure of. Finish them? "What exactly do you mean, Richard?"

"I want you to let me fund their completion."

Basil's head was shaking even before he had finished speaking. "No, Richard. Of course, no. I don't need you to do that."

"I know that."

His face was burning, his mouth was as dry as week-old bread. How could he think he would accept something like this? Was he looking down on him as if he was some pauper that needed to be brought up to scratch? "I'm not the richest man in the world, but I can finish my house on my own. I can take care of my wife and my family on my own."

"Your wife is my baby sister."

"I know who she is," Basil snapped, rising to his feet. He didn't know where he'd expected the conversation to turn but this wasn't it. "You're annoying me now. I'm going to go home and forget you said this."

"Basil, please just listen. I knew that Ada would marry one day and make a family of her own and for her sake I was prepared. I had her dowry, the funds which you knew about but there were things as well. Things—" His voice cracked, and he paused looking away almost angrily. He closed his eyes and took a breath, his jaw clenching and flexing against some emotion.

Basil watched in horrified fascination, still annoyed and yet terrified of seeing tears in his friend's eyes.

After a tense moment, Richard spoke again. "Things our mother wanted her only daughter to have. Silk brocades I made for her trousseau. Jade bracelets and hair pins from our mother. Ink sticks and brushes from home. I wanted to give them to her at her engagement party, on her wedding day. I wanted to give her a wedding where she would feel not only my love but theirs. Now, because of that man, I've missed all of that. My parents couldn't give her away and neither could I. Her wedding day was an act of desperation instead of a happy occasion."

Richard never spoke about his parents after their deaths, let alone their hopes. He made it easy for others to forget the loss he'd suffered at a young age and the responsibility he'd taken on willingly out of love for their memory. "You can still give those things to her, Richard."

Richard shook his head irritably, "It's not about the things." He looked at Basil with eyes that were bloodshot and glistening. "I missed her wedding, Basil. I don't have another sister. I can't get that back. Let me give my sister a house."

His throat was burning. *Fuck*, he looked away, shifting his weight awkwardly. What the hell could he say to that? Was he allowing his pride to rob Ada of a proper home? She was staying with him currently, but once work began, how could he expect her to live there? Was he being unreasonable? He sighed heavily and stalked back over to the chair, dropping into it. "A house," he conceded, knowing that in the end he would agree to anything. Anything for Richard to put those sad, fucking eyes away.

Richard blinked in surprise, then shook his head, clearing his throat. "Country house then."

"The city one needs more work." The words came out before he could stop them.

The tears were still there but now a smile was there, small but genuine. "Take my sister on her honeymoon and leave the blueprints with me."

Basil cleared his throat again, refusing to smile back. "I'm still not comfortable with this, mind."

"I know, but it's something I can do for you as well, for both of you. After all, you risked a great deal for my sake."

"Leo risked as much as I did, are you going to buy him a house as well?"

"First of all, Leo is a trained veteran, and you are not, secondly, Leo didn't nearly blow up his reputation by marrying my sister while engaged to a daughter of the nobility. But since you mentioned it, I am well aware that I will owe him for the rest of my life."

"So, I'm meant to consider this a favor?"

"Yes, if you like that better?"

It was a novel concept, if wildly disproportionate. "You and I have different ideas on what constitutes a favor."

Footsteps came fast and heavy down the hall and then the

door opened to reveal Leo, looking harried and exhausted.

"Speak of the devil," Richard murmured."

"You look absolutely gorgeous, Kingston," Basil joked. Leo rolled his tawny eyes and shook his head.

"I have had a bitch of a week, Thompson. I'm in no mood for you."

"You came here for succor and companionship?" Richard tilted his head and practically batted his eyes.

Leo pinned him with an exasperated stare, "I came here to make sure you two were all right and to ask if you've seen Trent."

"Not since we left him in your capable hands," Richard replied, all humor melting from his face.

"Not my hands—the local constabulary," Leo hissed in frustration. "Apparently he had friends in there. He's in the wind."

Basil and Richard shot to their feet in alarm. "I beg your pardon?" Basil said as he felt his blood pressure spike.

"Donald Trent is missing. I just came from questioning the sergeant who let him go. We can't find a trace of Trent anywhere."

"We haven't seen him, but frankly we haven't been looking."

"How long has he been gone?"

"It was noticed that he was missing three days ago."

Three fucking days? Basil's stomach pitched unceremoniously as a cold sweat coated his body.

"Three days?" Richard repeated in alarm. "And you've only thought to tell me this now?"

"I've only just heard of it," Leo replied testily but it was clear he wasn't angry with them. Someone in Scotland Yard had no doubt received an earful. "I was looking into the group that he's been involved with, which has been a cockup from day one, thank you for asking. I just went to question Trent this morning and found out that he had been missing for days and no one had relayed it to me."

"So, he could have been gone longer than three days?" Basil

asked.

"Potentially, yes."

He had to get to Ada. He'd left her all alone with no one but Mr. and Mrs. Crouch to protect her. He glanced at the clock. Five o'clock. Crouch would be leaving soon to escort his wife home. If Basil wasn't there, Trent would have nothing but a door between him and Ada. Basil grabbed his jacket from the back of the chair and started for the door.

"He's been laying low for a reason, Thompson," Leo said laying a hand on his shoulder, "With the men Trent has on his tail, you and Richard are the least of his problems."

"But those men don't care where they get their pound of flesh from," Basil said. "If they can't get it from Trent, they may well try his method of extracting cash from his former employer."

"Go," Leo said, giving him a light shove of encouragement.

Chapter Seventeen

26 Grosvenor Square
London

By the time Basil arrived at his residence, he was on the edge of a full-blown panic. The idea of Ada being at the mercy of a man like Trent, or worse yet, the men he was hiding from, had his skin crawling. He knew she was formidable, he knew she was intelligent, but he couldn't bet on her against a group of thugs. He wouldn't be able to breathe easily until he had her in his arms again. Until he had undeniable proof that no one had put fear in her eyes again.

No one but him, of course.

There was no way that he could hide something like this from her. Not without endangering her safety. She was smart enough to avoid any situations that would put her or her loved ones at risk. Provided, of course, that they hadn't gotten to her already.

"Ada," he called softly, peeking into his study. It was a good deal more organized than he remembered leaving it and bore a few additional pieces which he knew belonged to her. Hopefully, she hadn't done too much damage to his system. He made his way through the house, calling out for her, checking the kitchen, the dining room, the additional sitting room at the back. The property had been built for a small family, only three rooms above stairs, two parlors, a dining room, and a kitchen. With himself as the only true occupant, Basil had focused his energy on the rooms he used: the front parlor which was, truth be told, big enough to section part of it as a study, his bedroom, and the kitchen. He imagined that Ada would be only too glad to sink her fingers into everything. She probably already had ideas to reorganize.

He walked up the stairs and heard a faint humming coming from his bedroom. So that was where she was. It was the largest room in the house, meant to be shared by the master and mistress. When he pushed open the door, he was graced with the sight of Ada in the bath. Her eyes were closed but he knew she wasn't sleeping. Her lithe limbs were flushed with the heat and slick with her violet-scented bathwater. All that gorgeous dark hair was braided and pinned on top of her head. He needed to touch that body, feel that silken hair in his hands before his heart stopped racing.

He walked towards her, careful to stay as quiet as possible, but just as he grew close enough to touch her, those beautiful eyes opened and fixed on him with fond amusement.

"Hello, you," she said quietly.

"Hello to you, how are you feeling?" he replied, loosening his cravat and shrugging off his jacket and waistcoat. He paused to remove his boots before crouching beside her.

"I'm fine, just relaxing really."

"How did you spend your day?" he asked, kissing her jaw, debating if he should simply climb into the bath with her.

"I made a catalog of the things in your home that need replacing or updating."

"No wonder you are exhausted."

She grinned, tilting her head to grant him more access, "I was surprised at how long it became. Why did you leave half of it undone?"

"It seemed a waste of time really, it was only ever me, and I was always in the country."

"I'd forgotten you have another estate," she said.

"Hardly an estate," he replied, nuzzling her shoulder as his hands moved over her slick arms.

"Well, no matter. It's ours," she replied, leaning back against him.

"It certainly is."

"When do we go back there?" she asked.

"Whenever you like, dearest."

"Is it as badly furbished as this one?"

"It's equally functional. But feel free to do as you like." He brushed a few errant tendrils from her alabaster neck, feathering his fingertips over her sensitive skin before cupping her soft breasts in his hands, and she arched into his touch with a sharp breath. He loved the slight weight of them, the sensitive rose-tinted nipples that were always eager for his touch.

"I want a garden," she said on a soft sigh as his fingers danced over her soft stomach.

An image came to him of her laid out in a field of forget-me-nots, her dark eyes shining, her body warm and supple under his, "A garden sounds lovely."

"I know what you are thinking of and it's not flowers."

"It's definitely flower related."

She laughed and shook her head, turning to wrap her arms around his neck. "You are incorrigible."

He wrapped his arms around her, his chin resting on her shoulder as he tried to calm the anxious feeling at the base of his skull. He just needed to stay there for a moment, breathe her in and feel her against him, warm, loving, and utterly alive. "Your brother has asked to finish the renovations while I take you on a honeymoon," he murmured.

"Did you agree?"

"I did." He pressed a soft kiss against her damp neck. It was right there after all.

She sighed, "Good."

He nipped lightly at her skin, and she shivered slightly, the tips of her breasts furling into hard pebbles he felt through his shirt. "Good? Are you trying to say something, Mrs. Thompson?"

"No," she smiled lazily. "He hates owing others. What you did…" she trailed off, "What we did for him, he wouldn't be at peace until that debt was paid. It's how Mama was as well. She believed that a favor unpaid created a karmic debt you had to repay in your next life."

It was something he hadn't considered. It was true that Richard never let a favor go unreturned, but Basil had always seen it as him being kindhearted. It had never occurred to him that his brand of reciprocity was rooted in theocratic belief. "But a house? Doesn't that seem a bit much considering what a delightful handful you are?" he asked.

She nuzzled his face softly before drawing back enough to meet his eyes. "It is not about the effort you expended, it's about how much he values what you protected," she replied. "I am his beloved mèimei after all."

"You are beloved," he replied, his hands spreading over her back, pulling her closer. He was tired of the copper barrier between them. He needed to feel all of her. "Are you done in here?" he asked.

She nodded with a sly grin, and he took her mouth with his. She turned into him fully, tangling her fingers in his hair while he slipped an arm around her back and under her knees, yanking her out of the bath. She gasped against his mouth before pulling away to see where he was heading.

"We'll make the bed wet," she protested weakly as he lowered her onto the silken coverlet.

"I don't care," he replied, shrugging off his suspenders and lowering his half-dressed body to hers. The relief of that contact, even through his clothes, sent chills through him.

"Basil," her eyes darkened, and her beautiful hands came up to unbutton his shirt.

"Ada," he replied and she rolled her eyes in amusement before tugging his shirt from his trousers and pulling it over his head, tossing it behind her. "Be a good girl and kiss me."

She giggled as he nuzzled her jaw, shivered when his hungry mouth moved down her neck and breasts, tasting salt and smelling violets. He nipped at her skin, and she gasped, curling her hands into his hair, writhing beneath him. He knew there would be marks on her skin from his mouth, from his teeth, but he couldn't stop. Couldn't stop touching or tasting her long enough to clear his mind. Every gasp and whimper she let out, every tremble, told him that he wasn't hurting her. His hands roved over her bare, damp flesh down her leg, pulling it over his hip, opening her wider for his fingers to test her readiness.

The desperate relief he felt when he found her slick and hot almost shamed him. He couldn't wait any longer to be inside her. Half-blind with desire, he met her lustful gaze before kissing her gasping mouth and plunging himself inside her. Both their ragged cries were swallowed as her hips churned against his, her hands pulled him closer, her nails digging into his skin.

He buried his face in her shoulder as vicious pleasure clawed through his body, leaving him breathless. Her uneven desperate breaths fanned against his neck as he twined their fingers together to ground himself. As he began to move, her legs wrapped around him, and her free hand stroked down his side. The comfort that feather-light touch gave had his eyes burning as she began to climax and dragged him over the edge too soon. Wrung out, he stayed where he was in her arms as she pressed gentle kisses to his neck and shoulder, nuzzled his cheek with hers. All he wanted was this: a lifetime in her arms.

🔥

SOMETHING WAS WRONG with him. Or rather, something had happened. Something that had sent him into a state of desperation. She didn't have a problem with the results per say, but if her husband was going to come home and ravish her, she'd prefer it was owed to her own allurements rather than something else. He shifted until he was lying beside her on his stomach, his arm flung across her chest, his chin level with her shoulder.

She watched his eyes drift closed, but the small smile he usually wore after was absent. She wrapped her hands around his arm, trying to comfort him as much as she could. Even now, with the last echoes of pleasure fading from her limbs like a dying ember, she couldn't allow herself to relax with that question on her mind. "Are you sleeping?" she whispered after some time. He hummed in response before one blue eye cracked open.

"Why, are you after another round?" he murmured with a devilish grin.

She rolled her eyes and slapped his arm, "No, you ridiculous man. I wanted to ask if you were okay."

He kissed her neck and pressed his forehead against hers, nuzzling her nose. "Barely. I think you broke me."

She giggled while his beautiful blue eyes glimmered with amusement. "You started it."

He chuckled and rolled on to his back tugging her against his chest. "So I did."

She followed, settling against his side, her hand stroking his lightly haired chest in gentle, even caresses. Did he not understand her question or was he evading? "Are you truly well? You seemed more excited than usual earlier."

"The sight of my wife in her bath was very stimulating," he replied, tracing his fingertips over her smooth skin.

"Mmmm," she couldn't help the instinctive smile those words produced.

"I missed you terribly."

He was avoiding the question. "So did I, but that wasn't the reason was it?"

He peered down at her, and she wondered if he would tell her the truth. His broad hand slipped up to cover her shoulder, pulling her even closer to him as if he was afraid she would disappear. What on earth had happened? Was it his father? Had he and his brother bullied him? For a moment, she was afraid he wouldn't tell her the truth. That he would deny it or use their newly found intimacy to distract her. She didn't know what she would do if that happened.

"No, that's not the reason," he replied. He took a deep, steadying breath and pulled her tighter, resting his cheek on her forehead.

"What happened?" she asked, adjusting her breathing to withstand his viselike embrace.

"Trent has escaped, and we don't know where he is."

Her heart faltered for a moment before it began to race in her chest. *Escaped*? Was that nightmare not over as yet? Her fingers tightened on his shoulder. "That's why you were so anxious."

"I barely have any servants. If you were here alone when he came, I'd never know until it was too late. I thought I was going to come here and find you dead or missing."

She nuzzled his chest and wrapped her arm around his waist. He must have been terrified. "He's going to come for Richard again."

"He may come for either or both of you," he replied.

"He could come for you as well. He knows that you helped." How much did he know? Did he know she had gotten married? He'd hurt Basil to get to her.

"He needs money, not my blood. But I don't know what he is willing to do to get it. I thought you were safe at last, but now it seems you are in more danger than ever."

"Yes, but we know the danger is there now. Before we were all caught off guard."

"If I asked you to stay here until he was caught, would you do it?"

She was silent for a long moment before letting out a deep sigh, "I know we have to be careful, but we can't just hide forever."

"I said only until they catch him."

"They already caught him, but he got away." She couldn't spend her life in terror like a cornered rabbit.

"I know."

"He's already taken so much, how much more must he take before we are finally free?"

"I don't want you to stay under house arrest, but we need to take precautions. No public or private events."

"That's fair I suppose."

"No errands without at least three policemen—"

"Basil, be reasonable."

He grumbled but said nothing more for a moment. "Two footmen but they need to be armed."

"Maybe we can stay with my brother for a while."

"You mean seeing as he has footmen and we don't?"

She loved how easily the 'we' rolled off his tongue. "Yes. And perhaps Mr. Kingston has a few acquaintances who can help stand in. That way we know they can defend themselves, and they'll be able to take him into custody at once if he shows himself."

He frowned down at her, as if annoyed that he hadn't considered that first. She leaned her head back to meet his eyes and wiggled her eyebrows.

"Well? Do we have an accord?" she asked.

"Have I mentioned lately what a brilliant and beautiful woman you are, Mrs. Thompson?"

"It could bear mentioning again."

Chapter Eighteen

Three days later

THERE SHE WAS, that sneaky little slattern. She thought that he was done but she had no idea. None. Trent stayed where he was and watched as Ada and that jumped-up Miss Hawthorne—as she called herself—stepped out of their carriage. He couldn't believe that he'd ended up like this, hunted by villains and abandoned by those yellow-bellied cravens he thought were allies.

That gent would only get him his money if he got the job done now. Wouldn't lift a finger to help any more now that The Yard was out lookin' for him. Now Trent could barely move without looking over his shoulder. And look at them, laughing and smiling in their fine silks as if they had any right. In London.

His London.

He'd been born to roam these streets freely, to make his way and his fortune as an Englishman. No one had more of a claim to the wealth in this country than a true Englishman. Especially not that oriental whore and her mulatto bitch of a friend. She thought she was so clever getting out from his clutches, and her brother and his toffee-nosed shit of a friend. So fucking clever breaking that uppity little Chinaman out and ruining all of his plans.

And that half-breed bitch with the coloring of a rotten apple, how was she the daughter of a viscount? How could she enjoy the privilege of the nobility while a son of England toiled under the rules of an immigrant? How the hell did they have a claim to prosperity when he was stuck on the streets?

Miss Thornfield was brought up short by the Hawthorne girl who had paused to stare at something in the pawnbroker's window. Miss Thornfield turned her attention to the bustle of the London evening and Trent hid behind a stationary carriage. He had to be careful if he was going to get out of this bind, and he had every intention of getting out. He waited, watching her dark eyes scanning the street before turning back to her friend. Then she walked the remaining feet to the modiste and entered, leaving her friend by the pawnshop.

How was it possible that he was left in the shadows, and they got the sunlight? How was that the natural order of things? *Miss Thornfield, Miss Hawthorne...* ridiculous that he had to be deferential to them just because she and her stupid mother knew who to fuck. They were picky little bitches, that was for sure. Not any man would do, it had to be a man with money. And Mr. Thompson was too stupid to see what rot he was letting into his house, into his family legacy. Miss Thornfield was even more of a social climber than her mother. Fucking the son of a viscount, she got herself into the nobility. A good match. As if she could ever be meant to be there. He watched as the Hawthorne girl entered the pawnshop, and he pondered if he should make his move now or later.

The fact was, he had only one real shot at getting free and clear and it would take both of them. Fuck the gent. Trent didn't need him if all he was there to do was get in the way of his money. He knew his mistake the first time; it was waiting. Waiting for the gent to get his ducks in a row. Waiting for lawyers. Waiting too damn long. He was a man of action; he didn't need all that other nonsense. His plan would be foolproof: Grab those girls, demand a ransom and once he got the money, get the hell out of town. If they caused a ruckus, he'd keep 'em quiet the best way he knew how.

All he needed was a clear path and he would move. Best to wait. Wait until they were back in the carriage. Then he'd strike.

He'd show them they weren't the only ones who were clever. He'd show them that they would never be welcome, never be safe. They would never be able to pull one over on him and then go on about their lives as if he didn't matter, as if he didn't mean anything. They weren't going to leave him in the dust to hide and scrape a living like a hunted animal. He'd take what was due him and he'd start with those two nobodies. Once he milked Thornfield and that viscount dry, he'd give them back what was left of those whores. After he taught them some manners and reminded them of their place.

He'd get those evil fuckers off his back and live large like he'd always been meant to.

CHAPTER NINETEEN

A DA STARED AT herself in the full-length mirror, admiring the gown she had come to try out. It was one of several dresses commissioned by her brother as part of her trousseau, all in a special brocade designed for the occasion. With all the uncertainty and fear surrounding her, receiving these gifts had been a sweet reprieve.

This one in particular, fashioned into an evening gown with triple flounces at the skirt, was a deep hunter green brocade. He'd gifted her five brocades, but her favorites were the red with blue and pink peonies and a golden phoenix, the cerulean blue satin with lotuses and mandarin ducks, and the mustard yellow with white lilies and cranes. Those she would save and use for dresses in the future.

Each one represented his wishes for her: peace, wealth, fertility and marital bliss. Her family was mocked and looked down upon for being of the merchant class, but there wouldn't be another woman in the world with a dress like this, or with that pattern. If she was going to be unique, an aberration, then she would be envied as well.

"What do you think, Ellie?" she asked, glancing at her friend who had been silent with a secret smile ever since they left the pawn broker. Elodia blinked at her, then took in the gown for what was likely the first time.

"I like it. That pattern is unusual, isn't it?" She stood and walked over, running her fingertips over the floral motif of lilies and orchids in robin blue and pale sunshine yellow. She admired the flecks of red from hidden pairs of magpies in flight along the hem.

"Yes."

"It's the only one like it in the world," the modiste boasted.

"Oh?" Elodia glanced at Ada questioningly.

"Richard made the brocade. He commissioned the brocades last year for my wedding gifts."

"Does it mean anything in particular?"

"The lilies symbolize happy long-lasting unions, the orchids love and fertility."

"And the birds?"

"The magpies, when they are in a pair like here, they mean 'two happinesses'. He's congratulating me on my wedding."

"In a dress?"

"In a dress. They all have different meanings, but they are all happy wishes."

"How do you like the fit, madame?" the modiste asked.

Ada smiled and struck out her foot from where it was hidden under the draping material. "I think the hem at the bottom needs to be taken up an inch and the neckline could be a touch lower. What do you think, Ellie?"

"I think your husband is going to be delighted," Elodia replied.

A slow smile spread across the woman's face, "Alors, Madame, you think like a Parisienne."

"The other evening gowns will need the same."

"As you wish, Madame."

She would be needing more gowns for her honeymoon, which was happening within two weeks. She was resolved. Her life would not be derailed any longer by Trent and his schemes. She stepped down from the stand and began removing the dress carefully before changing back into her calling dress.

"Was that the last one Ada?" Elodia called.

"Yes, we can leave now, unless you had another mysterious purchase to make," Ada prodded, glancing again at the small package Elodia had on the seat with her reticule. Elodia ignored her and sipped her tea. "Are you going to tell me what you bought in that shop?" Ada asked as she finished fastening the front of her dress.

Elodia slipped the small package into the reticule hanging off her wrist and drew it shut before looking at her friend again. "Since you got married, you've become rather nosey."

"It is a state secret or something? I can't imagine what you would need at a pawn broker's shop."

"That's because you have a relatively limited imagination," Elodia replied cheekily.

Ada rolled her eyes in amusement, "Fine, then keep your secrets."

"Is your gown finished?" Elodia asked.

"Yes, as a matter of fact it is. They will deliver it within the week."

"It's very good of your brother to throw you a wedding reception."

"It was a compromise, believe me. He nearly insisted upon another wedding."

Elodia smiled softly, a strange light in her eyes. "He loves you. He's a good man."

Ada watched her friend carefully, noting the softness of her expression and the tightening of her hands on her reticule. There was something going on there... "He's a wonderful man." She considered ignoring the obvious tenderness in her friend's voice but then thought better of it. "Ellie—"

"We should get back. It's getting late in the day and my father has been a stickler for punctuality ever since our jaunt to Gretna Green."

Ada nodded and exited the modiste, heading towards the waiting carriage a few feet down the pavement. "You must thank your father again for me. I was going mad inside that house. If he hadn't agreed to lend us three footmen, I would never have gotten out."

"Mr. Thompson is right to be cautious, Ada."

"I never said he wasn't. I said that the walls had begun to close in."

The footman gave her a nod and opened the carriage door for them, but as they sat down, the sounds of a scuffle were heard outside. Then the carriage took off with a lurch and the door slammed shut. Through the window, Ada caught sight of Thomas chasing after them and the driver, John, lying on the ground. Elodia let out a startled sound before knocking on the ceiling.

"Have a care, John!" she snapped, incredulously.

"Ellie, that's not John," Ada replied.

It took a second for Elodia to understand what that meant. "Oh, damn."

IT TOOK MORE time than Ada was willing to admit for her and Elodia to understand that they had been kidnapped. They kept imagining that perhaps someone had jumped onto the wrong carriage, that perhaps the horses had been startled, anything. But none of that explained the fight they'd heard or the alarm on Thomas's face as he ran after them.

The second issue was who on earth had taken them. Their best hope was that Trent was trying to attempt another kidnapping, but it could also be the men Basil had mentioned. The ones who were hunting Trent down. What if they had decided to cut out the middleman as Basil had feared? Trent could be reasoned with, she hoped, but those men…

She and Elodia had limited options. It was either stay in the carriage and see what happened or make a jump for it and risk injury. Neither was particularly appealing.

"We have to jump, Ellie."

"No."

"Ellie—"

"I am not jumping out of a moving carriage to break my neck on the filthy streets of London."

"He could be taking us anywhere. How would we even be found?"

"Maybe the carriage will stop."

"Stop where?"

"Buckingham Palace, how the devil should I know?"

"There's no use sniping at each other. We need a plan."

Elodia peered out the carriage window and went still. "Ada, he's taking us to the river."

"The river?"

"I'm not jumping out there. Who knows what filth would be there?"

"There are fewer carriages at least."

"That is true."

They positioned themselves at the doors on either side of the carriage and waited. "When you hit the ground, remember to roll, Ellie."

Then the carriage came to a stop. Had he heard them, or had they run out of time? She looked at Elodia and saw her gripping her reticule in her hands. "What do we do now? Should we make a run for it?"

Ada opened her mouth to respond but then the door was flung open and a grimy faced man with a mean glint in his eyes stared back at her. She stared, frozen in terror, then quick as a snake he reached out and grabbed her hand, yanking her out by her arm. She landed awkwardly on the uneven ground, wincing as a sharp pain twinged up her leg from her ankle. Her arm was twisted behind her as she struggled to find her footing and take note of her surroundings.

They were indeed near the Thames as Elodia had said, but the wooden structures beside it caught her attention before the ships did. The holding yards.

Was this where they'd kept Richard?

"Who are you? What do you want?" Elodia asked as she was wrestled out of the carriage by a second brute.

Was it not Trent then?

She turned her head to look at the man holding her arm pinned. "Where are you taking us?"

He grinned but only tightened his grip to a painful extent in response. Ada took in his rotten teeth and soft belly. Perhaps they could outrun them if they got enough of a head start. The men started walking them towards one of the holding cabins, and Ada counted three steps before feigning a stumble. She caught Elodia's eye and nodded, the silent agreement clear.

Fight and run.

Drawing on all her strength, she slammed her head backward into his face. She heard a crunch and a satisfying howl. The moment his grip loosened she picked up her skirts and ran back towards the carriage. Out of the corner of her eyes, she saw Elodia following her. Should she take the carriage and ride away or continue on foot? Did she even have the time to climb up onto the driver's seat? Could she count on her own stamina to out run them?

She glanced behind her to see if they were still on the ground, and she saw Elodia's eyes widen.

"Ada!" she called out and Ada turned to collide with Trent. Filthier, angrier but unmistakably him. Her heart sank as she saw her last chance of escape evaporate.

He grabbed her by the arms. "You aren't outsmarting me again you little bitch," he snarled.

Pain exploded across her temple, then everything went dark.

🔥

SHE WAS LATE. Basil was trying his best to remain calm, but every instinct in him was screaming that something was wrong. Ada had gone into town with Miss Hawthorne to fit her new dresses. It had been a risk he wasn't fully comfortable with, but after nearly a week inside, he'd agreed under the condition that they took no less than three footmen. It wasn't his finest moment, he'd half expected Miss Hawthorne's father to balk at giving over three footmen for a mere errand. Unexpectedly, the man had agreed without any questions as if he knew the reason for the request.

Now, Basil was wondering if he should have insisted upon five footmen, or if he should have forced Leo to strong-arm two constables instead. They had moved to Thornfield House for the time being until Trent was located. More servants meant more barriers of entry and Richard had hired additional guards to watch the house in the event Trent made an appearance. It had seemed foolproof, but now he'd been expecting her for nearly an hour and with every minute that ticked by, he grew increasingly uneasy.

He heard the front door open, and he ran out of the sitting room. Finally, she was home. When he saw Richard removing his gloves instead of Ada, his stomach dropped to his feet as his heart began hammering away.

Richard gave him a quizzical glance before rolling his eyes. "Why is no one ever happy to see me?" he grumbled.

Basil walked towards him on unsteady legs, "Have you seen Ada?"

"She's not back yet?"

Basil shook his head as his heart tightened in his chest. "She's been due for over an hour. I don't mean to be histrionic but—"

"No, she wouldn't be late, not with Trent about." Richard snatched his gloves back from the footman and looked Basil up and down. "You aren't dressed for dinner as yet, so I assume you are coming with me."

"Go," Basil said shoving his shoulder, past the point of jokes. As they left, they saw Leo climbing out of a carriage. He caught sight of them and sighed, shaking his head. "We were just coming to find you."

"I know where they are," Leo said before stepping aside for them to climb into the vehicle.

"Are we going straight there?"

"Yes, but I'm bringing more help this time. With Trent escaping prison and all, I couldn't keep the police out of it. They want a chance to salvage their reputations."

"Kind of them."

"But there's another angle to this Richard, just as you suspected."

"Oh?"

"Trent keeps meeting with someone. At first I thought it was the loan sharks he owed money to but it's not. This person is connected. It's how he got out of prison to begin with."

"Are you going to tell me it's my uncle?" Richard asked calmly. Basil's head swiveled between the two of them as his brain struggled to comprehend what he was hearing.

"I don't have that confirmed, but he does stand to gain from it." Leo's head tilted. "How did you know?"

"It's as I said earlier. Trent is a greedy fucker but he doesn't' have the means to pull this off on his own. Kidnapping me was one thing, but breaking out of Newgate," Richard shook his head. "His backer would need money and influence. The only person I can think of who fits that bill and hates me enough for this is my dear Uncle Simon."

"How did you know all this, Leo?" Basil asked, "We only just realized they were gone."

Leo fixed those light brown eyes on his and smiled wryly. "I've had men trailing all three of you every time you left the house."

Basil's heart was still pounding, but the laugh that escaped him was pure relief.

"What?" Richard looked at him in shock.

"I called in some favors with other colleagues in my business. I left it to Scotland Yard once and they fucked it up. I wasn't about to leave it to them alone again."

Chapter Twenty

Ada didn't know how long she lay on her back, sprawled out on the dirt floor before she awoke and registered the pain. Everything hurt, from her hip to her head. Ears ringing, skull pounding, she tried to raise herself up. That was when she realized her hands and feet were tied. There was barely any light infiltrating the spaces between the wooden walls. Was it already dusk? How long had they been there? Her breath shortened when she thought of how much darker it would get once the sun was fully set. She looked around the dim room waiting for her eyes to adjust to the lack of light. Where was Elodia?

"Ellie?" she croaked out. Silence. Oh God, had they separated them? Was she here all alone? "Ellie," she called out again, a thread of panic leaking into her voice. Finally, she heard a low moan in reply. She caught sight of Elodia's golden-brown dress and slowly moved over to where she lay flat on her back. "Ellie, are you awake?"

"Unfortunately," she grumbled in reply.

Ada laughed, wincing slightly at the stinging sensation on her lip, and helped her up. "Are you all right? Can you move? Did they tie you up as well?"

Ada was only just able to make out the baleful look Elodia gave her before attempting to adjust her clothes. "Just the one question at a time, if you please."

Ada knew it wasn't a time to be laughing, but if her friend had the energy to grumble, she couldn't be too injured. "Are you all right?"

"That depends entirely on your definition of the term. My head is splitting and this floor is... not fit for humans. But I can move, and yes, they did tie me up as well."

Ada closed her eyes and leaned her shoulder against her friend trying to block out the pain and anxiety long enough to assess the situation. They were no doubt filthy, and captive for the moment, but they weren't seriously injured and most importantly they were together.

"They used rope, Ada," Elodia whispered.

"What?" Ada turned to her.

"To tie us up. They used rope."

It took her a moment to register the importance of what she was saying. Rope... they needed a blade. "Ellie, do you have our hairpins?" she asked.

"Always," she replied, pulling the six-inch pin from her voluminous curls. The silver filigree detail on the handle made it pretty enough to pass as a trinket, but the shaft hid a rapier thin blade tapered into a wicked point sharp enough to rival any needle. Regina had presented them with it in their third year at school as a Christmas gift.

"While we have the light," Ada said, pulling her own from her hair and placing the scabbard between her teeth to extract the blade. Holding it between both her slightly numb hands she nodded to Elodia, "You first." Within moments she had cut through the thick ropes binding Elodia's hands. Then she flipped the blade towards her and began sawing away at her own bonds as Elodia removed the ropes binding first her feet and then Ada's.

Once that was done, she put the pin back into its scabbard and stuck it back into her hair. Then she gathered up the ropes and hid them under her voluminous skirts.

"What do we do now?" Elodia asked, hooking her arm through Ada's.

"I don't know," Ada replied. She knew Basil and her brother

would come for her, but she didn't know when. They no doubt already knew she and Elodia were missing, but would they know where they were? Would Mr. Kingston be able to help on such short notice? She couldn't only rely on them to find her, but she didn't have much to work with in order to devise a plan of escape.

She didn't know how many men were outside that door, or how to get home from where she was. She didn't even know if the carriage was still there, or how far away it was. All she knew was that she wasn't tied up anymore, and she now had a weapon. She wasn't going to allow Trent to take her anywhere without the fight of his life.

"They are going to come back eventually. We can't stay here. Should we try the door? Maybe it isn't locked."

"What if it is and there are men guarding it from the outside? Then they'll know we are free. They'll probably end up watching us even more closely then."

"Right and we'll lose the element of surprise." Which would be lost already the moment they realized their hands were free. "Maybe we should..." Ada pulled two of the severed ropes out from under her and handed one to Elodia. "Wrap one around your wrists so we still look tied up."

Elodia nodded, placing the dagger back into her hair and wrapping the rope around her wrists.

"When he gets close enough, we rush him."

"And we start stabbing."

Start stabbing. Yes—that about summed it up.

They heard the rattling of a chain. This was it; someone was coming back. Ada tightened her grip on the two ends of the rope and gathered up as much courage as she could muster. Beside her, Elodia straightened her posture, lifting her chin in defiance. The door to the room opened and Trent emerged, carrying a lantern. "Good evening, Miss Ada and... Miss Hawthorne, is it?"

"Mr. Trent," Ada replied evenly as her heart hammered away in her chest.

"I suppose you're surprised to see me."

"Not especially," she replied. "Bad pennies always turn up, do they not?"

"I ain't doing this for fun. I don't have a choice."

"You *don't* need to do this," she said, and he watched her with a flat expression. "You can take the carriage and just go. You don't need us."

"You gonna try to tell me my business, is that it? Cause you're so high and mighty?" The old mask was gone now, replaced by resentful anger. That thin lip curled into a sneer and those watery eyes narrowed into slits. He pulled a pistol out of his pocket with his free hand and gestured to both of them as Ada watched it in wary silence. "I've got people need paying, and you're going to help me with that."

"We are not going anywhere with you. If you let us go—" Elodia said.

"—Shut up."

"—you have a chance at surviving. If you insist on this course of action, your little mix-up with the underbelly of London will be the least of your problems, I assure you."

"I ain't scared of your toffee-nosed old man. He's soft in the 'ead as it is, parading his little West Indies adventure around London."

Elodia's eyes narrowed. "And yet he has more sense than you, chasing a worse idea to amend a bad one."

"Shut your foul mouth, you little bitch. You think a jumped-up *mulatto* has the right to talk to me like that? Men like me built this country, not animals like you. Just because your mother spread her legs in a field for the right man doesn't give you a right to anything."

Ada felt Elodia stiffen beside her. *Don't Ellie.* Beyond the disgusting allegations about her mother, there were a few words Elodia didn't condone in her presence and that was certainly one of them. If she lost her temper at the wrong time, they could end up in a worse situation than they were already in. But Elodia didn't move, only glowered at him with unbridled rage.

"The law would seem to disagree with that thesis. Perhaps *you* would have gotten further if you had given it a try, you might have had a hidden talent for it."

"You little—" he took a threatening step forward, his hand curling into a fist and lifting to strike her.

"The law, I mean. Of course." She gave him a mocking smile.

"You think I won't kill you?"

"Ellie," Ada hissed, watching the mad glow of desperate hatred in Trent's eyes.

"I think you're stupid enough for anything," Elodia replied with the composure of a dowager duchess despite her disheveled state.

"We'll see about that." He started towards them again, his pistol hand unsteady, his breathing erratic, and Ada tensed in readiness. She'd use the rope to strangle him. She'd use anything. She wasn't going to allow him to hurt them.

Then they heard the sounds of fighting outside. Trent turned towards the sound as it grew louder. Basil. Ada glanced at Elodia and smirked. They were here, so there was no reason for them to wait any longer.

Silently they rose to their feet, and Ada unwound the rope around her wrists as Elodia removed the dagger from her hair. She let out a slow, silent breath as they drew ever closer. In one motion, she and Elodia attacked. Ada jumped on Trent's back, wrapping the rope around his neck, and threw her weight backwards with all the strength she could muster.

Elodia grabbed the hand with the gun and set her knee on his wrist before stabbing downward with her hair dagger clutched in one tawny, bloodless fist. There was a moment of surprise when Trent went down with a pained roar but then she remembered the strategy Regina had learned from her father. *When you are smaller than your opponent speed is of the essence, you keep moving and keep attacking until they stop moving.*

Trent bucked his body ferociously in an attempt to dislodge

them, but sheer desperation lent her the strength to keep a tight grip on the rope as his face turned scarlet and then purple. All they needed to do was wait for him to pass out, but she was worried about what would happen if his strength outpaced hers. His free hand flailed backwards, aiming for her face, and instinctively she grabbed it. Big mistake.

In an instant he was free and backhanded Elodia so hard she hit the ground in a motionless heap. Ada pulled her dagger from her own hair and lunged at his back again, wrapping her right arm around his neck and her legs around his torso as she stabbed down repeatedly with her left hand, aiming for his stomach, his chest, his shoulders, his face, anywhere she could reach. He flailed again, but he was growing weaker, she could feel it. She removed her legs and pushed forward until he was prone on the floor and still her bloody fist kept moving.

He wouldn't take anything else from her, she would make sure of it.

A pair of hands fell on her shoulders, and she went wild, terrified that his friends had come to help him, she kicked and bucked trying to get her arm back far enough to make contact, then the voice registered in her ear.

Ada, sweetheart. Ada it's me, I've got you, you're safe.

The scent of cloves and lavender. Basil. It was Basil. She went limp falling against him as her body dissolved into shudders. His arms came around her tightly, his cheek pressed against hers, his mouth pressed kisses wherever he could reach.

"Basil," she whispered.

"I have you. I have you. You are safe now."

She nodded and turned to him, pressing her face into his chest.

"Did he hurt you?" he asked, and she shook her head.

"I'm all right," she choked out as her eyes filled with tears. "Ellie, he hurt her."

"Your brother has Miss Hawthorne," he said, and Ada looked up to see Richard carefully gathering up Elodia's limp body into his arms before rising with her and walking out the door.

Basil kissed her head, and she closed her eyes tightly, desperately soaking in the sensation of being in his arms, hearing his heartbeat.

"You're certain you're well?"

"Yes. Is he dead?" she asked, glancing at Trent's immobile body bleeding onto the ground.

"Not yet, but I'll see him hanged for this even if I have to string him up myself."

"Basil."

"I have never been so terrified in my life as when you didn't come home. I nearly dropped dead on the spot."

"I'm glad you didn't," she replied, leaning her head back to stare up at him in the growing darkness.

"So am I. But I'm tying you to the bed for at least two weeks while I recover, just in case."

"I wouldn't mind that too much so long as you stayed with me."

Chapter Twenty-One

Thornfield House
London

Three hours later, Ada was clean and curled up on the chaise in her bedroom, wrapped in her dressing gown. Her hair was clean and woven in a damp braid down her back. Every inch of her body felt bruised and exhausted. Her mind couldn't settle, and her emotions darted from sadness to anger and fear. It seemed as though it had been months since she'd been able to take a breath. There had been no rest from the anxiety and terror since her brother had gone missing, and just when she'd been certain it had all been over, Trent had returned. Every noise, every sound, set her skin crawling and her teeth on edge.

Images, sounds, and scents from earlier in the night kept surfacing without warning. The heavy weight of Trent and Elodia pressing her into the ground while her numb hands struggled to keep pressure on his throat. The stench of the river. The dull thudding of footsteps on the ground. The sinking feeling in her stomach when Trent cut off her escape. The rage and desperation she felt coursing through her veins in those final moments when she was on her own, gripping her dagger with bloody desperate fingers as she stabbed down relentlessly into Trent's chest. In that moment she hadn't been herself, rather she had felt like a vengeful demon releasing a lifetime of rage and fear.

Basil had been a joy, waiting on her hand and foot, helping

her bathe the filth from her body, combing out her hair and braiding it for her. Every time he stopped touching her a mild panic began to simmer in the back of her mind, and those images threatened to emerge. When he'd left the room the panic had choked her long enough for him to get away and she'd been sitting there, afraid to move, hoping he would return. How had her childhood room become a place where fears could reach her? She hated it. She was tired of being afraid, tired of looking over her shoulder. Tired of feeling displaced.

The door opened and Basil entered carrying a cup and saucer. Her sweet, wonderful husband with his bright eyes and warm heart. His hair was all over the place and he only wore his shirt and trousers and an anxious expression. She was tired of seeing that look on his face as well.

He handed her the cup before crouching down before her. "Drink all of that," he said softly.

"Is it tea?"

"There's tea in there, yes." He said just as she took a sip. Fire raced down her throat as the flavor of smoke and wood flooded her tongue.

Ada coughed and winced, "That's horrific."

"Drink it all now, don't be troublesome," he said, a shadow of a smile on his mouth.

"What will you give me if I do?" she asked.

He pretended to think about it, tilting his head to one side. "I'll let you sit in my lap," he replied.

She glared at him but finished it quickly. "Couldn't you have used brandy? I like brandy."

"I'll keep some on hand in case you decide to get kidnapped again," he replied dryly as he took back the cup and placed it on the side table.

Her mouth opened to give him an outraged retort, but then he gathered her up in his arms and set her down in his lap, wrapping his arms around her. The instant she settled against that hard chest and the heat from his body sank into her skin she forgot her outrage. This was what she'd wanted the most. The safest place for her, the place with the most comfort and care would always be right here in his arms.

"I didn't mean to get kidnapped," she mumbled laying her head on his shoulder, as his hands stroked up and down her body, cuddling and caressing her at the same time.

"I know, Sweetheart," he replied before kissing her head. "I was only teasing."

"Are you sure you want a wife as troublesome as I am?" she asked, nuzzling her nose against his neck, breathing his scent of cloves and lavender.

"I'll take my chances," he said. "After all, it's not every day a man finds a woman who will ravish him in his study."

She hummed in response, her own hands drifting over his chest, inside the open collar of his white shirt. She felt him take a deep breath as her fingertips traced spirals over the smooth skin dusted with dark hair. In a short period of time his body had grown familiar to the point of necessity. Every time the low timbre of his voice rumbled through his throat and chest a restlessness grew inside her. A kind of desperation to touch and be touched. For her body to know the nightmare was finally over and she was safe at last.

She pressed her lips to the side of his throat once, twice, before moving down to his collarbone. He inhaled sharply, his grip on her tightening.

"Ada," his voice rumbled against her lips, making her smile.

"I miss you," she said, sliding her hand up to his shoulder to cup the back of his neck.

"You are too injured for that."

She frowned, lifting her head to pout at him. "Why are you the one who gets to decide that?"

"Because I'm the one who has to look at you," he said, and the look in his eyes told her he was about to be difficult about this.

"Are you saying you don't want to?" she asked.

"I'm saying I'm worried. My heart hasn't recovered from earlier and I won't want to hurt you."

If he was hoping she would give up after hearing that he was about to be educated otherwise. She shifted to straddle his lap, resting her palms on his shoulders and pressing her sex to his through his trousers. He hissed in a breath, his hands sliding over her dressing gown from her waist down to her upper thighs. She felt him harden against her and knew her goal was in sight.

"I haven't recovered either," she replied sliding her hands into his hair, scraping her nails over his scalp lightly. "But I can't think about it anymore. I need to forget for a while. Can you help me?"

He let out a breath, his eyes heavy lidden and dark with restrained passion. "Yes," he replied. "Tell me what you need."

"I need your hands on me," she said. He nodded once and leaned forward, his arms coming around her again, his hands smoothing over her back and sides, lingering on her stomach. The relief she felt at the pressure of his first touch was immeasurable. She wrapped her arms around his shoulders, holding him closer to her, then his fingers unwittingly found a tender spot on her back that had her hissing in pain.

Basil froze before drawing her away from him, concern etched all over his face. "Ada."

She shook her head, desperate tears stinging her eyes. "I'm all right." She was so close to feeling like herself again. He gazed at her, a fierce battle playing out in the depths of his blue eyes but then he sighed and began pulling at the ties holding her dressing gown together. Inch by inch her naked body revealed itself to him and with every bruise his eyes darkened with concern.

His touch drifted over her flesh as he pushed away the heavy green silk, light and hot as a flame turning her skin to gooseflesh and hardening her nipples in one shimmering instant. "I'm sick of seeing bruises on you," he murmured.

What was he talking about? "This is only the first time," she replied, fighting back a shiver as his fingertips pushed back her sleeves, tracing the delicate skin of her inner wrist where the ropes had left dark angry lines.

"And I'm sick of it." His eyes, when they met hers, were full of somber intensity. She wondered briefly if she was asking too much of him. If she was being too selfish by insisting on this when he was so anxious about her well-being. Then his hand curled around the back of her neck and he drew her down for a deep kiss that made her breath catch in her throat. It felt like forever since she'd felt his mouth against hers and his tongue sliding past her teeth.

She reached for his shirt, tugging on the crushed linen until the hem pulled free from the waistband of his trousers. Then her hands slid under, eager to touch his skin and feel the body that had given her so much pleasure and would continue to do so for the rest of their lives. She pulled away long enough to lift the fabric over his head and throw it away. Then his arms were around her again, pressing her to his body with careful but unyielding pressure.

"Basil," his name came out on a sigh and he nuzzled her ear.

"Tell me," he whispered.

"Kiss me."

Slow and steady his lips and tongue marked a path down her neck, turning every tendon to water until her head dropped backward. Her fingers tightened convulsively against his shoulders as he tasted her shoulders, as his hand lifted a breast with one aching nipple up to his mouth. The soft fuzz of his beard scraped her bare breasts, making her groin clench and with every pull of his soft mouth the ache between her legs deepened and sharpened until she was rocking against his hardening sex desperate for some kind of relief.

With one arm around her waist he released her breast and reached between them, sliding his palm over her aching sex, earning a sharp moan. This was what she'd been craving, that unerring, instinctive ability he had to know exactly where she needed to be touched and leave her glistening and swollen, stroked to writhing, moaning life.

He lifted his head, "Ada?"

She shook her head fervently, bringing his mouth to hers, "Don't stop. Touch me, please touch me." She gasped as he slid two strong fingers inside her, his thumb tracing circles of wet fiery sensation around the aching nub of flesh he'd been courting. She moved against his hand, encouraging his fingers to thrust deeper, tearing her mouth away from his for a desperate gasp of air. His mouth moved over her cheek, down her neck, pulling her closer as his fingers thrust inside her with methodical precision grazing an area of electrifying sensation. She wrapped her arms around his shoulders and buried her face in them chasing every ribbon of sensation, every ounce of tension until it all erupted into a shimmering cataclysm of pleasure that left her shaking.

She felt when he pulled his fingers from her body, resting his hot damp hand lightly on her bare hip while the other stroked and caressed her back, those broad palmed long-fingered hands holding her together, pressing her back into a shape she was finally starting to recognize again. When she lifted her head after a few moments of reprieve he was still petting her. He leaned his head back and met her eyes.

"All right, darling?" he asked.

She nodded and kissed him, once in gratitude, then again, slower as her hands gripped his face holding him where she needed him. He'd brought her some relief but she wanted all of him and she wasn't going to let him get away with giving her anything less. She could tell he was only meeting her halfway, still unsure whether to give her what she really wanted. He was kissing her back but unwilling to escalate further. When she drew away his face was flushed, his mouth was swollen but his gaze was focused and clear. That needed to change.

"What do you need?"

She didn't look away. Somehow it felt perfectly natural to look him in the eye and say the next words. "I need you inside me."

He reached up and brushed a loose tendril of hair back from

her face, his thumb brushing tenderly over her cheek. "Show me."

That was all she needed to hear from him, a sign that he was willing as long as he believed she was able. She reached between them and unbuttoned the front of his trousers where she found him hot and hard. She wrapped one hand around his length, reconciling herself to its size now that she was taking a good look at it. She'd always felt it inside her but never noticed the darker hue compared to the rest of his skin, had never appreciated how smooth and soft that skin felt in counterpart to the hard pulsating flesh it enveloped.

She glanced up at Basil and found his eyes fixed on her, heavy lidded and dark with carnal appreciation, while his breaths came heavy and slow. That gaze alone had her core clenching with anticipation and heat radiating from her core all throughout her body. She kissed him again, taking first his lower lip and then his upper lip between hers as her tongue traced over his. He nipped her lip lightly and she smiled. He was getting impatient.

Perfect.

She lifted her body up onto her knees and lowered herself onto his swollen length, guiding him into her wet, eager body. Or at least she tried to. No amount of enthusiasm could make up for the fact that somehow it felt like there was even more of him. She couldn't lower herself any further and her thighs were beginning to burn. Was she doing it wrong? She looked up at him and saw his eyes squeezed shut and his jaw so tense it looked like a touch would shatter it.

"Basil," she whispered and his eyes opened slowly. "It won't fit."

The sound he made could have been a laugh or a whimper, but he leaned forward wrapping his arm fully around her waist. Then he kissed her neck and moved his free hand between them to catch that swollen nubbin of flesh between his fingers. Slowly he moved her up and down, easing his penis further into her body with each stroke, teasing her with fresh delight every time his fingers brushed the sides of that locus of rapture.

He nuzzled her breast, his tongue searching for her tender nipple and bringing it between his lips. On the first pull her eyes rolled back in her head, the combined assault on her senses too much to bear. He kept sucking, stroking, thrusting, teasing until at last she felt her thighs resting on his. He shifted his hips forward and leaned back further, adjusting the angle until she was leaning over him as well as against him.

She braced one weak arm against the back of the chaise and the other on his chest, her heart racing and her body one movement away from igniting, ready to claim her prize. His hand rested on her hip and pushed, firmly guiding her movements, showing her how to roll her hips and set a slow and steady pace to give them both what they wanted. He arched his back on her downthrust, making sure she could grind that sensitive bit of flesh right against his pubic bone. Then he wrapped his arms around her glistening, trembling body, pressing kisses and moans into her skin from her neck to her forehead.

Ada squeezed her stinging eyes shut, clinging to him as the first wave of ecstasy took her by surprise, dragging her into convulsions. His hands shifted to grip her bottom, keeping her in place as he buried a groan in her hair. She pushed him down further into the arm of the chaise, rocking her hips harder and faster until he let out a shout, his hips jerking against hers in spasms, sending them both into another explosion of pleasure that Ada felt skittering across every nerve ending in her body.

She pressed her forehead to his waiting for her breath to calm down to normal, for her skin to settle. Then she knew nothing more.

🔥

SHE WAS FINALLY asleep. Ada lay curled on her side, curled up in her unfastened robe, buried under the covers while Basil watched, wide awake. He was bone weary, but he couldn't close his eyes. There was an itch in the back of his mind that wouldn't let him rest or take his eyes off his wife. He knew it was over. It had to be over now, didn't it? Only now that Trent was dealt with his mind was turning to Ada's uncle, the one who had started all of this in motion to begin with.

How many times would he have to feel that terror of knowing she was in danger every time she set foot outside the house? How many more times would he see her covered in cuts and bruises with that wild broken look in her eyes? He didn't know what being her husband would turn him into in order to keep her safe but he knew that whatever it was, the metamorphosis had begun long before tonight. Time would make it even more complete and intractable. More and more the only identify he could think to define himself was as her lover, her protector, her safe haven, her *husband*.

If his father could hear his thoughts now he would think Basil had lost his mind along with all sense of male patriotism. Perhaps he had. But the fear he'd never shake came with a freedom unlike anything he'd ever felt in his life. Freedom to love and be loved as much as his heart could manage. Freedom to look himself in the mirror unflinchingly and know that every part of his life was anchored in a woman beyond the price of rubies, or social pretense, or familial obligation.

A light knock came at the door and Basil glanced down at Ada, wondering if she would wake. When she didn't he kissed her forehead and rose from the bed, grabbing his rumpled shirt from the floor as he went and pulling it over his head. He cracked the door open and saw Richard's butler, Lewis, standing in the doorway.

"What is it?" he asked quietly.

"There's a Mr. Kingston here to see you, sir."

"Leo? Let him in," Basil said.

"He's in the sitting room awaiting you sir."

Basil nodded and closed the door. He tucked his shirt into his trousers and pulled up his suspenders before rebuttoning his trousers. A rustle from the bed drew his attention as Ada sat up, looking around for him.

"Basil?"

"I'm here," he said crossing over to her and taking her hand.

She stared at him with a sleepy frown. "You're dressed again."

"Leo has a message for us, I was just going down to speak to him."

"I'm coming," she said moving to slide off the bed.

He shook his head and ran his hand over her braid. "No, go back to sleep darling."

"I won't sleep without you anyway. I don't want to be here by myself." She would never know how those words tore at his heart. No matter what it took she would feel safe on her own again. He swore it.

He nodded in silence, and waited as she re-tied her robe before leading her down to the sitting room where Leo was standing by the fireplace, disheveled and visibly exhausted but the calmest he'd appeared in days.

"Sorry to come so late, Bas," he said. "And you, Mrs. Thompson."

"I think you can call me Ada at this point."

"Ada then. I know it's late, but I have news and I imagined you'd want to know as soon as possible."

"Is it about Trent?"

"Yes, I just left the prison."

"Has his execution been scheduled?"

"No, but either way he won't be an issue for anyone anymore."

Something on his face gave the answer to the obvious question.

"He's dead?" Ada asked.

Leo watched her solemnly and nodded.

"Was it... did Ellie and I do it?" she asked and Basil slid an arm around her narrow shoulders when she shivered.

"No, although you both did quite a number on him, I have to say. What on earth did you attack him with?"

"Hair pins."

Leo's eyebrows shot up as his eyes widened. "Jesus Christ."

"He tried to kidnap us! He was threatening to hurt Ellie!"

"I'm not excusing his actions but perforated by hairpins is not a good way to go."

"Well, they are more like daggers really," she exclaimed.

Leo's laughter, though weak, lit up his dark amber eyes. "Either way, it wasn't either of those. Someone slit his throat."

"While he was in prison?"

"Apparently."

Ada winced at the image. Inexplicably, despite all he'd done to her and her family her eyes burned with fresh tears. "It's not exactly surprising."

"No."

"Do we know who?" Basil asked. It could have been one of the men he owed money, but it could well have been Ada's uncle, or someone working for him.

"Not yet, but I have my guesses." Leo rose to his feet. "I won't stay any longer."

Ada took a step forward. "I'm indebted to you, Mr. Kingston. I can't thank you enough for what you've done to help me and my brother."

"Not at all. It's nothing your brother wouldn't do for me. And if I'm using your name, you can use mine."

Ada smiled and tried to sit up straight. "Are you sure you won't have at least a cup of tea, Leo?"

"You're good, but my mother is expecting me back tonight. I don't want to keep her up any later than usual."

"Give the old dear my regards," Basil said.

"I'll tell her you called her old," Leo said with a smirk before heading out the door.

Epilogue

Sterling House
London, June 1851

"Aren't we going in, Basil?" Ada asked, nudging his arm. He hummed in response as he stared at the bustling entrance to his parents' London home with skepticism. He wasn't entirely certain he wanted to enter at all. They could just have dinner with Richard. Richard was lovely company.

When he'd received the invitation to dinner, he hadn't known what to do at first. His instinct told him it was some kind of prank. After the way he'd parted with his father and brother, he had expected the occasional letter from his mother. He hadn't expected an invitation to his mother's last dinner party of the season where several members of the ton would be in attendance. Especially not an invitation which explicitly named him and his wife.

He'd even visited his mother to ask if she had actually meant to send him an invitation, wondering if perhaps it was some kind of plot set up by his brother. She hadn't been amused. When he attempted to explain the latest run of bad luck, namely the second kidnapping and the issues with security, she'd been furious at his refusal to keep her informed. Apparently, she and his father had heard all about the heroic raid by Scotland Yard from the commissioner. What they hadn't been aware of was that Ada and Basil had been at the center of it. This in turn triggered a second lecture about his poor taste in humor. And his refusal to see her as his mother, despite her acceptance of him and his family. Two hours later, his ears ringing, he returned to Ada with the invitation in hand.

After an hour of mulling, she had given him permission to accept. Now they were here at the London house for one outing before embarking on their honeymoon in Europe.

"Basil, I'm not staying in this carriage."

"That's fine, but we still don't have to go in. We can say that I'm ill."

"Mmm, I can see you've come down with a strong case of yellow fever," she commented dryly. Somehow, based on her expression, he could tell she meant something different.

"Are you trying to imply something?"

"What a coward you are."

"I am not a coward. I am only trying to avoid what is likely to be a very uncomfortable situation for both of us. You should be thanking me, you ungrateful little shrew." The fact that his palms were sweating was entirely immaterial.

"Weakling," she replied, shaking her head in the same pitying way Richard did.

He tried a different approach. "Father will still be cross and my brother will be there. You haven't met that bundle of joy as yet."

"Craven."

"Wouldn't you rather be making love in your bedroom?"

"Wouldn't you rather make love to me in your father's garden after dinner?" she countered.

He blinked, an image of Ada naked among the peonies springing to mind immediately. "Would you allow me to do that?" he asked.

"You'll never know if you don't *get out of the carriage.*"

"If only I'd known how much of a little bully you are."

"You mean kidnapping you wasn't your first clue?"

"Not you too. *You* did not kidnap me. I am a grown man."

"Apologies, husband. I won't forget again. However, a pillar of strength like yourself should be equal to enduring one night of food and conversation." She smiled and his eyes narrowed. *Minx.*

"Don't play the lawyer with me, Woman," he grumbled, but he opened the carriage door and the footman, who'd been waiting for nearly half an hour at that point, took down the steps before Basil stepped out and held out his hand for Ada. She was stunning in a green gown embossed with flowers and birds along her skirts. Her sleek hair was decorated with peonies and a coral hair pin he knew belonged to her mother.

"It's one night," she said, taking his arm. "If it goes badly, we don't have to return. If it goes well, you will still have your family."

"I already have that," he said resting his hand over hers.

"And now you are about to have more," she replied, wiggling her eyebrows and pulling him along with a cheerful smile.

"I'm going to have to talk to your brother about you."

"He's aware. Why do you think he was so eager to be rid of me? You're stuck with me now."

He winked at her and followed her lead to the front door where guests were still entering. As they arrived, he handed his hat to the footman and followed the line to his father who was greeting guests. When they reached him, their eyes met for a long, humming moment before his father nodded in acknowledgement.

"Good evening, Basil," he said.

"Good evening, father." Basil's hand tightened on Ada's as his father turned his attention to her. His beautiful little firecracker was watching the old man with a certain measure of arrogance, as if daring him to make a scene.

"Mrs. Thompson," he greeted her finally. "I am pleased you are here."

"I was gratified to be invited," she replied.

"I do not want to lose my son," he said by way of explanation. The words seemed lacking but there was a sheen in the old man's eyes, as if he truly meant it. As if he had sincerely been worried about it, as if he'd regretted his ultimatum. Perhaps it hadn't only been his mother trying to shoe horn him into an event. Perhaps it had been a genuine wish from his father to see him again.

"I have no intention of losing him either." Her hold on Basil's arm tightened. It was strange hearing his father express that sentiment, but it was even stranger watching her be his champion and stake her claim on him so blatantly.

"For Basil then," he said, glancing at him. It was an apology to him, he knew it, and an acknowledgement of Ada in a way. He glanced at her, wondering what she would make of it, but she was staring at him with a small smile.

"Indeed."

"Adelaide, I thought I'd heard you." They turned to see Basil's mother emerging from the crowd, glittering with diamonds, her face wreathed in a bright smile.

"Good evening, Mother."

"Hello dear." She patted Basil on the shoulder.

"Good evening, Lady Sterling," Ada replied before his mother took her arm, pulling her away from him and escorting her to the sitting room while he trailed behind.

"My dear, there is someone who is most eager to meet you."

"Oh?" Ada asked before glancing back at him in confusion. He shrugged in response. He had no idea who the hell she was referring to.

"Is that the new Mrs. Thompson?" he heard a woman say, and then none other than Miss Felicity Ashwood came forward, gloved hands outstretched to take Ada's. Ada glanced at him again this time in surprise and he fought back a smile. She was adorable.

"Ada, this is Miss Felicity Ashwood."

"Oh." Ada's eyes widened before she dipped into a curtsey. "I'm pleased to meet you, Miss Ashwood."

"And I am thrilled to meet you, Mrs. Thompson. Thanks to

you, I shall soon be Mrs. Halsbury," she gushed before shooting an apologetic look at Basil. "No disparagement meant towards you, Basil, of course."

"Are we doing first names now, Miss Ashwood?"

"You jilted me three weeks before our wedding. We're practically related now." She replied archly, before turning back to Ada. "I must introduce you to mama. What a beautiful dress you are wearing as well!"

"Where is Hamilton?" Basil asked his mother, as he watched Ada slowly warm up to the infectious energy the soon-to-be Mrs. Halsbury exhibited.

"Your brother wasn't invited," she replied. "He informed me that he couldn't pretend to be happy for you, so I agreed that any events you were invited to, he would not be."

"Oh." What on earth had happened when he left? "And he is at peace with that?"

"That's his business. He drew the line; I'm simply abiding by it." She patted his arm. "This is your home. It always will be so long as you wish it. I've spoken to your father, and he agrees. Despite everything, he wants your happiness."

He nodded and looked over at Ada, who was now smiling fully in the face of Felicity's earnest enthusiasm. "Ada is my happiness."

Ada was his home. So long as they kept that smile on her face, he would stay in theirs.

About the Author

Born in the tropical paradise of Trinidad and Tobago, Addy Du Lac moved to the US with her mother at the age of twelve. She began writing historical romance while she received a double major in History and Creative Writing from the University of South Florida. She enjoys writing books with diverse characters and steamy happy endings. When she isn't plotting her next series, she enjoys watching movies and Asian Dramas, traveling, and tempting her fate with new recipes.

Addy Du Lac lives in Florida with an eclectic library of books and a carefully curated wall of beautiful men.